GOING
TO THE LAST

Published by Modest Publishing

Copyright © 2013, 2018 K D Knight

K D Knight has asserted his
right under the Copyright, Designs and Patents
Act 1988 to be identified as the author
of this work.

All rights reserved.

ISBN 978-1-98658-689-4

Also available as a Kindle ebook
ISBN 978-1-84396-378-3

No part of this publication may be reproduced, stored in
or introduced into a retrieval system or transmitted in any
form or by any means electronic, photomechanical,
photocopying, recording or otherwise without the prior
written permission of the publisher. Any person who does
any unauthorised act in relation to this publication may be
liable to criminal prosecution

Pre-press production
eBook Versions
27 Old Gloucester Street
London WC1N 3AX
www.ebookversions.com

GOING TO THE LAST

K D Knight

MODEST PUBLISHING

Contents

1
Introduction

3
Going to the Last

17
A Grey Day

18
Without A Day

29
Yesterday's Magic

39
Second Consideration

47
Sentiment of Fools

55
Yes, I Fear He Is.
I Fear He Is.

62
One of the Reasons
I Am Now a Pinhooker

77
**The Mortgage, the Kids,
the Wife, the Dreams...**

86
A Private Matter

95
A Picture of Royland

104
A Sorry Tale

116
The Story of H

122
Pitchcroft Blues

132
Two Sides of the Coin

141
Veering Off a True Line

150
Mrs Underwood's Pony

156
Mischievous Jack

185
As Unbelievable as a Thriller

193
The Crux of the Matter

203
Christmas Surprise

211
The Fairisle Mystery

220
Heaven and Hell

234
The Golden Boy

250
Emily's Smile of Wonder

Introduction

Now professionally edited by a horse-riding professional editor with long-standing experience of both the correct and incorrect word, *Going to the Last* is now, at last, fit for human consumption. As an aid to digestion of this smorgasbord of racing and horse-related short stories, the writer suggests the moderate consumption of a good single malt or an over-indulgence of a medium-to-good Burgundy. I have it on good authority that the majority of writers are drunks, so it is only appropriate that their readers also enjoy the fruit of the grain or the grape whilst seeking enjoyment or detachment from the awfulness of life whilst reading the literary efforts of this particular writer.

To my shame I am not a drunk. I am a teetotalling tea addict, which I suspect explains why though bordering on competent I am not yet within thirty lengths of one of my literary heroes, Raymond Chandler, the greatest of the drunk writers.

Occasionally I am reduced to tears by the sheer magnificence of the racehorse, by its bravery and willingness to go beyond its natural endurance for the will of Man. Occasionally the sport can kick you in the solar plexus, when the reality of life and death is brought into sharp relief and the tears then represent tragedies that are not as insignificant as missed putts, missed penalties or a dropped ball.

I am of the opinion that the old philosophers' sore of 'what is the meaning of life' can be answered by the love that comes from deep within the heart and what stimulates the soul. To some it may be singing, politics, surfing or nursing the sick or elderly. My 'meaning of life' is horse racing. If I were Raymond Chandler I might be able to convey to non-horse-racing people the beauty of the spectacle that is horse racing and the goodness of the humans who own, train, ride or care for the horse, the most beautiful animal on the planet.

Going to the Last

Sarah walked out on me today. Just upped and left. No goodbye. No tearful au revoir. Just a scribbled note to tell me she had met a bloke who drove a BMW convertible and who appreciated her for who she is, indicating, with reference to the soft-roofed car, that she was already looking forward to summer. So in the spirit of what-the-hell I have driven down to Sandown Park in my prehistoric Morris Marina, where I am currently five losers closer to penury.

Sarah, bless her little cotton bud, tried so hard to change me into the sort of man she would find acceptable: to chasten me towards the married man's thrift. She attempted kindness, which was hard for her as kindness is not second nature to her. She also went in for bribery and hot-blooded, slapping-the-face, argument. But her efforts, obviously, to sanitise and organise my salvation, caused too many unnecessary silences to produce harmony and accord and, defeated, she has bitten the bullet to leave me to my weaknesses.

That was Sarah, bless her sensitive places, all the while acting in my best interests. She never, to give her credit, criticised me for spending my dosh on chocolate or flowers, which I did occasionally; or anything that was solely for her pleasure. Granted it was usually my predictable way to get back in her good books, but not once did she demand I stop wasting my money on her. Poor Sarah. She so believed I undersold myself; that I possess hidden, if subterranean levels of ability. If I were to exert myself, she told me frequently, I might make up into something respectable. How I must have disappointed her as much as I disappoint myself.

Hell's teeth! I need this winner. There is only enough juice in the car to get me out of the car park. But nothing ventured, as they say. It'll have to be a fiver each way. Pay out less than a tenner on the nose but with a bit of luck I'll at least get my stake back: a small blessing and easier on the shoe leather. Sixteen-runner handicap hurdle. Not the best of getting-out stakes. The maestro of Seven Barrows has the favourite – Irish Regent. What does the Tote board say? 2/1. No value, not at each way.

Tricky. Paddy, my old sparring partner, always advises to bet with the brain. He's right. A 2/1 winner is better than a 20/1 loser. Irish Regent. Won cosily at Kempton Park last time. Different type of track, of course. Flatter. Tighter. Less of a test of stamina. Now here's a horse that has done me well in the past – Phraseology. Last season, about this time of year, now I come to think about it, when Paddy was pulling that redhead, I backed it at Ludlow. Best pork pies in the world are to be found at Ludlow. He was 33's that day. Turned Paddy an appropriate shade of green. As rare as silver linings are days like that. Three hundred and fifty quid. Sarah made me stick the lot in the Black Horse, which took away that head-in-the-clouds sensation of having a wad of notes in the back pocket. It's still there. Miracle of all miracles, that.

It wasn't winnings, according to Sarah. It was a nest-egg.

She calculated the interest and what it would buy in the future. Hardly seemed worth worrying about, the future, I protested. But to give Sarah her due she never underestimated the strength of my weaknesses and to this day I have not found where she hid my bank book.

My luck is out because I'm on my own. Paddy is up at Warwick, chancing his arm with another redhead. She sent him home with a flea in his crotch when we were up there last week. She's a challenge now. To him, the chase is the thrill. He'll use any story. Tell any lie. One leg-over and he'll be content. Flash the cash and never mention the kids and the wife or that he works on the bins. I'll have my fiver each way on Phraseology, just for old times' sake.

Has my luck changed? To get rid of the loose silver in my pocket I treated myself to a quick half. And in the bar what do I see escaping from the back pocket of some nob? A folded twenty-pound note, that's all. Manna! Like a greyhound from the slip I had my size tens over it. No conjuror could have got that score into his pocket any cleaner.

Note to self: must ring Sarah's sister tonight to tell her my side of the story. Show concern. Plead my innocence. Bridget is sweet on me. Called her sister 'a lucky so-and-so' when I first met her.

Before Sarah I was going with a blonde called Michelle. Nice, Michelle. All home by ten o'clock and the Spanish Inquisition from her parents if I got her home five minutes late. A lot of hassle really for nothing, though her old man did introduce me to the Cottage. He's a diehard Fulham fan. Season-ticket holder. I stood on the terraces with him a couple of times. He told me about his tailoring business. He said he would take me on, show me the ropes, if I was serious about Michelle. I was serious. But not about the sort of commitment he was thinking about. We both had breasts as the central pivot of our existence, but his were of the pocket variety.

I still go to the Cottage. Every home game. Cheering and jeering. As loyal as Punch, that's me. At least that arm's-length courting done me some good in the end. If she hadn't slapped my face when I went in search of her bra strap I would never have driven home early and I wouldn't have picked up Sarah. She flagged me down. Stepped off the kerb and hoisted her skirt. She had a wicked smile. Still has. She was running away from home. I didn't ask where she was heading. I said jump in. And she did.

I remember now. That Ludlow race was only a seller. This race is a competitive handicap. And five furlongs further. Oh well, thanks to the nob I now have a saver on the favourite. I'll treat myself to a nice cigar if I collect. Long time since I had a real smoke. And I won't have Sarah boxing my ear lobes with talk about lung cancer and pollution and how her grandfather had to carry an oxygen bottle wherever he went.

She tried so hard to protect me from myself. No wife would have done more. She stopped me smoking, limited my drinking and even fed me on healthy food. She did try, bless her true blue eyes. Occasionally we indulged in Indian and Chinese takeaways. But only when she thought I deserved it.

Give Sarah her due she created an oasis in the desert of my life. I'll miss her. Madly. Truly. Every time I see a BMW with a soft top.

The horses are at the start. Phraseology is a grey. Easier to see where my money is going. Ah! He's got a claimer on top;

an inexperienced waif. Taking a bit of weight off; that might help up the notorious Sandown hill. Mind you, Irish surname. These lads from across the water are lean and hungry to prove themselves. Ready to ride for their lives. Born in a stable, most of them.

The starter is calling them in. Soon be off. The light is fading. Soon it'll be dark. Roll on summer and those balmy evenings by the Thames at Windsor. I bet I'm the only mug with his bins trained on the grey. Always the man going against the tide. That's me. They're off!

I hate it when mine makes the running. All I get is false hope. Takes a good one to lead all the way. Front runners fade, like in life. Two hurdles out, you wait and see. Jumped the first well, though. Encouraging. Boy on top looks the part. Not going too fast, reserving something for the hill. The boy has it sussed. I like him. Jumped the second nicely. One fell. Long way to go.

Once, I never knew why, Sarah came to a match with me. It was a cup game. We were playing Hendon. They were non-league and we were near the top of the table at the time. I thought we would score six or seven. I thought it would be a crystal illustration of my devotion. We lost one–nil. The ignominy compounded by the purchase of two stand tickets. It snowed. The car wouldn't start and I had to take a taxi home. Out of the cup in the first round with Sarah a spectator to my humiliation. And I was on my best behaviour. Didn't abuse either the linesman or the referee. I done a tenner on a six–nil score line.

Poor Sarah! How she deserved a bloke who would wine and dine her. Ritz and glitz her. A nob with a good job. Instead of a roper-doper no-hoper. And now she has found him. Mr.

BMW soft-top. Mr. Wonderful.

A mile to go and we are still in front. The commentator keeps saying that Phraseology is bowling along. Three or four are sitting handily, though. Waiting to pounce. To turn on the heat up that hill. Irish Regent is one of them.

There is a ruckus going on behind me. A hysterical female is shouting at some poor sod. I know the feeling. Too much celebrating on an empty stomach. Through the sea of binoculars I cannot make out where they are. The commentator has called the horses entering the straight. Phraseology still leads. Behind me, a woman in a beige trench coat is elbowing her way down off the stands. Pushing people aside like a scrum-half. Her suitor is two lengths adrift. His pursuit is impeded by irate spectators with better things on their minds than a lovers' tiff. The bloke is tall, swarthy, Latino-looking. He has dark untrusting eyes and a bushy moustache.

The commentator is getting excited. He's just said the 50/1 outsider is still in front. He's not tiring. The Latin guy has just cried out 'Sarah'. He is begging her to wait for him. That she has him all wrong. I can see her face now. I wonder if she's worth the public humiliation. It is Sarah. My Sarah. What the Dickie Davies is she doing at the races? She would never come with me.

Her mascara streaks her face. Never a good look for a woman. I've never seen her cry before. It was something I had never driven her to. Too tough, I thought, to cry. But she's crying now. Her chest is heaving with the raw emotion of her situation.

They have jumped the second last and Phraseology still leads. Irish Regent is just behind, cantering. Looking classy.

Sarah and Mr. Wonderful are in my line of vision, overloading my senses. Mr. Wonderful has grabbed hold of her. She looks all-in. The whips are up and Irish Regent is poised to pounce. Just waiting to get the last hurdle out of the way.

He's trying to calm her. Remonstrating as if they were surrounded by walls. He wants to lead her away and a part of me is determined to intervene. But over the last and Phraseology still leads. I have fifty fivers on a win and fifty fivers at a quarter the odds riding on him. If he jumps it I might yet be in clover. The favourite could run out of steam up the hill. He's giving my boy a stone and a half. It might count at the winning line.

Phraseology didn't have to battle at Ludlow. Sarah has slapped Mr. Wonderful's face. I know how that feels. That'll teach him for messing with her. Shit! Phraseology has fallen. Sarah's cow eyes have found me. But what is she doing here? She hates gambling. Only this morning I gathered up her silk undies and stuffed them down the rubbish chute. How will I explain that to her?

Irish Regent has won. I've won forty quid. The day is over. I can get home. The screens, I see, have been erected around Phraseology. Perhaps his heart gave out. I know mine is about to.

Silently, through the milling crowd, we walk arm in arm. United. The dark is making small the world we know. In my pocket are my winnings. Safe and snug. And I get to take Sarah home, too. She has said sorry. And I have forgiven her as I know she will have to forgive me. We all make mistakes.

Luck has called again. Sarah has come back when I didn't think she would. I've found twenty and won sixty. Behind us there is a hearty cheer. It can mean only one thing. Phraseology has risen. He, too, will live to fight another day.

A Grey Day

The rain strikes the car without pity. All hope is washed away. He turns off the engine and slumps down into the seat. This day was supposed to be the culmination of a life-long dream; it was confirmed in nearly all of the newspapers. When last night he had turned out the bedside light everything seemed perfect. Now he wishes he were somewhere else. Now he wishes they had taken a different decision.

He looks back at the dogs. They are oblivious to the rain, to the consternation which dances a reel of horrible consequence upon the heart of their owner. They only see open space and the certainty of fun and intriguing scent. For half an hour he has kept them waiting, ignoring their canine persuasions.

The rain methodically and without mercy transforms into snow, vanquishing the last scintilla of hope for a God-given miracle.

He succumbs to duty, to positive action. Half-heartedly he replaces his shoes with wellington boots, buttons up his old greatcoat and pulls on woollen gloves. It is time to move, time to exercise judgement, time to be brave. The others rely on him, which is his awful obligation. He is their spokesman. He is expected to be better informed. They will expect knowledgeable advice, especially if David leaves the final decision to them.

He opens the car door and steps into a puddle. He reaches back into the car to remove the ignition key. Noticing his binoculars on the passenger seat he decides to take them with him. Not that he will be able to see very far with or without them. The visibility and his mood are sparse and inseparable; his expression will leave observers with the idea that going around his head is a eulogy he is writing on the death of a friend. He slams the car door but does not bother to put the key to the lock.

The dogs bound from the car with the enthusiasm of a summer romp. For once their joie de vivre fails to raise his spirits. Head down he walks across to the course, calling the dogs to follow. The snow settles on his shoulder, on the rails, on the fences. As he ducks under the plastic running rail a featherweight of the white menace finds its way down his neck. He shivers at its death-like touch and senses that it must be an omen. As he digs his heel into the turf he finds himself praying for it to be frozen, for fate to make the judgement call for him. It is soft, very soft.

"Bit grim," someone comments, passing hurriedly by. "I shan't be running mine," he adds almost cheerily.

"Hey," someone else shouts from the hurdle course. He looks up and recognises the face beneath the flat cap but cannot put a name to it. He waves in acknowledgement and smiles weakly, suddenly aware that he is not alone, that his plight is shared by trainers, jockeys, racecourse staff and other owners. "The Gold Cup in April, couldn't be better for you, jammy sod," the man shouts across to him, adding. "They'll abandon, run the race at the April meeting. They'll have no other option if this stuff keeps falling." The man brushes snow from the running rail with his bare hands and throws a snowball at an acquaintance passing in the opposite direction.

His spirits are raised. "The stewards will abandon, of course," he tells one of his dogs. "There will be no need for a decision." The weight, as if by divine intervention, lifts from his shoulders and he straightens his back and stares up at the leaden sky, up over the second-last and towards the grandstand. Lights pierce the gloom, the famed panorama thick with silent grey foreboding. Carefully he looks around him, at the men and women inspecting the ground, assessing the situation and taking decisions on behalf of their connections, hoping to spot the clerk of the course or a steward.

Someone comes up from behind and slaps him on the shoulder. "Mine will love it. Been waiting for the ground to be this heavy all season. Those bookies are in for a right skinning."

"But they will abandon, surely," he argues, committing the heresy of verbally suggesting the Gold Cup should be postponed.

"No, why should they? The horses will gallop through this. It's just wet. Anyway, this is the Gold Cup. They will race if they damned well can, mark my words."

He calls the dogs, looking around to see where they are, his optimism torn in half. They are at a workman's hut, begging for food. He strides across to them, cursing their effrontery, apologising to the groundsman. "Shame about the weather, eh? I should think you are pig-sick," the man says, snapping a digestive biscuit in two and sharing it between the dogs. "Wrong course, wrong way round, wrong distance and now the wrong ground. You got the full set, congratulations. And it's been beautiful all week. If it doesn't stop snowing in the next hour we can all go home and get warm."

As he makes his way towards the grandstand, towards the fateful meeting with his father, the other owners and more importantly David, people, professional and racegoers alike, offer their opinion and their condolence at the abrupt and cruel change in the weather. The professionals are unanimous that they, or he, should withdraw. The racegoers, though, maintain the faith and urge him to run.

A television interviewer with a cameraman and sound crew in tow begs a few minutes of his time. Doubtfully he agrees. "Does he run, sir?" It is a polite question and the viewers at home, the fans, deserve an answer. He stares at the microphone as if it is a Kalashnikov and digs his heel once more into the snow-topped turf, unable and unwilling to commit to running or not running. "The ground is against you," the interviewer needlessly reminds him, wanting to get a scoop for the one o' clock news. Raising his hands to the heavens he mutters ambiguities that place the burden of decision at the feet of David. "You would not be upset if the stewards abandoned the meeting, I dare say?" the interviewer hastily continues, adding to the agony of the ambush interview.

Back at the car the snow has mercifully called a halt and a pale sun blinks through the murk. He rubs the dogs dry, offers them water and returns them to the car. He cannot put off the moment any longer; he must go and talk with his father, and with David.

On his way he rehearses in his mind what to say. The horse must be withdrawn. There will be no argument about it. It is the decision they would take on any other day. It will be unpopular with some and to others it will be a grave disappointment. But for the true fans, those with only the horse's best interests at heart, it is the only acceptable decision. No one will want to see him vanquished, pulled up or worse. They might be accused of cowardice, of wrapping the horse up in cotton wool. But it is not a case of winning and losing. It is about caring. And there will always be next year.

"There you are. Let's go and have a reviver. We have to talk." It is David, unworried, as ebullient as ever. David is not the man he wants to see. It is his father he needs to talk with, to form a united front to defeat David's blind optimism. They are going to disagree; he knows from the expression on his face that David still wants to run.

"Now let's have that drink before you lot get together and frighten yourself into making a stupid decision."

He leans against the weighing-room door, unwilling to be pummelled by David's infectious optimism. He needs his father; he needs his fellow owners to help safeguard him from logic that when said by David is akin to sorcery.

"I know the ground is on the soft side but let's not worry over that," David assures him.

He feels his jaw drop at this adjustment to usual opinion. But he steadies himself. He knows he must concentrate. David might be indulging in one of his wind-ups.

"Our horse is the best-balanced horse in the race. On this ground that will be worth lengths to us. Trust me, we can't be beat."

He is too bemused to reply. His well-rehearsed acceptance of the twist of fate is now worthless to him. David has sprung a reason for running which had not for one moment crossed his mind.

A journalist joins them, in want of first-hand knowledge, only for David to take him by the arm as if he were an errant schoolboy to frogmarch him from harm's way.

"If you bastards start on him we will never agree." The journalist, sniffing disagreement between owner and trainer, pursues the matter. "No," David answers him, opening the weighing-room door and pushing the journalist inside. "There is no difference of opinion, so stop fishing. We both want what is best for the horse. And when he agrees with my opinion we will have come to a decision whether to run or not."

"Have you collared David yet?" It is his father, standing outside the owners' and trainers' marquee. The weather has improved, though it remains cold and dismal. "The bugger's hiding from me. I keep spotting him walking in the opposite direction."

He is told David's upbeat 'Trust me, we can't be beat' speech. "So he has collared you." His father laughs out loud, slapping his son on the back, demonstrating togetherness. "Let's have a drink. You look like you need one. After all's said and done, we still have the favourite for the Gold Cup and we never thought that would happen a few years ago. And I suppose as we normally leave the difficult decisions to David we might just as well leave this one to him. And to be honest, and you know how hard this is for me to admit to, the bugger gets it right more times than he gets it wrong."

David's logic is beyond reason, beyond what is written in the form book. Yet without David's expertise where would they be? He cannot accept that it is correct to run the horse on ground he has always hated but at least they have the option of pulling up if it is too much for him. The public will understand. Their love of the horse will be strong enough to accept the disappointment.

Ruefully, he smiles. His father also smiles. They all agree. Though only David believes they will be lifting the Gold Cup. Quite possibly David is the only person in the country who believes the grey horse cannot be beaten.

Without A Day

He has fallen. But from where? And how?

There is a swelling lump on the back of his head, tender to the touch, and as he tries to rise it feels as if the ground holds a great force over him. At first, as he attempts to make sense of his predicament, he is heartened by the sensation of being in close proximity to a large gathering of his fellows, though his eyes cannot locate confirmation of the noise, for the hum and babble is very much like a concert before the curtains go up; a confusion of discord laced with a cacophony of static electricity. In conclusion, though, all there is to hear is silence.

He looks up to the sky. It is a shade of cornflower blue flecked by feathery, insignificant cloud. For a moment he thinks the sky is calling to him but when he reaches up to touch it his only awareness is a sharp pain in his chest. He is hot, with his shirt sticking to his sweating body. He looks at himself and is surprised to find that he is wearing a mackintosh. Carefully, he sits upright, unbuttoning the inappropriate garment. Underneath he is wearing a grey sweater. Restricted by pain he removes both the mackintosh and the sweater, falling back onto the grass in another attempt to make sense of his situation.

Yet it is hopeless. He cannot keep a thought in his head for a moment. He cannot even recall his name.

With the caution of a grievously wounded man he stands up. Unsteadily, his legs in danger of buckling, he surveys his surroundings. In front of him there is a paddock. He steadies himself against the chestnut fencing. Beyond the paddock there is a hilly field. The paddock is empty, the grass neatly tended. A driveway enters a large red-brick complex through an archway topped by a clock tower. In the near distance there is a lane fronting a steep escarpment and above that a belt of trees.

Nothing moves. All is quiet. It is as if nature is in mourning.

It is eleven-thirty. The cool and shadow of the archway entices him to move. Once moving, walking becomes bearable. He would like to linger, to stay out of the hot sun. But his head throbs and his chest hurts. Hesitantly he makes his way out into open view, expecting confrontation at any moment. His body demands medical intervention. And inherently he knows there is danger in this separation from companionship and logic.

He is in a large quadrangle with a stone trough at its centre. The enclosure echoes recent abandonment. The yellow gravel is even and clean, with the concrete path around the perimeter gleaming white and unblemished by either muck or straw. The yard appears ship-shape in its preservation.

The first stable he comes to is set fair and he collapses into the luxuriant straw bedding. He is unaccountably tired, his legs as heavy as if they have carried him without pause up the highest mountain. Again he tries to determine what has happened to him. He remembers the mackintosh and the absurdity of wearing it on such a hot day. He can remember the mackintosh but he cannot remember where he has left it. It is another predicament to daunt him. Without the energy to fight the sense of having fallen from reality he allows his eyes to close, allowing sleep to wrap him in the comfort he desires.

"I thought Johnstone terribly unlucky. If he was not forced to switch to the inside he would have surely won a good length."

"Well, Henry, I saw it differently. I watched the newsreel as you did yourself and my thought was that Elliott was damnably fortunate not to have been disqualified."

"Which is the same, Bartram, as agreeing with what I said."

"It is not, Henry. If the stewards had disqualified Elliott on Nimbus, then I reckon Smith would have got the race on Swallow Tail. He was, you surely agree, the main sufferer in the argy-bargy. If he had got the race it would have pleased me no end, Henry, as I had a couple of pounds on him."

"Hah! It's not known for the first and second to be disqualified in the Derby. Wait till I tell the governor, he'll chuckle."

"Mr. Fennerloe is a fair man, Henry Greaves, as you well know. If he thought they had transgressed the rules of racing he would be in favour of both of them being thrown out."

The sleeper is roused from the black depths of slumber by the genial dispute of old friends. He sits upright, too quickly for his sore head. Trying to ignore the throbbing discomfort he listens to ascertain the direction of the conversation. But all he can hear now is the hush of solitude, the disappointment triggering a flash of pain in his chest and he slumps sideways, clutching at his heart. The pain assaults him in volleys. Bang. Bang. Bang. Then he vomits, the excreta mingling with the bright straw to disappear from view. The pain diminishes.

He staggers from the stable, violently pushing open the large door, desperate for someone to hear or see him, to demand to know who he is and why he is trespassing.

He reels crazily across the gravel, unable to release the scream that is trapped in his throat. He rests against the trough, staring into the crystal-clear water. The face that confronts him reviles him. It is a face contorted by fear and confusion and he cannot recognise who the reflection might belong to. Repelled by his own likeness he thrusts his head down into the water.

The baptism revives the need for explanation, easing the pain in his head. As he sits on the edge of the trough he tries again to gather reason from the madness of his situation. But still he cannot even recall his name. Indeed his only memory is the two men talking about the Derby.

He looks about him, hoping to see either Henry Greaves or Bartram. The quadrangle shimmers under the hot sun, its secrets a history beyond his imagination. Opposite the trough are the archway and the four-sided clock. It is eleven-thirty. On three sides of the quadrangle there are stables with broad panelled doors secured from damage and blemish at the top and bottom with aluminium as polished as silver. At any moment he expects to see a brass handle turn and someone appear leading a glossy thoroughbred. But no one appears. No horse whinnies or neighs. The world is as still as a frozen pond.

He slips off the trough to quench his thirst. The water is sweet, the refreshment an elixir to the spirit. He must find Henry Greaves and Bartram or whoever Mr. Fennerloe might be.

"But, Tilda, the master has me running like a shot hare. I think he has me in training for these bloomin' Olympics. I hope not. I couldn't face those Jerries again. So go on, Tilda, I needs a second round of bread 'n' jam."

"Haven't you 'eard of rationing, Joshua Mills? And why 'as Mr. Fennerloe got you running like a shot hare? Punishment?"

"He reckons it'll make me a better jockey. A thinner one more like it. He says it'll make me understand what it's like for a horse to run when it's tired. The way the governor tells it, it kinda makes sense but when I'm halfway up them banks it's just seems a bonkers idea. And he makes me wear winter clothes."

"If Mr. Fennerloe reckons it'll do you good, Joshua, you keep at it. I'll see what I can rustle up for you."

"Thanks, Tilda, I'll make it up to you when I'm as famous as Rae Johnstone and Charlie Elliott. The latest thing is giving the 'prentices piggy-back rides. It's about balance and centre of gravity. He'll have us doing three-legged races next. He forgets. I was in the army. I fought Hitler. I thought I'd done with drill and combat fatigue."

"There, one round of bread and dripping. Best I can do."

"I was wanting to take my Joan to the dance on Saturday but the governor says I have to be in bed by nine if I want that ride at Warwick next week. Life isn't fair. I'll lose Joan at this rate."

He crouches below the window sill, listening. Through the lace curtains he can make out two silhouettes, one seated, one standing. The conversation excites his curiosity, levering ajar a door on a long-forgotten memory. Hearing a chair scraped over tiles he straightens himself, wincing as pain re-enters his chest. Allowing the discomfort to pass, he rattles the windowpane. He is unanswered, unrecognised. He knocks louder. Exasperated he finds a door and enters without knocking.

The kitchen is empty.

The sun remains hot and overhead. Sequentially he has inspected each stable and opened every unlocked door. There is no vestige of life. No explanation. No man. No beast. No rat, no sparrow. Everything is organised and in its place. The quadrangle should bustle yet it is vacant of life.

In the tack room he finds a full-length mirror and he realises he is wearing thick khaki jodhpurs. He stares at his reflection in fear and disbelief. "Who are you?" he asks himself. Looking deep into the mirror he tries to extract a single fact about his appearance, any remembrance which will trigger a clue as to who he is and where he might be but the sole contact he has with solid reality is the conversation between Tilda and Joshua.

He returns to the trough to again quench his thirst. In desperation he cries out, "Tilda! Joshua! Help me!", his despair echoing around the red brick with the resonance of a siren, igniting abruptly the spectral emergence of horses and people. First there is sound and then vision. Sleek, muscled horses adorned with monogrammed sheets and guided by riders in tweed and khaki. As they circle the trough a man dressed in cavalry-twill trousers, hacking jacket and cloth cap inspects each horse, directing their riders with a cane crop to go one way or the other out of the yard.

"Simes. Clayton. Mills."

"Yes sir." "Yes sir." "Yes sir."

"Walk and trot up and down the banks. And only walking and trotting. We are still muscling these two-year-olds. They are not ready for anything more strenuous. Ten minutes on an off lead, ten minutes on the near lead. You understand."

"Yes sir." "Yes sir." "Yes sir."

"Bartram will be close by to observe you. Henry."

"Yes, Mr. Fennerloe. This lad's a bit pepped this morning."

"Coming to hand, Henry. As we want him. Take him to the water meadow and work him at speed for four furlongs. Warm his muscles first, mind you."

"Let him bowl out of my hands, sir?"

"Yes. Do not pull him about. Sir George would like to go for the Goodwood Cup with him. He'll be fit enough to do himself justice, shouldn't he?"

"Yes sir. It will be nice to win the cup again."

"Bartram. Ride your horse across to the Halfyards and inform Wilson that the shearers are due to arrive tomorrow week. Then proceed home by way of the banks. The apprentices are to dismount at Strawberry Cottage to lead their horses home."

"Young Haslet is ready with Mr. Colville's horse. I've checked the tack, sir."

"Thank you. Colville would like him prepared for the Middle Park."

"He thinks him a classic horse, then?"

"He believes every two-year-old he owns will develop into a classic horse."

But too soon the eruption of activity fades from sight and solitude and emptiness reign once more. He spins round, hoping to see another glimpse of the clairaudient and ghostly apparitions. Yet there are no marks, no hoof-prints on the gravel to provide evidence for what he saw. No trace of life. Nothing but the glowering brick and the haze of a fiery sun.

He slumps exhausted to the ground and looks into his mind to dredge a semblance of sense from the madness. Sweat drips from his brow and once more his head and chest pulse with pain. He is tortured by a desire to retch, to evacuate all life from his body. Angry, he clambers to his feet, expecting everything to have changed again. But it remains the same. It remains eleven-thirty.

He walks with renewed purpose along a leafy lane, passing a tumbled-down cottage that reflects on the back of the eye with teasing familiarity.

At a junction he stops, unable to decide which direction to follow. In the hedge there is a name-plate, partly covered by foliage. A close inspection tells him that the lane he has just walked is called Fennerloe Road, the name rising up to assail his mind's eye with the speed and ferocity of a fiery rapier.

His feet take him to a long street of stone houses bookended by a pub and a shop. Two men roll out of the pub, their arms entwined. "Fennerloe?" he asks hopefully. He is ignored and their good humour stuns him like a smacked cheek. He would like to shout after them but the words stick in his throat. Three schoolgirls with straw boaters on their heads come from a churchyard and he dashes across the road to ask them the same question. "Fennerloe?" They too walk on, indifferent to his presence. Fennerloe is important. It is his only penetrative memory.

He sits on the bench in front of the Norman church. He is baffled and beaten. The name Fennerloe dances a reel of confusion inside his head.

A group of men come out of the pub. They are orderly and

smartly dressed. They each have a coat folded over their arms. The creaking of the pub sign takes his attention: The Fennerloe Arms. The men seem happy with life. "Well," one of them announces as he lights up his pipe. "All the same, I'm mighty glad Elliott didn't throw the race away. If it were a minor race at Birmingham or Hurst Park the stewards may have acted to the letter of the rulebook."

"It's my opinion they failed in their duty not doing so," his friend counters.

The first man pats his breast pocket. "This hundred guineas will pay the bills for a month or so." As if they are a conspirator's choir, the three men laugh, the play on words a familiar story to each of them.

"What you mean, Colville, you scoundrel? It will keep the lovely Lady Caroline in silk stockings and champagne for a week or two."

The pipe-smoker taps his pipe on the heel of his shoe. "Nice, though, to keep the blue riband in England for a change. The French have conquered too often for my liking.'

"Oh. I don't know. Pearl Diver was extremely rewarding, much to my liking."

"If Fennerloe can work the oracle it might be Colville who vanquishes the old enemy at Epsom next year."

"Hurrah to that possibility."

"Look, chaps, we ought do the decent thing and give Fennerloe a few quid to pass on to the dependents of poor Joshua Mills."

"Absolutely. It's the least we can do. Awful thing to happen. To think he survived Hitler only to perish under the hooves of a bally horse."

"It's the twist of fate that bothers me. Old Hopkins here was only saying last week on the train back from Newmarket that they should wear some sort of protective hat. Dangerous business, riding at full tilt."

"Tin hats, like soldiers wear?"

"On those lines. Modified, of course."

"He rode a winner for me, you know. Chester. Tricky course to ride. Rode it damn well. He had a future. Fennerloe didn't want him to enlist, you know. There was no need, not by then."

"What do you say, Colville, shall we go up and pay our respects? He was one of us, you know. One of the racing fraternity."

"We should. Fennerloe would expect it of us."

At a distance he follows the men to the churchyard. He is now aware of his destination. Explanation beats all around him like a drum. Amour Drake had finished second. He remembers giving Henry half a crown and calculating his possible winnings. And he remembers Joan; his winnings were all he needed to afford an engagement ring. And he remembers the banks and the horse bolting as Bartram appeared over the brow of the hill, hollering at Clayton for allowing his horse to break into a canter. In his mind's eye he can plainly see Bartram riding across his path, trying to break the stride of his bolting horse, his best efforts in vain, but only succeeding in making the horse shy violently to the near side, catapulting him into the grassy bank. He remembers the taste of the grass, the hooves of the two-year-old, Bartram demanding he be okay and the pain in his chest and head.

He looks to where Colville and his friends look but all he can see is the darkness of peace and he realises all pain has deserted him and that he is now without a day and without a care and that there is nothing left for him to know as he now knows all he will ever need to know.

Yesterday's Magic

Do you remember a horse called Ile de Chypre? At Royal Ascot, a good while ago, in one of the handicaps, he looked all over the winner only to veer dramatically, without warning or provocation, across from the running rail to the centre of the course and beyond, losing a race he had all but won. It was a talking point at the time, with many a theory as to why it happened. One of the more unorthodox explanations was that someone blasted him with a sonic gun mounted within a pair of binoculars.

Sonic guns were in vogue at the time. It was claimed that the Walls of Jericho were rendered to rubble by a similar device and according to several authors the technology had been reinvented or rediscovered. Certainly a burst of high-frequency sound fired directly into the ear of a horse would cause erratic behaviour, an instinctive act of avoidance.

A marksman, though, would require the aim of an Olympic archer and the foreknowledge of a clairvoyant to succeed in whatever devious plan he was involved in. As a jockey with ambitions to move into journalism the sonic gun theory exercised my mind. I hunted around for evidence to substantiate the technology. I drew a blank. No acoustic engineer I spoke to would take the subject seriously. It was my father, though, who finally disabused me of the idea. He had worked with horses for fifty years, though he was in an old people's home by then, virtually made an invalid by fibrositis and rheumatoid arthritis. He's dead now but to the end he remained a fund of horsey knowledge, even if not all of his stories were what you wanted to hear from your own father.

"Sonic guns, my ass," was his typical response to my consideration of the theory. "Folk either jump to the easiest conclusion or the most stupid. It's a case of too little education or too much of the wrong sort. Think about it, my boy. Animals live in an alien world – ours. It's not the world of either their choosing or nature. It's no wonder they behave in a way humans can't always fathom."

My father lacked stimulation in the home. It was nobody's fault; he just didn't fit in. He was well looked after but he was a racing man. Horses and racing had made him the man he was and surrounded by suburban housewives with Alzheimer's and men for whom life stopped with the arrival of the pension book, he was as much an alien as the animals that were so big a part of his working life. I was the only one he could communicate with and the hardest part of my visits was leaving him to return to a similar life he had lived and still yearned for.

"Folk are quick to think horses spook at what they see or hear. Some do, I can't deny it. But a horse's nose is bigger than either its ears or eyes. In the wild they smell trouble long before they see or hear it. I could tell a tale to prove what I'm saying is right, though you mightn't think so much of me for hearing it, what with your views on cheats and what should be done with them."

I was too aware he was no saint. He was a part of a period of racing when the successful coup was an event to be celebrated. The history of the turf abounds with legends of fortunes won and lost, of horses pulled all season to land the Cambridgeshire or November Handicap at fancy odds in the autumn. Times have changed, if not the perception of the public.

I understand the shaping of his character, mind you. In fifty years he must have worked for a dozen trainers and in every yard he was probably the most knowledgeable and doubtless the most independent. Unfortunately his understanding of what made individual horses tick was not matched by an understanding of the form book. He did not stem from racing stock. His father was a ploughman, as was his father before him. He came into racing because the war took horses off the farms to be replaced by tractors. He was lucky in one respect as he was too young to be conscripted, whereas all his brothers perished in the trenches. I cannot recall how my grandfather died but I can remember my mother saying, "They might as well have cut his heart out when they took the horses from the farm. What use was a tractor to a man whose whole life was held together by the lore of the Horseman's Word?" It was my first introduction to the ancient equine knowledge.

My father did not receive his true inheritance, the passing of secret knowledge from father to son. The secrets of my grandfather's private cabinet accompanied him to the grave. He was a member of a secret society with its roots in antiquity. He knew Horse-Magic. He knew how many links there were in a Horseman's Chain. He knew the chief points of horsemanship. He knew the five points of a horse. My father only knew the rudimentary basics of the Horseman's Word from observing his father at work with his potions and lotions, his whispering and, perhaps, trickery. My father knew that the liquid in the small blue bottle calmed a frightened horse but he had no more idea than me what the constituent parts were. This is the inheritance lost to me and which the war stole from my father.

He was present at some of the feats of the Horseman's Word carried out by my grandfather and yet even as a keen observer and helper (he was a boy at the time) he was neither able to work out for himself how the feat was performed nor was he given any insight by my grandfather. He could raise a stricken horse from a ditch simply by whispering in its ear. He could stop a horse and keep it motionless for as long as it suited his purpose by commanding it to do so. Today he would be termed a horse whisperer but to him, according to my father, it was what he whispered that was the magical constituent.

I suspect his lotions and potions, his jading and drawing oils, were natural remedies, pacifiers and stimulants, known only to the equine-shamans of the time. During my grandfather's life the horse was a vital cog in the merry-go-round of life, the internal combustion engine of antiquity. Today we rely on the skills of the local vet to diagnose and treat our animals but in history it was only the certain few who could provide the remedies and get the animal back to work. Today good stable husbandry is thought of as the ability to plait a tail or secure a poultice. This is why my disinherited father could amaze people; he could draw on a well of knowledge undreamed of by his contemporaries.

He astounded a leading breeder by getting a young and valuable broodmare to accept her foal after both the senior stud-groom and the vet had failed to do so. The call for a foster mare had gone out by the time my father turned up at the stable door with a ferocious bull mastiff. There was, as you can imagine, a brief and hearty debate before he was allowed to enter the stable with the snarling brute. The mare was bred in the purple and her colt-foal was by a Derby winner; there was a great deal of money and expectation involved. To the consternation of everyone my father unleashed the dog and provoked it towards the foal. As my father expected this aroused the mare's maternal instincts and she immediately acted to protect her offspring by turning on the dog, kicking out to such effect she killed the poor beast. The mare immediately allowed the foal to suckle and everyone was amazed and happy. Everyone except the owner of the dog, I suspect.

On another occasion he heard that a famous trainer was having trouble keeping his hunter in its paddock at night. The horse was late to be gelded and in his head, and elsewhere, he was a full-blooded male. In and around Newmarket there is always a mare on heat and seemingly there was no railing, fence or gate high enough to keep this horse penned. "A horse will never leave a donkey," my father advised and sure enough on putting a donkey in with the hunter the problem was solved.

I suppose he bathed in the reflected glory of the Horseman's Word. He was not initiated into the secret society, and the true and intimate knowledge so closely guarded by his father was denied him. His own tricks, his knowledge, were repetitions of what he had observed, what anyone present at one of my grandfather's feats might also have achieved if they had thought to do so. Perhaps it was his failure to replicate what the observers had not witnessed, his inability to continue the Horse-Magic of his forebears, which caused him to drink too freely, to gamble too heavily and to steadfastly refuse to call a spade anything other than a spade.

Let me quote a story my father related to me to illustrate the power, magic or trickery of my grandfather. "'He [my grandfather] was laid up in bed with influenza. People died of influenza in those days. The doctor told him to stay off work for two weeks. He wasn't happy about it, not that he had the strength to argue. Mother had never seen him so poorly and was convinced he would die. His place on the farm was taken by his second horseman, who your grandfather didn't care for. This chap was army trained and was prone to overwork the horses. My father bore his illness with good grace but as he regained strength he started to worry about the plough horses. Finally he could stand the uncertainty no more and he sent me to spy on the second horseman. I reported that the horses were stumbling and looked pale in their coats and needed encouragement to go about their work. That was it: measures needed to be taken. 'Those horses need rest,' he told me. 'And we're going to see they get some.'

"He sent me to fetch some chimney soot, a jar of linseed oil and a handcup. 'I shall need the red tin in my cabinet and don't spill any out. And fresh water.' This was the first time I was allowed the key to his cabinet and was the most exciting thing I'd ever done. Father had one sacrosanct rule – no one was to go near his cabinet. It was kept locked and it was treated with the respect of a shrine. He combined the soot and linseed oil and added a small amount of white powder from the tin. He stirred the mixture in the handcup and tipped it into half a bucket of water. At midnight I was sent to the field where the horses were corralled to paint the solution on the gateposts. It was odourless and soaked into the posts like ordinary water and what it was supposed to achieve he wouldn't tell me. That would have ruined the magic, I suspect. In fact nothing happened, other than those normally obedient horses could not be persuaded or cajoled to pass through the gates. For three days they defied all encouragement to go about their work. The squire knew who was responsible, of course, and eventually told my mother that 'unless the magic was undone by the end of the week we would all be homeless'. So under the cover of darkness I was sent to wash the posts and the next morning the horses walked from their field without fuss.

"It's easier to stop a horse than to get it to go faster," he assured me several times. "I've stopped a few in my time. Didn't get paid much when I married and there was always some trinket or other that needed buying. I'd proved on the Heath which of your grandfather's potions were the jading oils, the stuff he must have used to get horses to stand for him. I had to dilute them, of course, and there was a bit of trial and error before I got to know what I was doing but when I got a classic colt to work like a selling plater I knew I had cracked it. When I worked for Captain Black we had a lovely colt called Albioni. He was a backward sort but a fine good looker, a real athlete. From early spring the Captain was training him for the St. Leger. I looked after this horse but never got to ride it. A lad called Stan Lake rode him every day, on the roads or on his own on the Heath. The horse was headstrong and Stan was good with that type. The Captain liked a tilt at the ring and he didn't want the touts seeing this horse work with other horses. The Captain was cute like that. One day this horse came home loose, his eyes popping out of his head, in a right lather. He was headstrong but he didn't drop people. When Stan hobbled back to the yard he said the horse went berserk over nothing and reared. As soon as I heard that I knew the cause. Smell. God didn't give horses them great nostrils without reason. 'Pigs,' I told him. 'That'll be the cause.' Stan wouldn't have it. Pig farm was two miles away, you see. Said there was no way Albioni could smell pigs from two miles away.

"Two weeks later the horse won his maiden by a country mile beating one with Piggott up; 20/1 and nobody had a penny on. He wasn't supposed to win, you see. We had another in the race that was there to win. Albioni was only there for the experience but the young lad who rode him would have had to jump off to stop him winning and he wasn't brave enough. Hadn't worked with another horse. The Captain had no way of knowing how good he really was.

"I was having bother with a bookie at the time and I needed to get him off my back. I'd asked the Captain for a loan but he sent me away with a flea in my ear. He didn't approve of the working man gambling, apparently. I didn't take kindly to that, as you can imagine, what with him pulling horses when it suited him. So I thought I'd get one over on him. I didn't have long to wait.

"The next time Albioni ran, we again ran another of ours, Fightmaster, as inappropriately named as any horse could be as he had no fight in him whatsoever. There were only four runners, Albioni having frightened away the opposition. Fightmaster was a rogue. He wore blinkers and knew every trick there was about not winning. At home nothing could live with him. It was the perfect scenario for your grandfather's oils. I told everyone that Albioni was not as good as they thought and that Fightmaster would beat him. To back my boast I had twenty-five quid on him, a king's ransom in those days. On form Albioni was a certainty. At the furlong pole Albioni was ten lengths clear, his head in his chest. Then, just like your Ile de Chypre, he veered sharply across the track, unshipping the jockey, leaving Fightmaster with no alternative but to win."

When you preach on television or in the newspaper on the integrity of the sport; when fellow jockeys are arrested and then acquitted of fixing horse races; when rumours abound of money laundering in the betting ring and a needle-man nobbling favourites; what you do not need to hear is your own father confessing to similar actions.

"You might think I spread pig-muck on the furlong pole. You'd be wrong. Our race was the first, so I had plenty of time to paint the running rail with a thin solution of jading oil. But the real trick was to get a stronger solution on the jockey's whip. You or I wouldn't smell it but it scrambles a horse's brain. At the furlong pole Albioni caught a whiff of the oil, as did the three behind if anyone noticed. But it was the jockey pulling his whip into his other hand to straighten the horse up which fired the lethal blow. Suddenly the smell was all around him, in his eyes, on his skin. I wish I knew how to make the stuff, I'd make a fortune. I won the best part of two hundred quid that day. Justice, though, prevailed, you'll be glad to know, as I dropped the bottle in the racecourse stable and Albioni stood on it. I had to wash it down a drain or they wouldn't have got a horse in that stable yard for a month.

"What do they test for these days; steroids, growth hormones, that sodium bicarbonate they pump into their stomachs? Mind you, that isn't new. They call them milkshakes, don't they nowadays. Such an innocent name for a deceit. They'd never think about an oil made in part from the crotch bone of a toad. The cure-bone as the old man referred to it. Not that he told me anything about it. The gamekeeper was always bringing livers of rabbits and stoats to him. I suppose that must be part of his old-fashioned milkshakes as well."

Hocus-pocus? Was he having me on? It would not have been the only time. Or did the society of the Horseman's Word really exist? One day I will get round to a thorough investigation. Occasionally I still bump into people who knew my father and they all have a tale to tell about him. No one speaks of jading oils and cure bones, though. And no one has ever spoken of the Horseman's Word or Horse-Magic.

The last time I spoke to him – he died a few days later – to tease me one final time, he said quite coherently, even though he was incredibly frail and bed-ridden. "I once watched your grandfather bring down a skewbald pony just like what happened to Devon Loch, you know, as if jumping an imaginary fence, simply by whistling a single note. He'd do that, your grandfather, when he had nothing better to do. Just to prove he had possession of Horse-Magic."

Second Consideration

Chris Purser, Purse to his friends, lies on a bed in the corner of the first-aid room. In an adjacent corner, thrown hastily into a heap, are his riding boots, blood-splattered breeches and the blue and gold silks he wore in the novice chase in which he met with his accident. Nearby a doctor paces nervously, wanting to hurry time, glancing out of the window, at his watch, at the broken body on the bed. Every thought, every scintilla of medical insight implores him to do more, to do something to overturn the bewildering adherence to the rules. He is, though, powerless. He has done all that he is medically capable of doing to improve his patient's chances of survival. All he can do is wait in hope that the paramedics will get Chris to hospital with enough time to spare for the surgeons to successfully do their job.

A steward also concerned at the delay half opens the door, wanting to air his sympathy without appearing to seem at conflict with the decision that has caused the holdup. "Won't be long now," he reassures. "They're at the start."

The doctor looks stony-faced at the steward. The two have coincided with an amiability bordering on friendship for many years but now, because of the delay, hostility brews within the doctor's normally urbane nature. "I should bloody well think so," he snaps. Immediately he feels he should apologise for the fervour of his sentiment, yet his emotions are entrenched. The situation he is expected to abide with is wholly unacceptable, wholly avoidable.

The steward is taken aback by the sharp response, unused to having his authority slighted. "We must have two ambulances on the course or we must suspend racing," he replies in support of his superiors. "It is the rule, as you must be aware."

The doctor remains unapologetic. He cannot extend camaraderie towards the steward, towards the rulebook, not with Chris now moaning, his pain and torment apparent to both men. "With all due respects," he answers, his patience threadbare, looking not at the steward but at Chris, "in this instance your rule stinks. This man's life is jeopardised by your adherence to the printed word."

Guilt also beats at the steward's heart, yet he must remain loyal to the judgement of his peers. "But you declared his prognosis as extremely poor."

For the doctor it is the final insult to his professional pride to have his words quoted back at him. "That is hardly the point of contention, is it?"

The steward, his conscience pricked, returns to his official duties. The doctor has not allayed his fears and the worst-case scenario remains vivid in his imagination.

The closing of the door, the draught of air emanating from its closure, or a primeval instinct to survive, brings Chris to confused consciousness. He becomes animated, his arms flailing, his knees jerking, as pain contorts his body. He is an intelligent man, with a foresight not given to the majority of his colleagues to look beyond the immediate future. He had been aware that, barring a miraculous breakthrough in his stagnating career, sooner or later he would have to look elsewhere to earn a living. He had enrolled on a journalism course. He accepted that life existed beyond the compelling thrill of race-riding. And he knew from the very moment he was catapulted into the ground that his injuries on this occasion would not be commonplace and that his future had concertinaed into uncertainty.

Pain and medication inhibit speech and muddle thought. In his mind's eye he can see flashes of Cheryl, his girlfriend, and the desire to tell her he loves her is as great as his pain. He wants to reinforce how much the previous night meant to him. Yet he cannot hold her to his presence. A more dynamic instinct intercedes: he must tell someone about the splenectomy he underwent as a teenager. It is important. But the effort to gain the attention of whoever is in the room tires him and he slumps back into comfortless sleep.

A roar of enthusiastic urgency invades the stillness of the prefabricated room. The doctor is caught by surprise and is not a little dismayed by a world which continues to revolve unaffected by the tragedy which will become the focal point of the day. Life goes on, as it will for him. Another winner for someone, a host of losers who will lose far less than the price Chris will pay for a day at the races. He rushes to the door and opens it wide in readiness for the paramedics. Once again he takes Chris' pulse and with resignation pulls the pink blanket up to his chin. The seconds tick by; long seconds which allow him time to ponder whether the thrills of race-riding truly compensate the jockeys for the sacrifices they must endure.

As the paramedics transfer Chris to their stretcher he

momentarily slips back into consciousness, flailing his arms, hitting the doctor holding aloft the intravenous drip in the midriff. Aidan Malone, still dressed in gaudy lemon and purple silks, the sweat of exertion in finishing unplaced in the previous race evident on his gaunt face, sees Chris moving and his worst fears are assuaged. They are friends. Chris is godfather to his daughter. As Chris is wheeled past him, he asks the doctor. "Will he be okay?" He expects to hear a favourable reply and is startled by the foreshadowing silence of the ashen-faced doctor. He is too concerned to have Chris conveyed speedily to hospital to issue medical reports which can only be pessimistic. As the ambulance doors are slammed closed he returns to Aidan.

"Bad," he answers succinctly, his honesty a delivery of sorrow and trepidation.

Aidan has a ride in the final race, a hot favourite, for his retained stable. He will have to fulfil the commitment, of course. He must remain professional, to do his best for the owner, the trainer, the stable staff, the punters. He would prefer to go home to his wife and daughter, where the awful testimony to his daily worship of the thrills of horsemanship will be cushioned, where familiarity will help him come to terms with a day he will never be able to forget. Yet even the simple procedure of going home is made difficult, the sadness extenuated, by having travelled to the races in Chris' car, along with Tim and Dave. To get home he will have to rifle Chris' pockets to find the car keys. Then there is Chris' dog. Fred goes everywhere with Chris and was only left behind today because of Tim Youell's allergy.

In the weighing room Aidan reports what he has seen, what the doctor said. Gloom and disbelief transform the boisterous, energised assembly into contemplative reflection. This is no time for the usual banter, for gallows humour, for the latest tale of derring-do or sexual impropriety. One of their kinsmen has been taken from their ranks and suddenly the unthinkable haunts their step.

Aidan's mobile phone pierces the silence and the prayers. It's his wife. She witnessed the fall on the Racing Channel, watched in horror as the horse galloped into the fence and shot Chris into the ground and trampled on him. Aiden listens intently to his wife's graphic description. He had ridden the horse the last time it ran and suggested to the trainer that Chris would suit the horse perfectly. He had warned him that it was an ignorant so-and-so, in need of strong handling, and the sort of educational ride he was so good at. Chris was a fine horseman, noted for being able to give horses confidence.

"It's bad, Vick," he tells his wife. "The doc reckons he's a goner."

The private conversation is a sombre broadcast for valet and jockeys alike. Oaths, curses and expletives begin to drop like leaden autumn leaves as the crushing burden of loss takes root. Those with rides in the next race go without enthusiasm to meet their connections, soldiering on, not because they want to but because it is what is expected of them. Like Chris, race-riding pays the bills.

"Vick," Aidan continues, watching Tim Youell hurry back into the weighing room for his whip, "I'll be late home. Tell Lucy I'm okay. We came with Tim and Dave. If they can't get a lift back I'll have to drive them to the service station to pick up their cars. Oh, and I'll go to Purse's house and pick up Fred, so lock up the cats. I ought to go to the hospital ..."

But Vicky has heard enough. She tells him to do whatever

he feels must be done and then to hurry home. Aidan and Purse have known each other since Aidan first came to England. She knows Chris's death will be worse than an amputation to him. It will be for her, too, as it will be for everyone. Purse was everyone's friend; the first to offer advice to the inexperienced, the last to envy those more successful than himself.

Aidan easily wins the final race. A steering job befitting an odds-on favourite, which, as Aidan admits to the owner, was all to the good as that was all he was capable of in the circumstances.

As he is gathering up Chris' belongings, the quest for glory and a winner's percentage suspended for another day, with only the valets cleaning tack in preparation for the following day for company, Chris' mobile phone rings. It is Cheryl. She has been at work all day and is unaware of what has happened.

She wants to talk about last night, about tomorrow's dance and the holiday they discussed. She is happy, in love for the first time. All day she has yearned to talk to Chris, to be with him. Hearing Aidan's voice she immediately suspects he has had a fall. "What's he broken?" she asks, her ready laugh constricted by concern.

Aidan stalls from imparting the dreadful truth. It is not yet confirmed, of course. But he knows. The emptiness at his heart tells him the worst has happened. Cheryl insists on hearing every detail and he reluctantly repeats what the doctor said to him. In the ensuring silence as she digests the dire consequence of her life ripped apart, Aidan recalls what Purse told him in confidence as they waited for Tim and Dave at the service station. He ponders whether now is the right time to tell her? What purpose could it serve? It is just something else to make the journey home more harrowing, knowing that in the glove compartment is the engagement ring Purse intended to surprise Cheryl with at the Jockeys Association Dance.

"Come over to our place, if you can't face being on your own," he tells her, implying, unwittingly, that there would be little use in her going to the hospital.

On the drive home the three hardened jockeys can only speak of Purse in the past tense, no matter how hard they tried to be optimistic. All three share the same agent, the same agent as Chris, and he has not phoned to discuss the day, to discuss tomorrow and beyond. It is the clearest indication that their prayers have not been answered.

With Tim and Dave out of the way, with Fred curled up on the back seat, Aidan knows he must phone Carl, his agent, to be told what he must be told. They talk briefly about his four rides, his two winners, his prospects for a tomorrow which cannot be avoided. The subject matter is the very bread of life, yet now, for obvious reasons, it is unpalatable, the very words tainted with disloyalty and disrespect. Carl, too, has no enthusiasm for the mechanics of their working relationship. He has already e-mailed his condolences to Chris' parents and to no avail phoned Cheryl. He has booked one of his other jockeys to ride the two horses Chris would have ridden the following day.

"It was severe internal bleeding," he informs Aidan. "There was nothing that could be done for him."

"He hadn't a spleen. Did you know?" Carl did not know. "He had a fall hunting, before he finished school. He broke a wrist and lost his spleen. He had to have a flu jab every year and take tablets for it. Something to do with his immune system, I think."

"Why isn't that sort of thing recorded in your medical book?"

It is a question Aidan has never considered and cannot answer. As a teenager he had his appendix removed and that is not recorded in his own medical book.

Near his home, at the exit off the dual carriageway, Aidan is stopped by an accident. A car has overturned, two more have collided. Police cars, a fire engine and two ambulances block both lanes. As he surveys the wreckage a thought of brilliant intensity enters his head. As a body is taken from the upturned car the thought gathers momentum: if Chris had suffered his injuries in this car accident he would be taken straight to hospital, not kept hanging around waiting for a convenient moment for an ambulance to be made available. The thought hounds him, plucking at his heart. He loves the sport which is the essence of his life. He cannot envisage a life without horses. Yet an alarm bell sounds in every pore, every blood cell, every nerve: Purse deserved better than second consideration.

Suddenly, from out of a blue yonder he never believed existed, he is confronted by a crystal-clear reality: Vicky and Lucy deserve better than second consideration. It could have been him on that horse, not Purse. Perhaps it should have been. It is an original and traumatic revelation.

Up in front the road remains blocked. An ambulance, its lights flashing, moves off at speed. Aidan picks up his phone to contact Carl. But he changes his mind. He will speak to Vicky first. She should be consulted. She is his wife and she deserves better than second consideration.

Sentiment of Fools

"Aren't you gone yet," his wife admonishes, chivvying him towards the back door, a duster in her outstretched hand.

"Give o'er, woman. The boy's gone to look at that heifer, ain't 'e." He moves out of reach, keeping the kitchen table between his best brown suit and his wife's lavender-scented rag.

"The boy, as you calls 'im," she continues to scold, "is nineteen and it's time you learnt 'is name."

Yesterday she had accused him of being 'a mean old bugger' and being responsible for their other sons leaving the farm to work elsewhere. In forty years she was never so upset with him, suggesting that Dylan, too, 'could sling 'is hook if he 'ad a mind to'.

"There's a lot of time hanging around, woman," he blusters, sitting back down at the table. "But takes no time to get there, don't it? Always mitherin' and frettin', in want of getting things done before their time." Casually he pulls his watch from his waistcoat pocket and checks its accuracy against the mantle clock on the Welsh dresser. Satisfied there is still time to squander he picks up his morning paper and turns to the racing pages.

"You ain't time for that," she castigates, flicking the duster in his direction. "And you let Dylan drive. You piddle around worse than a cow with corns." She glances out the window, out across the orderless, mucky yard, searching for her youngest son. "You're only fit for 'earse and Fordson Major."

"I always get where I'm off, don't I, woman?" he demands, his eyes not rising from the newspaper. "And I've bin to sales more reg'lar o'er the years than yer tongue has had rest. Not that it's worth a ha'pence of spit going. Too much spare cash about this time of year." He grabs hold of his battered trilby and plonks it on his bald head. "I warn you, woman," he declares, making his point stand proud, stuffing the paper into a side pocket, "I won't be wasting my hard-earned cash, not in celebration of forty years or anything like it." For a moment they glower at each other with the ire of heavyweight boxers at a weigh-in. Finally he says, hoping to bring the vocal sparring to an end, "Best go see what's keeping the boy."

"Cedric Cowmeadow!" she bellows, thinking to send a cup hurtling in his direction. "You come back here. I ain't finished with you."

"While yer thinks on," he replies with an air of flippant indifference, "keep a lookout yonder for vet. I can't be doing yer bidding and tending to farm, can I? I'm not Superman."

Cedric and 'the boy' sit silently in the canteen, each chewing on a bacon roll. Both are brooding. Dylan would rather be at home, driving the pick-up into town, fetching cattle feed, chatting up Suzy in the office, not chaperoning his father. Too often he feels the walls of the cow shed closing in on him, limiting his prospects, enslaving him to the poverty of a farmer. He is envious of his older brothers, all of whom have escaped their father's niggardly ways and are making a life for themselves away from the dead-of-night mornings and seven-days-a-week year.

Cedric is reflecting on previous visits to the sales, on horses bought and sold, on the good horses who for the want of one final bid might have been his, and the one good horse he bred and sold, the one who has made his name known throughout the racing world.

Dylan is bored. "I'll go and make sure he's here, shall I?" he asks, rising from his chair, uncertain of his father's assent. "Mum won't care for it if I don't at least have a peek at the old boy."

"Aye, lad, if that's yer instruction." Cedric watches him leave, stepping heavy-footed around protruding chairs and tables, squeezing self-consciously past slim-line stable girls. He smiles ruefully, perhaps reflectively, at his son's crimson face, at his relief at reaching the door and the open air.

Like generations before him Cedric Cowmeadow is a traditional hunting farmer. At Dulver he rears Devon Reds and Cluns, his income and interest supplemented by the breeding and selling of horses. He governs the farm in the unquestioning way of his father, unfettered by modern wisdom or ambition. Stock is sold when he can make the most profit, be they cattle, sheep or horses. "Sentiment: friend of fools. Money: friend of all," is his favourite saying. The adage was learnt from his father and he cannot understand why his sons and their mother can think differently.

On his way to the sales ring Cedric pauses to appraise the horses in the collecting ring. Little attracts his eye. He hears lot 28 called into the ring and casually looks up its pedigree in the catalogue. A mare: he has enough mares. Two city types draw his attention and he eavesdrops on their conversation. It seems they are partners in a horse soon to go under the hammer and they are still in disagreement about whether to sell; the younger of the two vehement that the horse is sure to win races during the following season. The debate is an amusement and Cedric wishes he could offer the younger man a good bit of advice: Sentiment: friend of fools. Money: friend to all.

"You here to buy back the old horse, Cowmeadow?" Colonel Aitcheson asks, touching his cap in greeting and resting an elbow on the white wooden rail that Cedric is leaning against.

"Good heavens! You knows me more than that, Colonel, surely?" He doffs his trilby and toys with the feathered brim. "No, I reckons Featherstone has had best of 'im, don't you? Broken-winded, so I'm told. No, I'm here for summit cheap to keep the old woman and the boy occupied. Haven't a point-to-point horse on the farm to learn the boy, you know."

"I saw young Dylan looking the old horse over," Aitcheson tells him, keeping an eye on the matrix board. "Look, the one I'm interested in, Cowmeadow, is due in shortly. I'll have to scootle along."

"Sentiment, Colonel. It's the old woman encouraging the boy," Cedric confides, tilting his forehead in the direction of the advancing Dylan. "Can't be doing with it myself."

"He's here," Dylan informs his father, doffing his cap in acknowledgement of Colonel Aitcheson. "Better get ourselves a seat, oughtn't we?"

"As a matter of fact, Cowmeadow," Aitcheson interrupts. "If you don't mind me asking, how much did the horse make when you sold him originally?"

Cedric draws a breath, baring his brown teeth. "Oooh, only a couple hundred o'er the thousand. Gave 'im away. Not that any of us knew it at the time."

"Bought himself a tractor on the proceeds, he did," Dylan recalls. "Could do with a replacement now, the old one's as crocked as the horse. Poor bugger!"

"You would think," the Colonel observes, distracted from his own business, "that after the races the old horse has won for Featherstone he would give him an honourable retirement, not send him here to extract the last few pounds from him. If he was an owner of mine I would set the dogs on him rather than let him in the yard. He brings the sport into disrepute."

"Lot 52," the auctioneer announces as a sixteen-hand bay gelding is led into the ring. "Dulver Brook," the auctioneer informs his prospective bidders. "Thirteen years old, winner of numerous top chases amongst his twenty-one successes. You all know him, ladies and gentleman. So who will start us off at a thousand guineas?" His enquiry is met with embarrassed silence; as if everyone is leaving it to everyone else to ensure the old horse is given a good home and not left to the meat men to fight over him. Some of the audience look to Cedric, as does the auctioneer, to see if he has raised his finger. Cedric is indifferent to their curiosity.

By increments of one hundred guineas the asked-for bid sinks to three hundred. Finally one of the knackermen standing at the entrance raises his hand and a murmur of disapproval ripples around the auditorium.

"Right, we are away," the auctioneer announces, dismayed by the apathy which is greeting his efforts to find a home for

Dulver Brook. "How about four hundred? I'll take three-fifty. He must be worth three-fifty of anyone's money, surely. He's the winner of twenty-one races remember. He must be worth taking a chance with. He is undoubtedly one of the most popular horses of recent times." Another of the meat men raises his hand. "I have four hundred at the back," he reminds his clientele. "Four-fifty, then? Remember, this horse was unlucky not to win the Gold Cup. I'll eat this gavel without H.P. sauce if he can't win a point-to-point." A trickle of leaden laughter creeps around the auditorium and again people look to Cedric.

Dylan nudges his father's arm. "If mum finds out he's gone to knackers she'll never speak to you again," he whispers through clenched teeth.

"If only it were that simple, lad," his father replies, unruffled by the ripening of tension. "Sentiment is ..."

"Yes. And you're no fool. We've heard it all before."

"This grand old campaigner is sold without reserve, let me remind you," the auctioneer continues. "He is warranted sound in both limb and lung. You know his history, so how about one more bid? For only five hundred guineas you can take home with you one of the best chasers of modern times."

Reluctantly he raises his gavel, his eyes alert for one last bid. "So he's going for four hundred and fifty guineas to the man at the door." He pauses, the gavel high in the air, hovering like an executioner's axe. "For the last time then. Four hundred and fifty guineas it is." He searches the auditorium again, seeking guidance from his spotters. "Come on, gentleman, ladies," he beseeches, his professional poise in peril. He lowers the gavel, its downward spiral halted by a desperate cry of "Five hundred!"

Cedric straightens his back and glares resolutely towards

the auctioneer's rostrum, Dylan cowering at his side, shocked by the impetuosity of his actions. "I was wondering when you'd crack, boy," his father chides through the side of his mouth.

"Is that last bid genuine?" the auctioneer enquires, his fingers crossed.

Beads of sweat appear on Dylan's brow. He has not got five hundred guineas in his bank account. He cannot pay for the horse. This is the first time he has challenged his father and he can hardly breathe for the leaping of his heart. He stares at his father, fearful of rejection and reprisals.

"Aye, I reckon it is," his father answers the auctioneer and a collective sigh reverberates around the auditorium, cushioning and obliterating a call of six hundred from the entrance.

"Sold to Mr. Cowmeadow for five hundred guineas," the auctioneer declares, bringing the gavel down hard in unrestrained triumph. "Ladies and gentlemen, the old horse is going home. Please give Dulver Brook and Mr. Cowmeadow a hearty round of applause. I am sure Mrs. Cowmeadow will be truly grateful to see the old horse come off the lorry tonight, eh Cedric?"

Three cheers are proposed as Cedric rises from his seat and Dulver Brook, applauded as in the days when he was a big race winner, his attendant tearful and smiling, stops adjacent his breeder and neighs in appreciation of the forced kindness.

As he makes his way to the exit Cedric is waylaid by well-wishers. The attention startles him. To his astonishment he can see grown men hiding their faces behind handkerchiefs, some of them unashamed of their tears.

"I'll phone Mum and tell her the news, shall I?" Dylan asks as they break free of the throng.

"No, boy, let her be as surprised as me," his father tells him, putting a bundle of fifty pound notes in his son's hand."

"I can't wait to see Mum's face when old Dulver Brook arrives. It's not what she's expecting, not by a long mile."

"You think I'll get some peace, do you, boy?" Cedric asks, mopping his brow with the sleeve of his coat. "Well, boy?"

"It'll make up for forgetting your silver wedding anniversary, I should think."

"You'd better go sign for 'im, then." He spits on the ground and watches Dylan run like a schoolboy to the sales office. "Boy," he shouts after him, "and who said I'd forgotten anything? I'm no fool, you know. I've just bought a horse for less than half what I sold 'im for. Money; friend to all. Sentiment ..." But Dylan has run on. He's heard it all before.

Yes, I Fear He Is.
I Fear He Is.

Pat and Paddy ride along the narrow lane that leads to the schooling ground. Pat rides the horse all of Ireland refers to as 'Himself'. Paddy is aboard steeplechasing's pretender to the crown of 'best there has ever been'. It is remarkable on its own for two great horses to appear on the scene at the same time but for them to be stable companions reaches deep into the fantastic realm of fiction.

Pat is stable jockey, Paddy an ex-jockey of vast experience. Both are invaluable members of the team. Yet both are nervous. Racing's great attractions are to school together for the first time and both Pat and Paddy think it is chancing fate and speculate on why the boss has allowed himself to be talked into it.

Neither horse needs to be schooled and ordinarily would not be. But the Dublin press have sweet-talked Tom into staging 'a show' for their benefit, citing a need to give the public pictures of the great horses together. Pat and Paddy are far from convinced. The Duchess would certainly not approve and it is no surprise to either of them to hear that Tom has omitted to inform her of the day's happening.

"But all we will be doing is popping them over a few fences.

It'll be no different from coming back to the stables up the jumping lane."

Pat senses that 'Himself' is keen and unusually fractious, as if he knows the younger horse is a threat to his supremacy. The 'Pretender', by nature a more buzzy horse, champs eagerly at the bit, as if he too senses this cannot be an ordinary day. Their riders try to remain calm and chat away about the stable's runners for the week, assessing their prospects and gnawing over tactics and weaknesses in their opposition. But they cannot entirely forget they are astride two colossi of the sport that is the foundation and history of their lives.

The two horses are trotted around in a wide circle while Tom and the journalists up from Dublin exchange opinion on procedure. The photographers are adamant they need the horses to jump as many fences as possible, allowing them the greatest opportunity to capture for posterity spectacular and unique pictures. Tom is equally adamant that the horses will only be schooled once over the row of three fences. The debate continues; the disconnected massed intonations of the press and the lone calm voice of the professional racehorse trainer. All the while the bay and the chestnut jog around in a circle, their excited vitality contained by the soft hands and perfect poise of their skilful riders.

"I shouldn't be schooling at all," Tom tells his behatted adversaries, his eagle eye focused on his horses. Better armed, though, by dint of numbers the journalists rally their argument, declaring the exercise a waste of everyone's time if they go home without a satisfactory story and exciting photographs.

Alarmed by the lengthening of the delay Tom issues an ultimatum. "Once over the schooling fences or not at all."

His place in Irish racing history ensures him respect with even the most diehard journalist and begrudgingly they capitulate and the photographers scuttle away to secure the best vantage points – some favouring the last fence, hoping that by then the two horses will be in full, unrestrainable flight; while the majority choose the first fence. Only one man positions himself close to the second fence.

Finally Tom signals for the schooling to begin, his affirming nod of the head as anticipated by the small audience as the rising of the tapes at Aintree or Cheltenham.

"We had best go in upsides," Pat suggests, gathering up the reins.

"Ay, and heaven help us," Paddy answers as they set themselves for the short run to the first fence. "We'll need the help of all the saints if one of us gets half-lengthed."

Unbidden the horses break into a canter, straining to be let loose at the fences. Both men cry "Steady" but their steeds disobey as they are both intent upon gaining the ascendancy. The first fence looms up, small yet ominous, hammered out of its original dimensions by decades of constant use. Inside the wing of the fence both horses rise as one; the rivalry as competitive as any duel up the Cheltenham hill: the Pretender determined to lead, Himself as determined not to be led. It is a battle of equine wills; a dispute of equine pride. For the first time on the great horse Pat feels out of control. Both riders would like to stop and start again; the thrill negated by discord. Tom shouts for them to slow down but his plea goes unheeded, unheard. The photographers hold their breath and snap away, each one congratulating himself on achieving the occasion.

The two horses lengthen once more and sprint for the

second fence. Grasping the air they fly its inconsequential height in high-spirited unison: the Pretender inch perfect, Himself, in his exuberance to match the impetuosity of his rival, knuckling over, his nose scraping the earth, spilling Pat over his ears.

It is the first time the great horse has met the rising ground and for an immediate moment the world is put on pause, as if the Creator must take stock of the situation in order to remedy the calamity. The press, each and every one of them, exclaim profanities which only the confessional can excuse them from. Tom, his face ghost-like, averts his eyes, a prayer for forgiveness engraved at his heart.

The Pretender gallops on unnoticed. He leaps the final fence as impeccably as the two before and bowls along into the distance, his stride unchecked, still keen to prove his superiority. Finally Paddy persuades him to a trot and looks left and right, astonished and dismayed to find he is alone. "Merciful Father!" he cries, fearful of what he might see in the distance, his every thought a hope for the avoidance of catastrophe.

Pat is on his feet, his comments of more importance to the press than his health. The great horse is also on his feet, waiting for Tom to take charge of him.

The cold chill of alarm subsides and relief counters despondency. The photographers refocus their cameras and return to work, picturing for posterity the aftermath of near tragedy. The journalists, hyped up by the unique opportunity that has unexpectedly blown their way, pull out pencil and notebook and start to piece together the sequence of events, thinking of subtle ways to apportion blame, recognising that they are witness to something hitherto unseen, something of which the British press will be in ignorance of.

Tom struggles with his conscience. He knows that ultimately he is to blame – the horse and Pat could have been hurt. He tries to remain calm, in charge of proceedings. It was a calamitous misjudgement. But it is done. He cannot undo the tangled minutes that have passed his grasp. Yet he cannot help but think about the Duchess. What will she say when she finds out her beloved horse has taken a tumble schooling for the benefit of the newspapers? She has horses trained in England. She could transfer Himself to one of her English trainers. If that happens and the reason for it is made public his reputation would be as shot as a grouse on one of her highland estates. He must, he decides, have the incident suppressed.

He suggests to the journalists that the predicament that has befallen him has at its roots their arm-twisting but they are in no mood for compromise; a golden scoop has been gifted them, there is great profit and kudos to be gained from its exploitation. Newsworthy stories are their livelihood and any story involving Himself transcends the sports pages.

"Ah, but you see, Tom, now the majority of us would surely oblige you but it only takes one to break rank and the rest of us poor souls will look right ejits in the eyes of our hard-nosed editors. We also are in a predicament. Hasn't the pictures man of the Irish Times alone amongst us had a picture of the great horse falling?"

The man in question, his homburg hat askew above a sheepish look of pride, smiles to his envious, glowering colleagues; the power of the moment belonging solely to him.

"It would be a source of national shame if the Duchess took Himself across the water," Tom reminds them. "Who would benefit then? The English press, maybe?"

Reflection and second thought is now the new order. It is an incredulous supposition; a spectre too woeful to be speculated on for long. "Is that likely? After all you have won with him?" a journalist asks, speaking for the whole of Ireland.

"Why should she not?" Tom answers. "I am responsible for what has happened this morning. I may put the blame on you but she quite rightly will lay the blame at my door."

"Not after two Gold Cups, surely?"

"The Duchess pays the bills," Tom reminds them, deflecting guilt towards them. "But I am sure there'll be a compromise, don't you think, boys?"

A third Gold Cup is duly won. April brings sunshine and relaxation and with the height of the season achieved the promise is honoured to host a private celebration for those who witnessed that awful day when history might have been turned on its head.

The party is alfresco, in the stable yard, with journalists and photographers mingling with stable staff, drinks in hand, the stabled horses, Himself and the Pretender included, taking a keen interest in the invasion. Reminiscences are exchanged, good and bad jokes told, tales of gambles lost and won embellished and distorted by the passing of the ages.

The editor of a parochial magazine approaches Tom and Pat as they discuss the following day's work. Without preamble he interrupts their conversation, recollecting a race meeting at Navan before the war, imperiously assuming credit for introducing Tom, then a struggling farmer with only a handful of point-to-pointers to his name, to Edward Rank, a wealthy owner in need of someone to take charge of a rebellious young horse he had acquired. Tom easily remembers the occasion and the horse and instinctively looks across the cobbled yard to the stone stable which all those years ago had housed his first great steeplechaser.

"Unbeatable, nearly, over here, wasn't he?" the editor recalls. "If it wasn't for Herr Hitler he would have won more Gold Cups than any horse living. More than one, that's for sure." To Pat he adds. "Third in the Grand National after the war. Twelve-seven he carried and not beaten far. What would he have achieved if the English had raced throughout the war as we did? Best horse I ever damn saw and I'm older than the Mountains of Mourne."

Pat nods his head. He too knows of the exploits of Tom's most revered horse, the horse that won Tom his career, which has now peaked with Himself. He turns to his employer and friend for him to add his own recollection and is surprised to see tears forming in the old man's eyes.

A young fledgling journalist, an underling at The Field, joins them, a whiskey too large for his constitution in his hand. "Himself, sir, must now be the best horse you have trained. Or ever likely to, perhaps?"

To the three men gathered around Tom it seems an innocuous question, with the answer as obvious as the question is unnecessary. But in his mind's eye Tom can visualise what the others cannot. He can see Prince Regent and knows he can never repay the debt owed to him. Yet the truth cannot be denied. "Yes," he admits, his heart caught in an act of disloyalty. "Yes, I fear he is. I fear he is."

One of the Reasons I Am Now a Pinhooker

Jockeys usually retire because of either injury or financial necessity. Very few of us go voluntarily. Some jockeys start to see a red light at every fence, even the very best. Some just cannot face the consequences of another serious fall. Some cannot see where next month's mortgage payment is coming from. Occasionally a jockey must retire because his injuries do not allow him to walk unaided let alone sit astride a big powerful horse. Occasionally, thankfully rarely, a jockey will leave the sport at the same time as he leaves life itself.

Jockeys such as myself suffer tribulations that are all too easily glossed over by the media and those who police our sport. Visits to casualty departments are taken as part and parcel of the job. It is as if we were born to make sacrifices of our bodies. Cry not for us, though. We wouldn't have it any other way. We are heroes, even if some might think us villains or fools.

"Maxieee. Maxieee." I spun round. It was Melissa. Her demonstrations of affection for me come with too much verve for the public arena. "You were brilliant," she said effusively.

"No one else could have won on that old monkey!" It was high praise, if totally undeserved.

But who was I to contradict her? The jockeys coming out for the next race also heard her lavish praise and each and every one had their own contradictions. It was common gossip in the weighing room that Melissa Forbes had her eye on me but it was impossible and not exactly in my interests to side-step her on every occasion.

"Mrs. Forbes," I replied, emphasising her marital status. "Thank you. Sometimes we get the luck we deserve."

For all of her honey-blonde beauty and Cheltenham Ladies' College vowels Melissa was a fine horsewoman, winner of Ladies' Opens on the point-to-point circuit, and she did in fact know what she was talking about. Siren Sound was a bit of monkey, a horse with many ways of getting himself beat. Occasionally, though, if you allowed him to think he was in control, he consented to put his true talent on show.

"'Gently they go, the beautiful, the tender, the kind. Quietly they go, the intelligent, the witty, the brave.' Do you think, Max, that Millay had jump jockeys in mind when she penned those lines?"

We were watching the lads getting mounted, sorting out their stirrup irons and knotting their reins as they circulated the paddock. "I doubt if any of them consider themselves beautiful, Melissa, though some of the females who now share our perils are worth a second glance." In the weighing room I had the reputation of being something of a scholar. Or knobhead, as some like to think of me. I could be found between rides reading proper books and not just the Racing Post. "On the whole American poets know as much about National Hunt jockeys as National Hunt jockeys know about American poets."

It was a characteristic December day: grey and cold. Trainers and stewards hurried past in their winter finest, while I stood glowing from winning the previous race in my thin breeches, boots, body protector and unzipped anorak. Melissa wore her sable coat and hat. She looked like a Scandinavian princess. As much as it was flattering my ego to be seen with her, I needed to find Paul Lickorish to see if he was still running his good horse on the Saturday. Having done all the schooling I thought he was obliged to have me ride it. Not that it always worked out like that. Owners quite often wanted the best and jockeys of my ilk were not really thought of as being in the big-race category. But Melissa was important; her husband had just started training and had the considerable advantage of being bankrolled by his father's sizeable fortune. "How are the horses?" I asked, noticing Paul at the far end of the paddock. "I haven't been down to school recently."

"You know how it is, Max, some are four-legged, others three." She laughed. It was the sort of laugh to warm the coldest day.

"You lost one yesterday," I needlessly reminded her, wanting to preserve my connection with, if not her, her husband.

"Yes. Hill of Joy. Poor thing. I used to ride him at home." Her bright face clouded over and I knew she was about to confide in me whether I wanted it or not. "Big Daddy not happy." She forced a smile but I could see something unmanageable was tugging at her heartstrings. "It's the third this season. We could do with some luck. I wish I could distance myself from the bad side of things but I can't. The horses are my babies. Not that Big Daddy sees it like that. To him it is his investment that is dying, his reputation dragged over the coals of our bad luck."

I had the misfortune of riding their first casualty, a nice chestnut called Capricorn. I was schooling and riding for the Forbes yard on a regular basis at the time. It was how I met Melissa. It remains a sad and bad memory. I was counting my lucky stars that I had got away from a dreadful fall without injury when I saw the distressed stable girl running across the course to get to her old friend before the vet could do his torrid duty.

I was about to go after Paul when Melissa laid a gloved hand on my arm. "Max, will you do me a big favour? It will be worth your while, I promise. Adam is being beastly about my mother's young horse. It's an involved tale, not worth the telling. I need someone to get him going. I know he's worth persevering with and it would please my mother. Adam says he's dangerous and unbreakable. But you have such lovely soft hands. I'm sure you will succeed where everyone else has failed."

Which is how The Maverick came into my life, and how I came to be involved with Melissa Forbes.

The Maverick was a chestnut gelding with three white socks and a four-pointed star on his handsome head. He was a nice sort, compact and racy, with a kind nature, though as fractious as a kite, with a box of tricks when spooked, which was, seemingly, a hundred times a day. But there was a lot to like about him even on first sight: good bone, nice big ears, athletic and related to a whole host of good horses. His problem, as it is with many troublesome horses, was that he was overdone and over-indulged: too much grub and not enough work, as anyone with half an Oxo cube for a brain should have recognised.

The attraction to the project was not wholly the horse, though. It was not even Melissa. I had enough casual relationships on the boil to keep me happy. No, the attraction was her husband and the empire constructed on his behalf. I had ridden a few for the stable earlier in the season. Bottom of the handicap types, horses in need of an educational run, the type of horse top jockeys were either too heavy to ride or did not want to ride. Perhaps because of Capricorn, though that was not my fault, I had lost favour.

Adam was not an established trainer and despite the quality of horse in his stable his winner to runner ratio was poor. He would always train winners, though; he couldn't fail to given the facilities he had at his disposal and the quality of horse his wealthy owners could afford to buy. If I could get my feet under his kitchen table it would do wonders for both my career and my bank balance. The Maverick was, I suppose, a sprat to catch a mackerel.

Adam's father was someone big in the International Futures Market. He was an elusive man. He was never seen at the races, even when a horse he owned was running. Sladely Park, the private estate where Adam trained, was an investment, a safe haven for money he did not want the Inland Revenue to get their hands on. I read in the Financial Times that he intended to develop it into a training facility to rival any in Europe. I heard that George Soros was there one day, which was believable as that was the type of financial wizard Victor Forbes was known to hang out with.

Because of the wherewithal Adam had access to he was envied and his successes, as minor as they were in comparison to the ammunition he had to take aim with, were disparaged, which I thought unfair and not wholly deserved. He was a young man under pressure, a good deal of it thrust onto him by his father, or 'The Big Daddy' as Melissa referred to him.

The Maverick was stabled away from the main yard, in a disused cow shed, the large corrugated-steel gates tied open to allow the horse limited exercise to a high-walled crew-yard. It was the antithesis of the solid brass bolts, clock tower and surveillance cameras of the red-brick stables of the main yard. Melissa was unhappy with the discrimination and her first instruction was to get the horse back to the stables.

"Look, Jacobs, the horse is a nuisance. His antics upsets the other horses. You must be on your uppers to be bothering with it, that's all I can think."

I had caught Adam at a bad moment. A frazzled housekeeper had told me to go straight into the kitchen. He had a mobile phone embedded in his ear, his face a perplexity of concern and frustration. His introductory welcome was made as he poured himself a whiskey. It was a quarter to one. It must have been a demanding morning. Outside, lads swept the concrete frontage of the stables and raked the yellow gravel. It was almost a scene from the nineteen forties or fifties. "I suppose out of good manners I should offer you a drink," he continued, his plummy accent softened by a long gulp of Jack Daniels. "But too many calories for you to accept, I suppose. My one advantage, I suspect, I have over you." He poured himself a second glass and sat down at the kitchen table, remembering my Christian name as he did so.

"Max. That horse weaves, box-walks and we waste too much ruddy time chasing after him as he pisses off across the estate. No one can ride him and I am fed up having to take people to hospital who have fallen off the bugger. Melissa may not like it but he's off to the sales in March. I only wish I could get rid ..." But the phone interrupted him, leaving me dangling, wondering whether it was Melissa he wanted to be rid of.

The kitchen still bore evidence of breakfast, which indicated all was not well with the domestic arrangements. "If this horse is going to the sales why is your wife paying me to break him in?"

"Max. The horse is broken in. It's a bastard to ride. Why are you risking your neck, that's the question, not what is Melissa's motivation?"

As I watched him brooding over a glass of whiskey at one in the afternoon I could not help but wonder how he managed to attract Melissa. He might be wealthy but he was not an attractive man. What handsomeness he might possess was tarnished by an ugly crescent-shaped scar under his right eye and his smile was as crooked as a Great Train Robber's tax return, giving him the appearance of sneering even when he was happy. He also was never seen without gold cuff-links, a gold pocket watch and chain and three-piece woollen suit. He was thirty years old and dressed like a fifty-year-old from the nineteen fifties.

"She's a bitch, you know. If I were you, Max, I wouldn't mess with her. It wouldn't be worth it, not for one crazy horse."

It was then, as he stared at me over the lip of a whiskey glass, that my opinion of Melissa as being nothing more than a man-hunter changed, as did my opinion of Adam. The one thing I like to see and hear in a trainer is for them to ask why a horse behaves as it does and to have a burning desire to find a cure, a solution.

"I have influential people on my books," he said as I left.

"You would do well to remember that."

* * *

Rides became scarce: extraneous interference or too many good young riders coming through? I had an agent but I was just one jockey amongst so many others he had to find rides for. I was suffering days without a ride and not riding regularly affects your confidence, and riding well is as much about confidence as it is about ability.

The Maverick kept me busy, though. Melissa had him moved to her parents' farm, which was closer to where I lived. I went back to basics with him, treating him as if he had never had a saddle on. I lunged and long-reined him until my arms ached. He was keen and responsive, with a light-mouth, and eager to work, if skittish. I prefer to break a horse on my own, without assistance, so that I can jabber to him any nonsense I like and so the horse is not distracted by the movements of someone else. Even when sitting on a horse for the first time I prefer to be on my own. I flatter myself that I am good at breaking in young horses. My main aim is to get their trust, much like these horse whisperers do, which is better achieved on your own.

The first time I attempted to ease myself across his withers he exploded like a jack-in-the-box, bucking and plunging as if he had hot plates on his feet. I landed on my backside. But the success was in the horse standing still, looking at me as if to assess how many bones I had broken, and not galloping off, even if he couldn't get very far in the enclosed space we were in. Eventually, to my surprise, perhaps due to an attack of conscience, the horse came to me, nuzzling my shoulder, inviting me not to give up on him. So I had another go, with almost exactly the same result!

There is a maxim that I subscribe to: 'never have a battle with a horse that you cannot win'. After a third failure to get across his back I decided to eat humble pie and ask Melissa's mother to come to my aid. With Kay Watts-Gordon at his head he consented to be led with me hanging across his back like a sack of potatoes. We did this for three days. I got to know every shred of the artificial surface of the small manège.

On the fourth day I sat astride him. I sat like a limpet as he Catherine-wheeled around the ménage. If I loosed the reins he plunged forward. If I gathered up the reins to take hold of him he bucked like a bronco.

If I kicked him the belly he went off like a bullet.

"That horse has got a back problem," Kay said as I pulled myself up from the ground. "When he tenses his muscles it hurts him. I'll phone Lydia Spink, she'll put him right. She got the Captain's brother on his feet when the doctors at the hospital couldn't."

I didn't know who Lydia Spink was, though I assumed she was someone who specialised in putting horses' backs right. She came the same day, closing the stable door to allow herself privacy, perhaps to protect whatever magic art she practised, to emerge half an hour later to say the horse was now okay and for me to proceed with caution. What she did, what she manipulated, I don't know but a week later I was riding the horse around the farm, in and out of buildings that before would have frightened him to death, past tractors and along country lanes. He still managed to drop me but old habits are hard to dislodge. But he never once reared, which in a horse is a sign of cowardice, and never ran off when loose.

It became routine before I dashed off to the races to have a cup of coffee with the Watts-Gordons in their cosy farmhouse kitchen. The house was a menagerie, swarming with cats and dogs, a parrot flying free in the conservatory with a tame jackdaw for company. They treated me like family, which was something new to experience. Sometimes Melissa joined us, a Melissa I had not seen before, a loving daughter who obviously doted on her parents. Captain Watts-Gordon, or 'the Captain' as he was referred to, was in a wheelchair, paralysed in a hunting accident, and yet in spite of his disability he was as cheerful a man as you could wish to know.

"Need something to occupy the old mind, Max. Any ideas? Nothing like the risk of losing your hard-earned to concentrate the mind. Thought about buying foals to sell as yearlings. What do you think? Kay reckons it's too risky but that's what I want. You're an expert, or that's the line Melissa is spinning about you. So it's now time to prove your mettle. As you can see, Kay fritters away what money we have buying what can only be described as tat, so it's up to me to demonstrate how to turn a profit."

"And that, Max, from someone who cannot pass a second-hand bookshop without seeing a book he simply must have even though we both know he is unlikely to ever get round to reading it," Kay remonstrated. But the exchange of smiles told the true story of their relationship.

"Pinhooking," I suggested without elaboration.

"Another damn Americanism! But yes. Money in it?"

"Sandy McEvoy lost a packet, I know. But others make a fair living at it. You need luck, as with all things equine, but it is also about having a good eye for how a foal will develop and knowing what first and second-season stallions are attracting good quality broodmares and the type of stock they are throwing."

It was easy to see that I had not impressed Kay. "Too risky for greenhorns like us is what you are saying, isn't it, Max?"

But it was not for me to advise them on ways to lose their money.

By the time we got The Maverick to the racecourse Melissa and Adam had separated and on my recommendations the Watt-Gordons sent the horse to Paul Lickorish. It was May and all of Paul's good horses were out to grass. I had ridden a couple of winners for him, including pulling off a bit of a coup at Market Rasen which the press made a big deal out of. We were asked by the stewards to explain the horse's previous run, his first for two years, and why I had pulled him up. They recorded our explanation, which meant they didn't believe us but had no evidence to disprove our case. The horse had a history of respiratory problems and it was in fact a brilliant stroke of training on Paul's part but that was overlooked because the owners had taken a sizeable amount of money off the bookies. Paul was incensed and who could blame him.

The owners may have won a suitcase of money but all I got out of it was my riding fee and seven and a half percent of two grand. Paul gave me rides and occasional winners but I had to drive to Hexham, Sedgefield and Cartmel to get them and if you don't know where those racecourses are believe me they are a long way from where I live. So you can understand why The Maverick had become my white hope. He was my ride. Only bad luck could lose me the ride when he matured into the good horse I was sure he would become.

Worcester is a nice track for a young horse: two longish straights, two easy bends. I regarded it as a lucky course.

I was told to drop in, take my time and to organise and educate the horse. Paul kept reminding me that The Maverick was a horse for next season and that I was not to use my whip on him. "Better an easy season than a hard-ridden winner," he reminded me as I left the parade ring.

For the time of year it was a good bumper. Adam Forbes had a runner, which added spice. To show he was a bad loser even before the race had started he said as I passed him. "Fall off, Max. It will make my day."

In the parade ring The Maverick was on edge but once on the course he settled down. Horses that are excitable at home can sometimes be amenable on the racecourse. As the tapes went up he hung back, caught by surprise, and we lost a few lengths. We went a sensible gallop. Young horses, which bumpers are for, can be as clumsy as teenagers and it can test even the best of jockeys to keep them straight and settled. Being in a pack, with jockeys urging and hustling, shouting for room, goading, squeezing, asking questions not before asked, is a new experience for them. Nothing they do at home can fully prepare them for the racing experience.

From last place I moved upsides the horses immediately in front of me. I shortened my reins and squeezed him into the bridle and I was excited by the response I got. Lengthening his stride he passed a few. Pat O'Sullivan came with me. He's the chatty sort and commented how well my horse moved. I steadied and allowed The Maverick to fill his lungs. I wanted him to run to the line, to impress the Watt-Gordons.

Turning into the home straight horses were dropping back and I found myself closer to the lead than planned. I was happy, even if I was twenty-five lengths off the leader. I was mid-division, letting him run in my hands, on the bridle. All up the straight I passed horses. At the line we were sixth of nineteen runners, a pleasing first run and not beaten more than ten lengths by the winner.

Everyone was pleased. So to say I was surprised to be summoned by the steward's secretary is putting it mildly. "The stewards are not convinced you made sufficient effort to obtain the best possible placing," he said curtly, as if it was my intention to keep him from his supper. "Rule 152," he added, as if I didn't know what rule I was accused of breaching.

I had come to the races with Bobby Leavy and he wanted to get home. "Be a good boy, Max, and call them sir, agree with everything they say, plead guilty and thank them kindly for depriving you of your living," he advised, putting his own interests before natural justice.

Paul was also summoned, to explain what instructions he had given me. We had nothing to hide and he confirmed what I had already told them. The Market Rasen affair still rankled with him and he unwisely reminded them that we were 50/1 outsiders and that no punter could have lost money even if I had ridden an injudicious race. We watched videos of the race from all angles, all of which told the story of my hands and heels effort. I did not pick up my whip once; in a handicap hurdle it would be a hard case to defend but this was a bumper, a race designed to educate young horses and to be honest I could not believe I was being asked to defend my ride.

I regaled the stewards with The Maverick's history and

reiterated my instructions and tried not to think of the names Bobby would be calling me for dragging out the enquiry. Our defence, though, fell on deaf ears and I was suspended for seven days and Paul fined £1,500 for not instructing me to gain the best possible placing. Even though sixth was probably the best the horse could have done.

"This is about the Market Rasen race," Paul fumed. "They had no evidence then, so they've saved it for now."

He may have been right, many thought the same, but that is how the system works. I thought about appealing but as Bobby said on the way home. "They'll only add two days for the temerity of questioning the decision. You would do better to have a holiday."

Undeniably it was a poor decision, probably born out of malice. It was premeditated, a decision which undermined the principles of justice. It was like being robbed at knife-point. They declared me a cheat and there was nothing I could do about it. My previous good character was not even given an airing.

When I got home, to add insult to injury, there was a letter from the bank suggesting an interview to discuss my overdraft. A bad, bad day was just about to go viral when Melissa rang. "The Captain wants to know when you are going to give him a decision on this pinhooking venture. He's quite keen and he's got more money than he lets on."

I had not realised that the conversation we had had was in any way a business proposal but the more I thought about it the more it seemed fated that I should hand in my jockey's licence and do something else with my life. And then Melissa suggested we, even though I had also not realised she thought of us as a couple, should go on holiday to Mustique to dot the i's and cross the t's of her father's proposal.

And that is the reason I am now a pinhooker and not a jockey.

The Mortgage, the Kids, the Wife, the Dreams...

The children are noisily, messily, eating their Sunday roast. Their mother looks on disapprovingly, watching their food spread outwards from their plates. She reproves them once more, wanting them to have the manners of their grandparents, to be well-brought-up children. She also cannot stop looking anxiously at the clock: Mickey, her husband, is late.

It has crossed her mind several times to phone him, to phone John Heath to make sure the schooling session has gone without incident. But she knows Mickey would be offended and that if word got round the weighing room that she was leaving messages for him, as if she did not trust him, he would be ribbed without mercy by his fellow jockeys, many of whom remain, despite his close proximity to them, his heroes.

She takes a deep breath and cajoles Edward, her eldest, into finishing his meat and encourages Patrick to eat his roast potatoes. She turns her back and they pull faces at one another and attempt to push a marrowfat pea up one another's noses, further extending the circumference of their meal. In resignation to her failure she picks up their plates and scrapes their leftovers into the dog's bowl. Outside a car passes by and she looks up but it continues down the lane.

"Here, she tells Edward. "Take Davey's bowl out to him. He'll appreciate that nice meal I cooked if you two mongrels don't."

"Where's Daddy?" Edward asks, his tone demanding.

"I've told you where he is, he's schooling horses for Mr. Heath," she replies negligently. Edward catches her agitation and stares dumbly back at her, uncertain if he has upset her. Penitently she adds. "He won't be long, sweetheart. You know Daddy, nothing ever hurries him."

Another glance out of the window and she removes the rice pudding from the oven and places it to cool on the window sill. As long as she is occupied she can keep her concerns at bay. Mickey getting himself hurt is never far from her mind and today he is schooling the horse he calls 'the big boat', a raw-boned horse with no mouth and less sense, a horse the stable jockey refuses to ride, and it takes little imagination to think it has trampled on Mickey, reared over with him, or thrown him off, breaking who knows what bones. Injury-wise the season has been kind to them, the best since they were married. But the law of averages, of diminishing returns, ensures that sooner or later it will be his turn to take a ride to hospital in the back of an ambulance. And Mickey is not getting any younger.

Since the turn of the year the waiting around for his homecomings have become unbearable, with every phone call in his absence firing dire warnings at her heart. Yet she knew what she was getting involved with when she married Mickey Galloway. From grandfather onwards the Galloway boys have been jockeys and there is nothing she could say which would dissuade Mickey from wanting to ride over fences. But she is determined to do all she can to persuade Edward and Patrick away from racing.

Finally she hears the familiar sound of Mickey's car coming to a halt in the drive and with a quickening heart she steals a look out of the window. As he alights from the ageing saloon he notices her suffering expression and flashes the warm, disarming smile that always, or nearly always, dissolves the tension of being married to a journeyman steeplechase jockey. She waves in acknowledgement of his safe return and with festooning relief clears a place at the table for him.

"How's my boys?" he asks playfully, pushing open the back door with his foot and dropping his kit-bag next to the washing machine. He pecks his wife on the cheek and pats her bottom. Washing his hands at the sink he tells the boys to clean his car and takes their silence as an affirmative.

"You're late," she reminds him, producing from under the grill a plate of mixed vegetables and a small steak, only slightly spoiled.

"Sorry, Kath, but you knows what it's like. You goes to school one and you ends up riding four. T.B. was there on his crutches, rattling on about his wedding. I suppose we chin-wagged a bit long as well. He'll not ride again this season." He sits at the table and grins and winks at his mischievous sons. In turn they mimic him and laugh at their effrontery.

"They don't need your encouragement to be silly," Kath scolds.

"Sorry, love. Go, boys, and get me car washed. Standing there getting me into hot water with your mammy."

"How many of these four horses will you actually get to ride on the racecourse?" she asks, upset by how few rides he gets from John Heath despite all the work he puts in.

"If its owner don't put the block on I ride the Dalakhani gelding next week at Hereford," he informs her, perversely pleased by the opportunity to ride a horse that has fallen in its last two races. "Perhaps all of them. Who can tell? A ride is a ride, you knows the score as well as I do. And I got paid for today. That's sixty quid."

Kath turns away, her silence representing her argument, and serves the boys their rice pudding. "If you get around to presenting an invoice?"

"I'll get some paperwork done this week. I promise."

"Hear that, boys," Kath addresses her sons. "Daddy will be using his office this week so you had better get your bikes out of there."

"This Dalakhani horse is good, believe me. As mad as a wet hen but really good," Mickey defends himself. "It's the sort of horse that might lead to something."

Without responding to his enthusiasm Kath switches on the kettle and starts to load the dishwasher, recalling all the other dodgy no-hopers he has ridden that have not led to something. Waiting for the kettle to boil she watches Mickey eat his frugal meal, the biggest meal he will eat all week, knowing that nothing will tempt him into eating even a spoonful of the rice pudding, even though rice pudding is his favourite dessert.

Kath issues the boys with buckets of soapy water and sponges and directs them towards the car. It is certain that they will soak each other and the car will be little cleaner for their efforts but the chore will keep them occupied long enough for her to talk about the future with Mickey.

She makes them both a mug of black coffee and joins Mickey in the living room. He is seated on the floor with the week's Racing Posts scattered around him, a Spin Doctors CD playing. She hands him his coffee and sits beside him, content to have him to herself for a few moments, content to enjoy the tranquillity of the melodic silence, ignoring together the piercing shrieks of her boys at play. Seeing Mickey's attention wander from hoped-for rides to come she begins the discussion she has put off for weeks.

"I suppose the owner will want a top jockey to ride," she suggests, harking back to the Dalakhani gelding.

"Possibly but it is Easter Monday. A lot of meetings. And not many of the big boys will be going to Hereford."

"Why can't trainers train their owners as they train their horses? Why doesn't John Heath tell his owner that a top jockey won't risk his neck for such a moderate horse?" she argues, arguing with no one in particular, wanting her husband to be given the chance he deserves to further his career whilst at the same time harbouring the guilt of wishing he would quit being a jockey and settle for a more prosaic but more rewarding job.

"This horse ain't moderate, believe me, Kath. Trainers like John can't afford to offend owners. They pay the bills and for two pins an owner will take his horse to another trainer. We've done too much work on this fella to let someone else reap the rewards. I've been in several different counties all at once with this fella, believe you me, Kath. I'm some man not to have been put on the floor, I can tell you." He looks up, his cheery face momentarily serious. "If this horse doesn't break his neck first, he'll be the best I've ridden in a long time."

He returns to marking off horses he has ridden in the past and Kath regroups, revises what she must say, what she must ask, perhaps even get round to mentioning the bills which require paying, the jobs around the house which must be attended to. To Mickey it will sound like a litany of unnecessary necessities.

This matrimonial crossroads is rooted in dreams, dreams which diverge but which start out from the same loving spot. Their home is decorated with photographs that chart Mickey's progress from a child riding ponies to where he is now, on the same rung of the ladder as he has been on for years. His first winner, a horse owned by Kath's father, hangs above their bed. A picture of him riding out his claim hangs next to a photograph of them taken at their engagement party. Over the mantle-place is their wedding portrait, encircled by pictures of the boys and interspaced by winning horses that history will forget but whose names remain in the memory of the Galloways for the cherished glimpse they provided of the limelight that once upon a time was on the horizon. There are no reminders of the stays in hospital, plaster-of-Paris, physiotherapy and broken promises.

"The immersion heater is on the blink," she tells him matter-of-factly, as if its repair can wait a while longer. "And the mortgage repayments have gone up and the insurance on my car is due this week and there is a rumour circulating at the factory that there are more redundancies coming up." Not that any of those important concerns are as important as her desire for him to find another way of earning a living.

"Everything will be okay," he reassures, rubbing her cheek with the palm of his hand. "Now that T.B. is off John will give me plenty of rides."

"It will be summer soon, Mickey, and most of his horses will be out in the fields."

Mickey's mobile phone rings and he goes into the kitchen where reception is better. He can see Edward spraying his brother with the hosepipe, the car neglected while the war by water is enacted. He smiles, excusing their dereliction of duty for no better reason than they are his boys. It is his agent. He has a ride for him at Newbury, if Mickey can ride at ten stone. Mickey has never ridden for this trainer before and to cement the new association he tells his agent to volunteer him to go down and school if he is required.

He informs Kath. She is pleased but not exuberant. It may represent a new line of hope but it will inevitably be false hope. A win, even a win at Newbury on the television, if indeed the horse does win, will not solve their financial dilemma. Ten winners, a hundred and ten rides, will not divert them from the parlous road to financial ruin.

She wishes she could put into words easily understood the uncertainly building within her, to place before Mickey the unease she experiences every time he leaves home. At twenty-nine his life is ahead of him. Edward and Patrick's lives are ahead of him.

Yet she appreciates Mickey's desire to be recognised as the equal of the heroes he rides against, to prove to the critics in the stands that he possesses the verve and ability to be trusted with horses of promise, that he is too good a rider to only get on dodgy jumpers, runaways and slow no-hopers. She loves him and she feels his pain when he is looked over, when a younger rider gets to ride horses on the racecourse on which he has done all the work at home. She even shares his ambition, his dream, to give the boys something to be proud of. Yet deep down she would prefer him to take up her brother's offer of a partnership in his taxi business.

"Mickey," she says softly, taking his hand and pulling herself up from the floor. "I know this is bad timing." She pauses, to give herself time for a deep breath. "I don't know how it happened exactly but I'm late this month."

The implications of another mouth to feed are immediately clear. Kath will have to give up her job; their income will be drastically cut. Mickey has often brooded on how he could unburden her from the obligation of shoring up the family finances, juggled with the facts and the dreams and the hopes. Now there are no options left to juggle with. "I'll talk to your brother, shall I?"

The enormity of his commitment thuds hard against her heart. "What about your 'big boat'? John's promise of more rides?"

"I hope this one is a girl," he tells her, drawing her to him, his cheery face a riot of expectation. "It'll even the family up." He touches her belly and kisses her forehead. "Everything will be okay, you'll see." To the sound of approaching tears they hug each other, united by a force even greater than the fraternity that binds the varying social strands that is the world of racing.

"Look," she tells him, pulling her lips from his, scared by the imminent threat of upheaval, preparing herself to comfort a blabbing child. "Let's not rush things. Wait until after Easter, see how things go with this Dalakhani gelding. You never know, do you?" Patrick runs in. He looks like someone who has been swimming in his clothes. He is keen to expose his elder brother as a bully and a cheat. "By the way," she adds, pulling Patrick away from the sheepskin rug. "What's the name of this horse?"

A Private Matter

The horse lies motionless upon the hallowed Cheltenham turf. Whether it is dead or merely winded Pritchard cannot determine from his lofty vantage point in Lord Grey's private box. As he raises his binoculars to gain a clearer view the ground staff erect a large green screen, removing the pitiful sight from curious and concerned onlookers. Resigned to hearing the inevitable crack of the humane-killer he drops his binoculars to dangle from his neck and braces himself for a nervous afternoon amongst the socialites he has elected to share this second day of the Festival with.

"Not so Lucky Man, eh?" an old soldier cackles as he passes by, the regimental crest embroidered on the breast pocket of his smart blazer signifying all that he wishes to be known of his past.

As Pritchard looks out on the cosmopolitan cauldron of sport, the exhilarated buzz of the milling throng rising up to engage his senses with the expectation of the day, it strikes him with cold clarity that his prospective revenge will have to be executed in front of thousands of potential witnesses. He empties his complimentary glass of Bucks Fizz in one quick swallow and turns his gaze to Lord Grey's invited guests, and wonders when his trespass will be noticed.

At length Lord Grey catches sight of Pritchard and in cordial acknowledgement raises his fluted glass, asking the blonde at his side if she knows the identity of the interloper. To emphasise his good nature he pulls two betting slips from an inside pocket of his jacket and mimes the word 'winners' across the room. Pritchard responds by similarly raising his empty glass and producing a winning betting ticket.

Under instruction the blonde picks up a glass of champagne from a laden table and advances upon Pritchard.

He views her strutting progress with detachment: events have turned him cynical and scantily-clad bimbos masquerading as personal assistants are unworthy of even a cursory glance.

"His lordship, love him, has for the moment misplaced your name." She offers the champagne to Pritchard, shaking her golden tresses and smiling with the calculated sharpness of a sniper. "Be a sweetie and tell me so that I can jog his brain cells." He suspects her smile is as plastic as her enhanced breasts, as false as her position in life.

Accepting the champagne, Pritchard offers his name, adding. "It should be familiar."

With time to kill, Pritchard lowers his lips to the champagne to indirectly scrutinise the luminaries who circulate with legitimacy around him. Although there are no formalities of introduction afforded him it is obvious he is in the company of highflyers and perhaps lower members of the aristocracy. Some of the women are dressed as if this were Royal Ascot in June rather than Cheltenham in March and he alone is dressed to match both the occasion and the inclement weather.

The party is too richly decorated for his suburban tastes. He hates it; hates having to be amongst it. The greatest faux-pas here, he muses, helping himself to a canapé, would be to mention the poor, the starving or the stricken horse on the landing side of the third-last fence. His socialist values demand he hate the depravity of endless wealth, the jewels that if auctioned would keep a hospital ward from closure.

Returning to the private box the red-nosed old soldier once more gravitates towards Pritchard. In his left hand is an unlit Turkish cigarette. His right hand wrestles with his fly-buttons.

"Bowled you a googly, old man," he apologises. "Not Lucky Man, ugh." He puts the cigarette to his lips and sucks reflectively. "Chap in the latrine, Carruthers, nice old boy, do you know him? Shouldn't think you would. Went to Kings or was it Keble? Nice sort. Has a horse in the big one tomorrow. Gold Cup would it be? Mind you, he thinks old Johnney Grey's will win. Not that I know a damn thing about the gee-gees. Anne's Revenge, not Lucky Man at all, went ass over apex. He was the winner, Lucky whatever its name. Funny old game, isn't it, racing?"

Pritchard knew all along it was Anne's Revenge lying on the ground. He watched the race closely and had harboured hopes of collecting from the bookies for a second time until she failed to get high enough at the notorious third-last. It was only a sentimental bet. He had not expected her to win. But it was not to be. Though by the close of racing he is determined that Anne, or Annie, will be revenged. He has both the gun and the commitment, and the twelve hundred pounds he won on the first race will even pay his expenses.

A loud cheer from the spectators takes his attention. Anne's

Revenge has clambered to her feet and the screens are removed. He smiles, pleased for the mare, relieved that the gods are seemingly on the side of the stricken.

He feels a finger stabbing into his side. "What the deuce is your name, old man? Bloody game going on trying to put a name to the face, ugh." It is the old soldier, a glass of whiskey now in his hand. "Well, what the deuce is it?"

"Lord Grey knows who I am. Ask him." He excuses himself. He has his expenses to collect.

It is his life-long dream to own a racehorse; to stand in the parade ring with his trainer and jockey talking tactics, appraising the opposition. The idea started back in Dublin when he ran to the local bookie on behalf of his father with accumulators and each-way doubles, and absconded from school to go down the road to the Phoenix Park. The dream, though, has outlived both his father and the Park.

He looks out across the magnificent panoply and logs for the sake of memory the florid movement of unified humanity. Tomorrow he will describe the kaleidoscope of sporting endeavour to Annabel, to put into simple words the supercharged sounds of a momentous day. He will tell her about the grand houses that look down on the racecourse from Cleeve Hill; the cold blue sky and aimless angry clouds; the great gamblers with their five- and six-figure bets; the ladies in their winter finery and the men in their hats, scarves and greatcoats. Annabel will smile at his descriptions of hat-tossing and the looks of anguish as odds-on favourites are pipped on the line. And he will tell her about the magnificent horses: most of all he will tell her about the horses. But not Lord Grey or his private box. That will be his secret.

The blonde P.A. sidles across to him to gaze out at the crowd, her bare arm touching the sleeve of his jacket, her expensive perfume an annoyance, and he wishes he could open a window to remove it from his nostrils. Her closeness annoys him even more than the cloying sweetness of her perfume. He requires space; his moment is near the horizon. Before she can speak he tells her.

"Anne's Revenge will be washed down by now. She'll be snug as a bug in a rug. Mind you, it was a bad fall, a right old purler as we say back home. Could take its toll, make her think about life differently. She's well bred, though, so she'll be a right prospect for the paddocks. Her owner will get plenty of babies out of her alright." He pauses to see if the blonde is at all interested in what he is telling her. "This is of no interest to you, is it?"

"Look, sweetie, my name is Donna and I just do what his lordship asks of me, get it? At the moment he is getting into a right stew about you. He thinks you might be from Lloyds, you know, of London."

"No, Donna. He needn't worry. I have no connection with Lloyds."

"Are you one of those clever financial regulator people?"

"Threadneedle Street is not my patch, Donna. I'm just a poor laddo from across the water. Though to stretch the definition of regulator a little it might be said that I am here to regulate the past."

He turns from Donna and the champagne unreality of her existence to look to the centre of the course, searching for the helicopter he has hired for the journey home, relieved to see it hovering above the landing area. The moment has finally arrived for him to interact with a destiny he has planned and paid for.

"Lord Grey, you see, is particular about who he invites to his parties. How did you get in? Bribed the guard on the door, I suppose?" Donna is showing no sign of leaving him in peace so he takes hold of her wrist, squeezing it hard enough to bring tears to her eyes but not so hard as to make her squeal.

"Congratulations, hole in one. So go be a good personal assistant and fetch Lord Grey to me." He releases his grip and adds in a whisper. "Tell him I have come to settle an account."

"You must make an appointment to see him at his office," she answers, rubbing her wrist as in want of raising a genie, unaware of the abyss before her. Pritchard pulls her back to him, his disregard for subtlety now attracting attention. "He's with the Dowager," Donna protests.

"I don't care if he is with the Archbishop of Canterbury," Pritchard tells her through clenched teeth, his heart now pumping with the excitement of what he proposes.

"What shall I say it is about?" she asks, her pretty face a picture of alarm.

"Tell him it's a private matter that is best attended to here and now. Tell him it's about a girl. That should take his fascination."

He needs to look nonchalant, in control of himself and the situation. But he can feel suppressed anger rising in his heart and mind and he takes a deep breath as he looks down on the emptying parade ring, the horses already on their way to the start. Time is pressing. Momentarily a white flag flutters amongst the agitation for revenge, wanting him to think again, to consider if this is the way he wants to be remembered by his family. In his pocket he has a photograph of Annabel swimming for her school. He takes it out to kiss it, to seek inspiration from one of the last active memories she was allowed to provide for him.

"What's all this about? Pritchard, isn't it? Dashed bad manners, you know." Lord Grey stands at his elbow, his face flushed with alcohol and indignation.

"You and me, old man, are going for a helicopter ride," Pritchard informs him, returning the photograph to his pocket.

"Don't be absurd! I have guests."

"And I have a loaded gun in my pocket. Look." He pulls the butt into Lord Grey's view. "I'm not good with guns, so who knows how many of your guests I might hit if you force me to use it."

"This is preposterous," Lord Grey continues to protest, trying to pull free of Pritchard's grasp. "I haven't an inkling who you are."

There is no time for explanation or negotiation. "Call for help and you are dead. Announce you are going to place a bet."

Hesitantly Lord Grey does as he is instructed. As he is cajoled down the passage and into the lift he pleads for his release. Pritchard ignores him, his only thought to reach the helicopter and to be airborne before the police arrive.

"This is madness. You won't get away with it, you know. My friends will already have alerted the authorities. They'll not be fooled, you know. They know I would have sent someone to place my bet." He continues to protest as he is bundled into the car that will take them to the helicopter.

"You didn't say it was like this," the pilot argues. "You said he was a friend."

Pritchard reaches into his pocket. "Here, I won twelve-hundred on the first race. It's yours." He throws the bundle of fifty pound notes into the pilot's lap. "If that won't persuade you perhaps this will." He waves the gun at Lord Grey, fingering the trigger.

In the air Pritchard informs his prisoner where he is being taken. "You are going to tea. I'll introduce you to my daughter, Annabel, and you can see close up what you have done to her." Lord Grey stares blankly at him, droplets of comprehension forming in his mind's eye.

As the chase for glory continues below Pritchard explains to the pilot how his little girl was run over by a red Bentley bearing the number plate G1 and how the driver had sped away, leaving the girl and her dog for dead.

"It's a matter for the Garda," the pilot remonstrates. "What will this solve? The Garda and the law will sort him."

"You would think so but so far they haven't got round to pressing charges." He points the gun into Lord Grey's chest. "Perhaps it has something to do with him being English and an aristocrat with connections in all the right places."

Lord Grey sits ashen-faced, unable to form a reply to defeat his kidnapper. He thought the incident with the silly girl was done and dusted; he thought his lawyers had succeeded in hushing it up. He had admitted responsibility and donated a large sum of money to a Dublin hospital. "I have a runner in the Gold Cup. It's worth a punt, if you are interested."

Pritchard cannot answer. He has lost control of the situation. The pilot is now in command of his destiny. He doesn't even know if they are flying in the right direction. All he needed to do was confront Lord Grey with the enormity of his crime; to have him sit at Annabel's bedside and for him to apologise. But now he doesn't know if he can make that happen. He just wants his little Annie to be like she used to be; for her to rise from the ground and walk, and just like Anne's Revenge to go on to have a life, to have babies, to go on being his little princess. He cannot shoot Grey, as much as he deserves to die, as he has no bullets in the gun, and he cannot release them as they are in the sky and there is no justice to be had in leniency.

Seeing Pritchard dissolve into tears, his fear plainly greater than his own, Lord Grey places a consoling hand on his shoulder. "I lost my daughter when she was five years old. I know how you feel." And he instructs the pilot to return to Cheltenham. "I will ensure no charges are brought against you. As you rightly said, I have friends in all the right places."

A Picture of Royland

With all the resentment of a child giving up the last sweet in the packet to a disliked grandparent, the heavy wrought-iron gates creak open and Lord John Fitzalen re-enters his world of memory. Before him, at the termination of the long gravelled drive, is Royland, his ancestral home, the place of his birth, the focal point of his thoughts and dreams.

The nightmare is nearly over.

Choking back two decades of suffering he allows himself the indulgence of savouring his triumph. The past is once more the future, with new hope encircling him with the gay abandon of a carousel. It is, for the moment, overpowering, so physically present he can feel his skin rippling with expectation, and yet at one and the same time he feels ephemeral, as if he is as light as a cloud.

The yellow gravel crunches like crisp snow as he walks purposefully towards the great house. Out of view, in the red-brick stables, his horses will be waiting for him. They will be different from those he gazed upon with pride and admiration the last time he was at Royland but they will descend from the same breeding line. Cowdray will have seen to it; Cowdray would never let him down.

He looks for Smithers, the head gardener. For a brief moment he thinks it odd for the grounds to be vacant of gardeners in early June but the reflection passes with the flight of fancy. It is what lies ahead of him that is important, not the absence of summer roses and clipped topiary. Elisabeth will be waiting for him: that is what is truly important.

Ascending the stone steps that lead to the oak doors he recalls his childhood game when he pretended the steps were Mont Blanc or Everest and he a mountaineer of world renown, his friends trusty Sherpas. At the top he rests, readying himself for what is to come, containing his anticipation with steady, slow breaths. When the joy of his surprise homecoming can no longer be held in check he walks to the great double doors and knocks firmly, stepping back and straightening his tie, to await Jenkins. He could have strolled casually in, of course, as if he had just gone out to attend to some small detail in the grounds, but he cannot know for sure how he will be received. Jenkins, he knows, will proceed in his usual dignified manner, and on opening the door his eye will mirror the reception he can expect from others.

He continues to wait for the door to be opened and as he waits he is bombarded by reminiscence: the hunt balls, the Christmases when the children of the village came for tea and presents handed out by Jenkins dressed as Father Christmas. The magnificence of his engagement to Elisabeth. Yet no one comes to acknowledge him. He knocks again, annoyed to think standards have declined in his absence. With a troubled heart he listens for a sound that will alert him to the approach of Jenkins.

"Damn strange carry on," he mutters to himself. "Where

the dickens has he got to?" Reluctantly he turns the large brass handle and the doors swing open and there before him is the billowing heart of Royland. The pink mottled marble stone floor and pillars, the sweeping staircase, the welcoming aroma of home. The troubled beat of his heart transforms into sweet refrain as his eye alights on the crystal chandelier he bought in Czechoslovakia, the last item he purchased on behalf of the estate before his departure. "Its installation, darling, is as spectacular as the birth of a new star." He spins around expecting to see Elisabeth, to have her arms around him again, but she is nowhere, at least for the moment, but in his heart and memory.

His favourite room in the whole house is his study. It is his treasury, his refuge. As he stands in the doorway he strives to reconcile reality with memory. The square room is, as always, sparsely furnished, with just the glass-fronted trophy case, brimming with the silverware of success, a filing cabinet to complement the Victorian writing desk, and the leather and mahogany swivel chair that as always occupies the centre of the room. It is as it is stored in his memory. No one has made alterations. It has waited all these years for his repatriation.

Nearest the door there are three photographs of his father's Irish Derby winner Myopic. The first shows the horse passing the winning post, the jockey saluting the crowd. In the second photograph Myopic is being led into the winner's enclosure by Lord John's father. In the third photograph he can see himself as a child, holding his mother's hand, a look of bemusement on his chubby face, as Myopic is fed an apple by his grandmother. All the photographs are autographed by Con Maher, the victorious jockey.

Suddenly reality is an intruder to calm reflective thought. He slumps against the doorframe, his optimism rendered impotent by the sound of Con's hearty laughter ringing in his ears, his incomprehensible tales of deceit and skulduggery reverberating around the marble hall. "Jays! Young John, dem gambles me ol' fader pulled off at dem pony meets. At Tralee one day dem bookies were beggin' me fader to try the horses and leave the ponies alone. I rode four and me li'l sister Patsy won the udder. Mind you, young John, she'd dress like a man cos the lasses in dem days were barred from racin' with us boys. Dem sights she saw in dem changing rooms weren't fit to be seen by a good Cath'lic girl. It's most likely what put her off men for life." Con's dialect triggers another memory, a memory more cogent and less pure. He straightens himself and moves on, to stop at an oil painting of Sir Randolph, with Sammy Flynn, dressed in the green and white racing silks, handed down generation to generation, on his back.

"What a fine horse you were, Randolph." Adding, pointing at the cherubic face of his rider, "But you, you devil!"

Hostility quickly fades as a moving picture thunders into his head of Sir Randolph jumping the last fence in the Becher Chase. "A National winner if ever I saw one," he can hear Bobby Renton saying again. "If he isn't the finest lepper I have ever sat on," Sammy enthused at the party the following day.

Lord John stretches out a hand to touch the painting, caressing again the smooth bay coat of his favourite horse. "You were the best. The best any man could hope for." But when he thinks of Sir Randolph he cannot but remember the terrible day at Hurst Park, the horse stricken on the ground, big oval tears running down Sammy's cherubic face as he cradled the horse's head in his lap. "He just never came up for me, my Lord. He crashed straight through it. That's the National done for us. We'll never win it now."

As if winning was what mattered! Closing his eyes he reassures himself that Sammy Flynn is history, a part of a past that can never return.

Opening his eyes he sees in front of him a photograph in a silver frame. It is what he has come for. The photograph always took pride of place on his desk, travelling with him whenever he went abroad. It is a photograph of the Lincolnshire winner Polyandrus. At his head is his owner, Elisabeth Venning. It captures for posterity his happiest day; the perfect prelude to their marriage in Lincoln Cathedral.

It was love at first sight. They met at Doncaster races. She strode up to him in the owners' bar, tapped him on the shoulder and without introduction asked if he would train Polyandrus for her. "I want you to win the Lincolnshire Handicap for me. You can do that, can't you?"

He picks up the photograph and hugs it to his chest, tears trickling down his face, and in a few incalculable moments he is outside the master bedroom listening to the unmistakeable sounds of lovemaking. Outrage consumes him as a tumult of indignation hammers at his senses. Despite his love of her he knows he will find Elisabeth entwined in the arms of Sammy Flynn. "Oh my God!" Elisabeth will scream and Sammy will turn to face him, expecting only to see Jenkins or an embarrassed maid. "Be Jesu, guv'ner, where have you sprung from?"

He will go to his dressing table and take out a revolver. Sammy will freeze in horror of his fate, one leg returned to his jodhpurs. Elisabeth will lean forward, the nakedness of her treachery a sight frozen on his mind, to plead with him to put away the gun. "It's not as you think, John. He knows something about me …"

He will raise the revolver and Elisabeth will cry out as Sammy cowardly dives under the bed. He will fire one bullet and Elisabeth will be dead.

Dr. Brook pushes open the rusted gates and with the loyal Mrs. French at his side they walk up the weed-ridden drive. On either side the neglected lawns and shrubberies grow wild, with nettles and thistles where once superbly cultivated roses stood proud. At the end of the drive a large country house stands neglected and isolated, black clouds mustering above its grey slate roof and crumbling chimneys.

"Stygian, isn't it?" Mrs. French suggests. This her first sight of Royland.

Hastily they mount the stone steps, pausing at the summit to look back to the car parked at the gates, at the besieging housing estate at Royland's boundary. They wait a moment before entering the plundered house.

"You won't be cross with Loran, will you?" Mrs. French asks. "She wasn't to know he would slip away. He's always been as good as gold."

"No, she is not to blame. This is my error. I can blame no one but myself." He smiles to reassure her, to reduce her apprehension. "We'll have dinner tonight. Gianni's."

Her eyes light up. "Thank you. It will be a special evening."

"Yes, it will."

"How dreadful," she comments, casting her eyes around the ruined hallway, the marble floor despoiled and disfigured by the invasion of nature. Plaster has all but completely fallen from the ceiling and walls. There are no light fittings and the doors are either smashed or covered with graffiti. Fragments of glass merge with a multitude of cigarette butts, lager cans, bottles and the assorted filth of squatters and vandals. "How can this be allowed to happen?"

"How the mighty can fall."

"But why? How can such a historic house be allowed to degenerate to this?"

"No one to inherit. No one to look after the place. And he has refused down the years to sell. If only he would give up the idea that one day he will return to live here again."

"To rest his bones and regain his spirit," she reminds him.

"Please, do not remind me. I have heard him say it a thousand times." He looks across to the staircase and wonders if it is safe to climb. "We had better get on. You search down here, I'll go upstairs."

She advances cautiously into a room without a door. In the grate she can see charred remains of a hinge and doorknob. The walls are daubed with offensive graffiti, the glass in the casement window smashed, providing a convenient entrance for swallows to build their nests, their guano as obscene as the graffiti. A broken leg from a once gilded chair in a cardboard box occupies the centre of the room. There are rat droppings and a large hole in the skirting board. She shivers and turns away.

Dr. Brook stands on the balcony, alert for any sound that will indicate the presence of Lord John. It is inconceivable that such a frail old man could travel so far unaided but they know of nowhere else where he might be found. His attention is drawn to a room at the end of the landing. The doors are open and he can see the roofs and gable ends of the modern housing estate through the window. As he gets closer he can hear Lord John. "Damn you, you fornicating devil!"

"Lord John," he says entering the room. But the old man is held in engagement within in a different, perhaps parallel, world.

"How could you betray me with a cur like him? How could you do this to us?" His eyes are red with a rage that the decades have never diminished, his face taut with a misery which took possession of him the second he fired the gun.

"No, your lordship," Dr. Brook assures him calmly. "It is over. We must go home now."

Ambushed from his living nightmare Lord John spins round, his imaginary gun pointed at Dr. Brook. Recognising who his intruder is, recognising the hopelessness of his situation, he drops his shooting arm and slumps to the floor.

"Has he ...?" Mrs. French asks, running into the room.

"Yes. I wish we could help him forget. It has been over twenty years now."

"At least we found him alive."

"I think that may be scant consolation to him." He takes a syringe from his pocket and Mrs. French gently removes Lord John's jacket and rolls up his sleeve. "He's a danger to himself. We must return him to the secure ward."

"He must think Elisabeth is still here."

"Who can say what goes on in his head? Come on, let's get him sedated. The sooner we get him back to the home the sooner we can get to Gianni's."

Mrs. French encourages Lord John to his feet. She tries to

make eye contact with him but his head and heart are beset by sights and sounds only he can comprehend. "Let's get you home. Dr. Brook is taking me to an Italian restaurant this evening. Won't that be nice?"

"This is home," Lord John tells her. "This is where my spirit is. Not that other place!"

"What's this?" Dr. Brook asks, bending down to pick up a silver-framed photograph.

"That's mine. I came for it. Elisabeth told me it would be here." Lord John snatches back possession of the photograph, covering it with his coat.

"He's not had that picture at the unit, has he?" Dr. Brook asks.

"No. I've never seen it before. What did he mean; Elisabeth told him it would be here?"

A gust of wind blows through the broken windows. Somewhere close by a door slams and there is the hint of a female voice carried on the crest of the blown air. Without noticing Lord John's departure Dr. Brook and Mrs. French are suddenly aware he is not with them. They run after him. But they are only in time to see him fall. They do not witness the smile that bathes his face as he embraces the air, the image in shadowed form that is a replica of the photograph. Nor do they find the silver-framed photograph that captured for posterity Lord John's happiest day.

A Sorry Tale

Once autumn was over, when the red squirrels and the purity of the air had become commonplace, before the mystical and impenetrable fogs descended from previously bright blue skies to baffle and alarm us, the differences in our backgrounds and philosophies emerged to dominate our working days. For all of us it was our first experience of working in a racing stable so far north.

They, Captain Corrie and his middle-aged head girl, Regina, were disciples of long leathers and hunting saddles, whereas we were enamoured of the short leathers of the work rider and accustomed to the racing way of doing things rather than the old-fashioned huntsman's approach to the job. We were assembled for a common purpose yet were unable in the midst of niggling setbacks and mutual suspicion to accept as inalienable the rights and differing knowledge of the other. Consequently respect was misplaced in the trajectory of their command, with the Captain and Regina as exasperated no doubt with us as we were with them.

Of all of us Dickie Corbett had the greatest grievance, though he was the most tolerant of our situation. In his younger days he had been head lad to a successful trainer in the Midlands and a private trainer in his own right, and when offered the opportunity of working at Kirkside he had been given to believe that someone of his experience would be valued by a stable graduating from point-to-points to National Hunt. Yet his experience, advice if you may, was rarely called upon and his dedication and knowledge was considered by Regina as contrary to her ideas on horse husbandry.

I started at Kirkside during the close season, a few weeks before Steve and Ronnie. Along with Dickie we were the paid hands, the workforce. I too had cause for complaint and whenever we were all together after work, usually bemoaning our plight, I felt compelled to tell my colleagues about the letter of employment given to me by Captain Corrie confirming my appointment as stable jockey. As with Dickie, my place in the hierarchy at Kirkside was more menial than I had been led to believe. We were working in lovely surroundings, if not for lovely people, and we took the devaluation of our talents with more restraint than perhaps we should have done. It has to be said that we let our wives do most of the moaning for us.

Steve Hix and Ronnie Kelsey were employed as stable lads and were treated accordingly by our employers.

Alexa, the Captain's secretary, was also a comparative newcomer to Kirkside, though she had been in residence since the summer. She lived in, in the Captain's manor house, and as daughter of a Lord Lieutenant of somewhere in the Highlands was decidedly not of our social standing. At Kirkside the horses were rarely exercised as a string, as would be the case in most racing yards, and on occasion, when she too felt alienated by her employer, she would exercise her eventer with one of us. I was riding out with her when I was forced to commit the modest act of insurrection which sparked this sorry tale.

I had been instructed to walk my horse for two hours and to cross the moor to a village called Bramley. The day before, Lovely Linda, the mare I was riding, had galloped in preparation for a race the following week and at Kirkside the day after workdays were long-walk days, and I mean long walks. We had gone no further than a mile when the mare broke into a white sweat. In literally a second she was awash. It was as if someone had covered her in a moist white blanket. I had never seen anything like it in all my experience. Alexa, too, was startled.

My instinct was to take the mare straight back to the stables but Alexa, as fearful as we were about going against orders, suggested we go on a bit further. "She still has a trace-clip and it is warm," she put forward as explanation. It was a valid point but I was convinced the problem was more serious than simply the warmth of the day.

I tried to turn the mare around but she was so wooden she almost knuckled over. I slipped off her back to lead her home. "It's could be her liver or kidneys are wrong," Alexa said, repeating what Dickie had suggested the previous day after she had worked rather sluggishly.

On the walk back to the stables I rehearsed what I should say. I was getting no rides for Captain Corrie and I was certain whatever I said would be taken as sour grapes, as criticism of them. In telling Captain Corrie and Regina that I thought Dickie was right in thinking the mare had something wrong with her I was putting my credibility and career on the line. I needed rides to establish myself up north and in leaving the security of the southern-based trainers who had helped get me started I had put all my eggs into the Kirkside basket.

Regina had dismissed Dickie's concern as 'nonsense' and criticised him for not being forceful enough with the mare on the gallops. "Perhaps if you all dropped your stirrup irons four or five notches you might be able to squeeze your horse into its bridle," she had barked, reminding us yet again of the poor opinion she had of our riding styles. There was no doubt in my mind that my unexpected reappearance would fan the smouldering embers of dispute.

As I finally made it back to the stables I tried to remember if I looked in the mare's manger before tacking her up or if her behaviour was different to normal. On both counts I could not be sure. I cursed myself for my negligence. At Kirkside you had to watch your back. The Captain was a genuine army man, unused to having his orders countermanded or queried and Regina was an exponent of the 'do as I say and not as I do' principle of management. As I stood at the entrance to the stables I feared for what I had let myself in for and wondered if I would have a job by the end of the day.

To my dismay, as I vacillated at the entrance to the horsebarn, the mare seemed a little brighter. My confidence waned further when I recognised she was not as glassy-eyed as when I last examined her. Just as I decided to take the mare to her stable the Captain came out of the tack room, straightening his old regimental tie and looking flustered. He was a commanding presence, straight backed and long striding. His customary clothes for working were cavalry-twill trousers, and hacking jacket, checked shirt and tie. His reputation for sacking people on the spot and demanding a higher sense of morality than he exercised himself streaked our fear of him with contempt and ridicule. His affair with Regina was common knowledge, yet they acted around us as if they were strictly acquaintances. It was both comic and unseemly at the same time and so obviously not our business.

"What are you doing back so quickly?" he demanded to know, picking up a cane whip from outside the tack room. I explained the situation, the mare standing as if made into a statue by my side. "What do you mean by 'she isn't right'? How can I deduce the problem, if there is one, by such a vague, inarticulate description?" After I had given him a chapter and verse report on what had happened, adding that Alexa would confirm my version of events, Regina appeared from the tack room, pinning her hair back.

"What's going on, Hugh?" she asked Captain Corrie, unusually using his first name, casting a suspicious glance in my direction and increasing my discomfort many fold. The Captain gave her an abridged account of what I had told him, leaving out Alexa, my invaluable witness. "She looks okay, wouldn't you say, Hugh? Trot her up," she demanded, ushering me to get on with things as if she had something more important to get back to. "It's still warm. We will have to get her clipped," I heard her say, her mind already made up that there was nothing wrong with the mare.

In their combined judgement all that was wrong was my attitude, which, given the comparative ease in which the mare moved when trotted up, might have been anyone's judgement. "If we all knew as much as you think you know," she said to me, the sneer in her voice as sharp as scissors. "You might forever get out of doing what you are told to do. We do things correctly here, the old-fashioned, tried and tested way. Where you come from, where you received what training you received, it was and doubtless remains slip-shod."

The slight amount of energy the mare used in being trotted up weakened her and quickly she began to lose flexibility in her muscles; her eyes glazed over and she became stiff and angular. I actually hoped she would break into a sweat so that they could understand I was not work-shy and ignorant and that I was acting responsibly. When I was told to take the mare and give her another hour around the roads I told them the mare would not leave her stable again until a vet had been called. I was outnumbered and terribly alone, but in this instance Regina was wrong and I was right. I just hoped the others would back me up. As I unbuckled the girth and pulled off the saddle I directed their furious gaze at the sweat-soaked numnah.

"That's nothing," Regina retaliated, trying to take the saddle from me to re-tack the mare. "We have known this horse for a lot longer than you. She is a free-sweater and lazy."

"Look," Captain Corrie intervened. I knew he would take Regina's side, he always did, but for a moment my hopes were raised that he would put caution before their own pride. "Either give this mare the exercise you are ordered to do or you are, regrettably, down the road. Do you understand?"

I reiterated my position and led the mare to her stable and hoped it would not be long before Dickie, Steve and Ronnie got back from whatever far-flung part of the moor they had been detailed to. Steve was Scottish, he would enjoy the skirmish but I was not so certain of Dickie and Ronnie backing me up. As for me, I had little to lose. We were having runners and my name was not in the frame to ride scarce few of them and my wife hated the isolation of Kirkside. As I tried to induce the mare to drink, I espied Captain Corrie and Regina in deep conversation, no doubt discussing what punishment my mutinous conduct deserved.

"Tetanus," Dickie diagnosed, watching the mare struggle to lift her head to pull hay from the rack. Lovely Linda was one of the three horses he looked after at Kirkside and his diagnosis implicated him in my mutiny. Of course being the dedicated professional horseman he was by nature he blamed himself. "I must have missed a small cut after she galloped yesterday. Up here, that is all it takes. The downside of exercising on the moor is the risk of tetanus."

To my mind, as it was with Steve and Ronnie, tetanus was a disease of the past. Not one of us had seen a case in our combined experience working down south. Dickie was putting me right when Captain Corrie came on the scene.

"Regina is very upset by your outburst," he told me, ignoring Dickie and the plight of the mare. "As jockey here you have a responsibility to conduct yourself in a respectful manner."

I almost laughed. It was if he was mocking me with his description of me as the jockey for the stable as only a few days before I had ridden a horse up to the schooling field expecting to school it only to find a better-known, older jockey waiting to take over. I had ridden twenty-five winners the previous season but that meant nothing at Kirkside.

I watched Steve and Ronnie skepping out stables in preparation for the horses to be fed. The question of whether they would stand by me had not yet arisen. For some reason I was envious of them as they had a choice in the matter whereas I was committed to my cause.

"We shall have a serious talk about your future this

afternoon," Captain Corrie continued, not making it clear who would be participating in the discussion. "Your attitude has done you no favours. You may be disappointed by the number of rides you are receiving from me but it is largely out of my hands. The owners pay the bills, though you make it difficult for me to argue your case when I do not believe you are committed to our values." He then advised me to apologise to Regina.

"Excuse me for butting in, Captain, but this mare has tetanus. We must get a vet to her straightaway. I had an old pony die of it and I never want to see another go the same, painful way." Dickie's intervention was greatly appreciated by me, though by the initial look in the Captain's eye it was clear he thought the mutiny was spreading.

Then I thought I saw recognition in the Captain's eyes. But he was compromised. To do as we suggested meant going against Regina. In his own closeted way he was, I suppose, a decent enough bloke. He trained winners, even if his methods were unorthodox to pure racing men like us, and I suppose that is what it is all about. He was officer class and we were not. As he stood in the passageway of the barn with Dickie's stinging, constructive censure ringing in his ears, I think the truth of the situation sank in: Regina was wrong.

Within an hour the vet had confirmed Dickie's diagnosis and had pumped a large dose of antitoxins and tranquillisers into her system. His prognosis was dire, though: if we did not keep her on her feet she would die.

We did not see Regina again that day and the Captain left us to organise a rota to ensure someone was with the mare at all times. We decided on two-hour shifts to go right through the night. We had a united cause: we would save the mare no matter what. Captain Corrie did not volunteer to have his name placed on the rota and left no instruction on what to do if the mare's condition worsened through the night.

As luck would have it, the mare took a turn for the worse during my occupation of her stable. For an hour I convinced myself the antitoxins were easing her condition; animals, though, seem able to bear discomfort with greater forbearance than humans and her apparent improvement was I suspect wishful thinking on my part. After hours of unsteady immobility she tried to move, to lift her head in recognition of a neigh from a horse further down the barn. She stumbled and groaned with pain from her unflexing muscles. Then she began to sweat profusely and convulse. Her bottom lip grazed the straw bedding as she stood precariously on three legs at an angle which threatened certain death.

I knew she was on the point of collapse and that I was powerless to prevent it. There was no such thing as mobile phones back then and all I could do was rush to summon help. I ran as I had not done for years, across the dark lane to the manor house. To my horror the drive was lined with cars. I tried the front and back doors without reply, so I let myself into the back of the house. I shouted to make my presence known but no one answered me.

From the depths of the big house I could hear music and the drone of a merry gathering. The light was on in the estate office and knocking on the door I waited again for a reply. Again nothing. I went in, looking to the phone on the desk and searching the directory for the vet's number with my heart beating as if I were burglar out to steal the silver. But that was all I could do. I felt puny, as menial as I was treated. I had no responsibility to call in a vet and wished I had gone to Dickie's house and got him out of bed.

What I needed was the courage to infiltrate the party and seek out Captain Corrie. He needed to know how desperate the situation had become. In fact he needed to be dealing with the problem, not me. But timidity overcame me. I was on the verge of losing my job and Captain Corrie was not the sort of employer to give a parting man a glowing reference. And to be honest I did not want to leave. In time Cathy, my wife, would have settled and grown to love the wild isolation of the moorland village. I thought I could even come to terms with the Captain's training methods. And I knew from what Dickie had said that it was unlikely the mare could be saved anyway. Kirkside was not the sort of place to encourage initiative. The mare would have to be put out of her misery but it was not my place to authorise her humane destruction. It was the owner's decision or the trainer's. It certainly was not mine.

I went back into the dark and fetched Steve from his bed. He told me in a language that was ripe and compatible for the night that I should have taken the initiative and called the vet. "Watch me, I'll take pleasure in joining the county set," he bragged, setting off for the Manor. As we walked back up the dark lane discussing the possibility of rigging up a hoist to get the mare back on her feet Dickie came out of his front door to take his place on shift. It was midnight, somewhere far in the distance a church clock chimed.

The mare had fallen. She was laid against the side wall of the stable, her neck twisted under her. I have never seen a more pitiable sight. Thank God Dickie was there. He tugged her head into a less uncomfortable position and organised her legs the best he could. The mare groaned and we all knew the battle was already lost. He sent me back to the house. As there was nothing more practical he could do Steve came with me. "Calls himself a trainer! I'll make sure he sees the state that mare is in if I have to drag him across."

He was spared having to act on his boast by the appearance of Alexa at the front door. She was about to accompany a grand-looking woman in a fur stole to her car and it was difficult to decide which of us was more surprised by the other. I explained our purpose and to her credit Alexa did what none of us had done; she responded quickly and efficiently. She went back to the party and came back with someone from the local hunt who by good fortune had a humane-killer in the boot of his car. "In case of emergencies," he explained. "Like tonight."

If you don't pray for a miracle in dire situations you pray for a speedy solution and the huntsman provided the solution. Within five minutes the mare was out of her misery. Big, belligerent Steve cried his eyes out.

Whether Alexa took the decision or whether she consulted Captain Corrie we were never told. During the whole sad night we did not see either the Captain or Regina and any respect any of us had for them evaporated because of it.

The following day, perhaps to his credit, Captain Corrie offered me a watered-down apology which I refused to accept. Regina remained tight-lipped and unapologetic.

One by one we left Kirkside and by the summer, when Dickie left to take a job as a private trainer, only Alexa remained. We all departed wiser, our experience broadened. During the two weeks of my notice Captain Corrie gave me two rides, one a winner. But it made no difference. I couldn't look him in the eye and I could not respect him. I came into racing because of a love of horses. For our sport, our pleasure, horses get injured and sometimes they die. It is horrible and no one cares for that side of the sport. But they never die through negligence and it is beyond the pale when one does die because of negligence, as did Lovely Linda.

Steve is now travelling head lad to a big stable down south and Ronnie is Dickie's assistant. And Captain Corrie married Regina, his wife dying conveniently not long after Lovely Linda. And he trained two winners at the Cheltenham Festival, two horses I might have ridden if I had stayed. I work for a horse feed company. The night Lovely Linda died a part of me died, too.

The Story of H

We will call him H, as he is now and forever legendary: at least legendary to those that know of him. He doesn't know he is a legend, of course, though the manner in which he lived always suggested he was never going to be one of the ordinary crew. So in telling his story we will refer to him as H. H for horse. Because that is what he is, a horse.

He lived a good life, as most racehorses do. As a foal he frolicked with his kith and kin in lush Irish fields, the only irritation to his idyllic life being the finicky administrations of the blacksmith whose job it was to keep his brittle feet in sound order. From foal to yearling, from yearling to three-year-old, H grew fat, not too tall, and with a nature that allowed him to go with the flow. In the spring of his third year he was gelded and for a week he was miserable and suspicious of people who till that unpleasant moment he had only thought of as kind.

When it came to being broken in to Man's use of him he accepted the rigmarole with the same equanimity of temperament as he did most things. He made an initial protest when the girth was first tightened around his stomach, as he has seen his comrades do when he had watched from the field, but all in all he quite enjoyed the attention.

People continued to be kind to him, though at times they were insistent he do things he was uncertain about. Walking up the ramp into the dark hold of a lorry made no sense to him, especially when they made him stand in the partition without taking him anywhere. And when he was long-reined around the roads the man insisted he stand still outside a house with snapping, yelping dogs when his instincts demanded that he shoot ahead to avert the danger.

At first it was strange to have a man vault onto his back but once he got used to the sensation he found it tolerable. He sensed, though, that the man expected him to misbehave, to jump into the air and rush about, as he had seen his less confident companions do. But H did not see the point in wasting energy; it only excited the man and delayed his feed. Even from an early age H liked to see matters in the long term and the quicker he satisfied man's expectations of him the quicker he was fed and returned to the field.

When he was four he was put into a lorry and taken with two companions to a place where a whole lot of young horses were congregated. It was a noisy, busy place and H sensed that some of the young horses were frightened by the strange routine and hullabaloo. To H, though, it was simply an interesting development. People had never done him any harm and he saw no evidence why it should change. People came into his stable, disturbing him from his hay, feeling his legs and generally inspecting him. He sensed they were unimpressed, though he could not understand why.

On the whole, as long as he was eating, he did not object to having people around him, especially people who offered him treats, though he often whiled away a long hour trying to figure out why his life should be the way it was. He tried to discuss people with his companions but they could not grasp the significance of the subject, taking the view that as long as people continued to feed them it was a waste of time analysing their reasons. But H was a thinker; he liked to occupy himself with such matters. He wanted to know where life was leading him.

He found himself at a stable with a tougher regime than he was used to. Not that it bothered him unduly. People continued to be kind to him and his new companions seemed happy. When the man asked him to trot, he trotted. When he was asked to follow in a string of his companions he obliged. When asked to gallop he put down his head and galloped. Why argue? When they put poles and things in his path, once he realised what was expected of him, he jumped. It was fun, in its way. Life was interesting. He only wished he could determine where it was leading.

Initially it took him to faraway racecourses. He tried his best, wanting to achieve whatever was expected of him, but it was all too fast for him. After consulting his jockey it was decided that H's best was not and never would be good enough to warrant his upkeep and he was dispatched once more to the sales ring.

At his new stable there were enthusiastic horses and in the morning he had to work devilishly hard to keep up with his illustrious companions. Consequently he got himself very fit, losing the puppy fat he had retained for so long. A few races later, he won. His people were pleased, which pleased H as all he ever wanted to do was please people.

They then put larger obstacles in his path which required greater effort. Again people were pleased with him. Next time he raced he had these bigger obstacles to jump over, which he preferred as they remained upright if he touched them with his legs, whereas the smaller obstacles swung about, making rat-a-tat-tat noises which distracted. He did not win but his people seemed happy with his effort.

No matter how hard H tried or how much he apparently pleased people he kept finding himself moved on to new stables and new people. They even put him on a boat and shipped him across the water to people who spoke an entirely different brogue. Yet even these people were kind to him.

His new people raced him more often and in longer races. Over time he enjoyed himself less and less and did not try quite so hard to please. He won a race, which pleased people, though his jockey was very hard with both his whip and his voice, which did not displease people. After giving the matter deep thought he decided that if he lagged behind and conserved his energy the jockey was kinder to him than if he tried to be up the front. So the obvious and natural thing to do was not to run fast enough to be a leader.

One day, at the time of year when the grass ripens and the birds fill the air with song, H found himself taken to an unusual place. The day had begun ordinarily enough, though his people, he sensed, were uncommonly excited, as if something extraordinary was about to happen.

The first thing he noticed was the amount of people. He had never seen so many people in one place. It made his muscles twitch to see the hustle and bustle and noise, and the excitement transferred itself to him and he could feel sweat breaking out all over him and his feet danced a jig of their own making. Then there were the other horses, all on edge as if they too knew something extraordinary was about to happen. There were so many horses they were beyond counting and all in his race. In the place where the people strapped on the saddle he began to sense that this was the moment his life was leading to.

The proceedings were so drawn out it tried everyone's patience. The routine was completely different. They had to walk in single file past people without number and then canter so slowly to the start H was convinced his jockey did not want to go there. Then they walked around in circles for a long time. Nerves were showing everywhere. Even H was nervous, though he did not know why. He sensed the air pulsating with expectancy and delay. He had been shown the first fence and it was unlike any obstacle ever put his way before. It was darkly green, as broad and long as a stable block.

Jumping the unusual obstacles was easy for him, though he had to concentrate very hard to avoid his companions all around him. The leaders were running fast. Too fast for H. A few horses fell, but not many. Some of the fences were particularly scary yet his jockey urged him to go forward and he responded, wanting to please. Slowly, though, as much as he wanted to please, jumping the fences was the best H could achieve.

Then, after jumping the biggest jump he had ever seen in his life for a second time, something strange and inexplicable began to happen in front of him, something he had never seen before.

Almost beyond his view, as if in slow motion, on the launch side of the jump, not the landing side where H might have expected, jockeys were falling off horses as if in sequence. Horses without jockeys were running hither and thither, jockeys without horses were also running around. One jockey was on top of the jump. H's jockey was unsure what to do. Should he go left, right or stop? H decided for him, doing his best to avoid his companions, looking for a gap amongst the mayhem to jump the fence.

He was the only horse to jump the fence that to this day bears his name, at least at the first attempt. From then on his jockey rode as if his life depended on staying in front and H offered him every encouragement. It was not an ordinary day and H knew if he stayed in front his people would be pleased with him. His jockey was kind to him all the way to the finish, only encouraging him with words. And the people, the hordes, seemed happy with him, and like in all good fairy stories H lived a long and happy life because in wanting to please people he was brave and belied the odds stacked against him.

Pitchcroft Blues

He is in two minds. He would like to go; he always does, yet the nagging torment that thinks itself to be common sense advises him that he shouldn't. The loans his advisors insist he should repay are as much an incentive to accept the invitation as to refuse. But Terry, as usual, persists. "Come on," he appeals. "Do something positive and stop moping. Chance your arm. See if Lady Luck comes a'calling."

As Terry came into the world undoubtedly a black cat walked by. He has no need of Lady Luck. He has a guardian angel with access to inside information.

Eddie's benefits must last the week. To come home potless from the races would make for a very thin week. It would be a week of sponging and going without: a week of battling the very worst of temptations. Without ever acquiescing to Terry's request for his company he gets into the van, his fingers as figuratively crossed as his conscience.

To make his capitulation ever more reckless the Pitchcroft has never proved a profitable place for him to visit. As Terry parks up, Eddie recalls an example of his poor fortune on the Pitchcroft. "This is the unluckiest place on Earth. See over there, the third-last, when I worked in racing I had a horse break a shoulder. I had to hold him as the vet put him out of his misery. In six years it was the only horse I lost."

"Some would say that sort of statistic makes you lucky."

"Well, if I have a bad night, I'll as likely as not jump in the river. If you try to hold me back you'll probably end up joining me."

"What are you on about? It's going to be a great night. Tonight is the night your luck is going to change. I feel it in my water."

In a self-absorbed sort of way Terry is a good mate to Eddie. When it suits him, when he would rather be at the races than at his market stall, he gives Eddie work, cash in hand. It is an arrangement that benefits them both. Terry earns more from betting than he does from selling cheap lingerie and for Eddie it is a boost to the pittance he is entitled to from the government. Raceform is Terry's bible, the Racing Post its daily supplement. Though booze, women and work have their places in his life, it is the racecourse where his happiest heartbeats occur.

"Eddie, my friend, what a lovely evening for it. The sun is shining, the going is perfect, the Almighty is in his element with a celestial brew in one hand and the Racing Post in the other." He slams the door shut and stretches his five-foot-six body so that his belly threatens to explode from his flowery shirt. "Worcester races on a balmy Monday evening. Where else would two red-blooded males like us rather be?"

"You should be bottled, your optimism is priceless." Eddie watches as Terry sets off with the strut of a peacock to be admired across the course, slipping underneath the running rail with a dexterity he displays nowhere else, keen for the fray to begin. He follows, not wanting to be left behind in case Terry offers to pay for him to get in, wishing in his own mind's eye that he could think of himself as worth looking at.

Eddie crushes a five-pound note into Terry's hand. "Put two quid each way on West Orient for me while I get the beer in."

"Oh, come on, Eddie, that nag pulled up in a point-to-point only three starts ago. It won't have the speed to win a hurdle, even a seller."

Eddie has studied the form and knows a likely outsider when he sees one. He, too, can be optimistic when the spirit of the fool moves him. "It was second last time in a similar race," he counters, wanting to have a beer in his hand before off-time.

"Believe me, the form is as out of kilter as a bent tuning fork."

"Look, J. P. McManus, the horses are at the start. You get the bets on, I'll get the beer in." He turns away, determined not to be dissuaded by Terry's Jehovah zeal, and bumps into a blonde of middle age. She smiles and Eddie mumbles an apology. They part. Eddie is badly in need of a drink.

"I said his luck would change tonight," Terry tells the blonde, winking, encouraging her to look out for him. "If someone were to take off the peel he's as sweet as a nut underneath."

They watch the race on the hoof, relocating to different vantage points as the race progresses. Terry once suffered a panic attack on the crowded stands at Cheltenham and now only spectates from inside the course. It suits Eddie as the cheaper enclosures are easier on his pocket.

"What have you done yourself?" Eddie asks, putting his beer at his feet to follow the race more closely with his binoculars.

"Come On Dancer. You've got fives. I've had a ton at evens."

"The 'back a John White's in a seller' method," Eddie scoffs.

"The form book never lies and it's a better system than your 'back a jockey with a fanny' system."

"I thought about Diane Clay's but it ran poorly last time."

"And you didn't like the name."

Eddie declines to continue with the repartee as the horses are rounding the far bend, entering the straight for the first time. West Orient is prominent, with Come On Dancer mid-division. "I'm happy," Eddie declares as they flash past the winning post to set off on a second circuit. "How about you? Yours off, do you think?"

"My ton is nearly two ton already. Mr. Bridgwater is sitting pretty, biding his time."

"If it's not odds-on the stable hardly think it a good thing," Eddie crows, his logic as watertight as a muslin cloth.

Terry concentrates on the race. This race, this humble selling hurdle, is business, the finishing position of Come On Dancer a manifestation of his credibility as a gambler.

As the runners turn out of the back straight West Orient takes up the running, with Come On Dancer making no progress. All the way up the straight West Orient is in the lead and Eddie becomes increasingly animated. At the last hurdle Criminal Record is his closest pursuer, the mirroring of his life lost for the moment in the excitement of the race. It is nip and tuck to the line and neither Terry nor Eddie can tell if West Orient has held on.

A few minutes later it is announced that Criminal Record has won.

"Bastard!" Eddie hollers louder than he intended. "Diane

Clay, too!"

Terry hands him his betting slip and tears up his own. "You got your stake money back. Mind you, each-way betting is for kids. It's like knocking on doors and running away." They wait for the weighed-in announcement so that Eddie can go and collect his winnings. "Criminal Record, eh," Terry adds. "If anyone should have been on it was you." Eddie ignores him.

Eddie had once been tall and dapper. Now his wardrobe is what remains of better days. Somewhere he has a wife and two kids. Somehow he contrived to lose them. In the night, when sleep is as slippery as good fortune, he sometimes tries to remember how old the twins are. It is a constant source of concern to him that Rebecca has not thought fit to get in touch, if only to claim child support. They had lived in a semi-detached three-bedroomed house; now he has a small subterranean flat courtesy of the council. He wonders how Rebecca supports herself, but mainly he regrets allowing her to badger him into giving up his job as a stable lad to better himself in factories and on market stalls.

He stands in line and watches the blonde woman collect on Criminal Record. "You done me on the line," he comments as she turns towards him, a clutch of ten-pound notes in her hand. She smiles and walks away.

It annoys him not to have backed a 10/1 winner just because of its name. Terry is keen on Jewel Thief in the third race and he knows he will not be able to back it because of its name. It is irrational but then Eddie is like that. He dislikes jockeys whose surname begins with a P or any food which has the word sour in its name. To back a horse with a name like Criminal Record or Jewel Thief is like referring to his past, to the loss of his wife and children.

According to Terry the second race is a foregone conclusion for the favourite. But Eddie cannot back odds-on chances, so he has two pounds each way on Frequent Vision at 14/1.

"Tilting at windmills, will you never learn?"

Shikeree, the odds-on favourite, duly obliges, with Frequent Vision a respectable second. Two races, two seconds: Eddie is ahead of the game.

"Jewel Thief," Terry insists. "This is the one I've come to back. Forget your six months at Her Majesty's Pleasure and have a tenner on."

They are seated on the steps in front of the bar, Terry with his Racing Post stretched before him like a prayer mat. Eddie leans across and points to Becky Boo.

"Windmills, Eddie Quixote. For once do what is right. Look. 'Shaped with promise in a recent flat race at Chepstow.'" He gives the paper to Eddie so that he can read the summary himself, wanting him to go home with a bulging wallet. "And McCoy can do no wrong."

"That was seven furlongs, Terry. Seven bloody furlongs. It's by a sprinter out of a sprinter. This is two miles over hurdles. I'm having a couple quid on Becky Boo and it's not sentimental because of Rebecca. I never once called her Becky Boo." He walks away, angry with himself, angry for Terry always plying him with advice he doesn't need.

Becky Boo is held up, makes good headway down the back straight and takes up the running turning for home. Going to the final hurdle she is still leading. Eddie jumps up and down with the sheer pleasure of it. Then the mare tries to duck out and Marston does well to keep her inside the wings. They lose ground, dropping back to fifth, leaving Jewel Thief in front, pursued by Noble Society. It is close fought, with Noble Society finishing fastest. Becky Boo rallies to finish fourth.

"Where the Dickie Davies did that come from?" Terry slaps Eddie on the back. "Our priest might as well throw his bible away after a result like that." They are both of the opinion that Jewel Thief was caught on the line, as is everyone else. It was a good, entertaining race, which seems to allow Terry to forget that he nearly won a thousand pounds. Then they hear the announcement that Jewel Thief had held on. Under his breath Eddie can only swear at the good fortune that follows Terry around with the devotion of a pet dog.

"What's up?" Terry asks. "You have a face longer than a fiddler's elbow. Three bets, three drawings." He hands Eddie a small whiskey.

"Thanks. I've been thinking about Rebecca and the twins recently, that's all," he admits, displaying feelings that he normally keeps wrapped and locked away. They watch the five runners come out onto the course for the two-mile, four-furlong chase.

"Wish I could help," Terry tells him without even a hint of sincerity. He doesn't want to pursue the matter. To him there is no fun to be had with intimacy. He knew long before Eddie that Rebecca was having an affair with a lorry driver. To his way of thinking Eddie is better off doing as he pleases rather than living at Rebecca's beck and call.

A grey canters past. "I was intending to back that old horse," Eddie says without enthusiasm. "But, 5/2, you know, not each-way value. He's well handicapped, though."

"Mr. Entertainer." Terry peruses the form in the Racing

Post. "He used to be useful. Won last time," he adds. "Might have a score on him."

"So you are ignoring this odds-on favourite, Crosula? Has won six on the bounce."

"McCoy can't win every race."

Crosula runs out at the first fence in the home straight and Mr. Entertainer wins easily. Eddie is so frustrated at Terry's luck he cannot even bring himself to curse or swear.

The fifth race, a novice chase, is the most competitive race of the night. Terry leaves it alone. Eddie has two pounds each way on Tap Dancing. It is an uneventful race which never gives Eddie any hope of collecting.

"It's been a great night," Terry decides as they walk across the course. "Not a good night, a great night. To celebrate I'll treat you to a tandoori." Terry is happy; his judgement has once again proved superior to Eddie's. "You leaving the last alone?"

"Are you?"

"No. I've had an interest on Milzig."

"What, the great Terry Docherty tilting at windmills? Milzig was beaten in a seller last time."

Terry taps the side of his nose. "This race is poor, less competitive than the seller he ran in last time. Let me mark your card: Welshman is light of former glories; Wings of Freedom is out of form; Goldingo, despite all the seconds and thirds in his form figures, is hard to win with. Here He Comes has only shown worthwhile form on soft ground. This ground is proper summer ground. Milzig likes the firm. I'm having fifty on the nose."

Eddie is tempted. Terry is rarely wrong when he is this confident and it would be hell on the way home with him gloating about how he should never ignore the advice of a punting genius. A tenner at 14/1 would do him no harm at all. But he knows he should stop betting while he is not losing. Yet temptation claws at him like bony fingers from beyond the grave. He leaves Terry to look over Milzig, to see if he can find something in his physique that Terry has overlooked. He goes to the bookmaker and sees 16/1 chalked up. At the end of the line of bookies he turns quickly around and almost knocks over a boy holding the hand of his father. As he is apologising the blonde woman passes by.

"People will talk, you know," she teases.

"Why?"

"Closest I've come to sex for a long while when you touched me up earlier." Eddie protests his innocence. "I'm only joking, my love. What are you on? I've done fifty quid on Welshman. I know one of the owners and he is very hopeful."

Eddie is unsure. Unsure which horse to back. Or if he should have a bet at all. Or even if the woman is chatting him up. Her clothes and jewellery suggest wealth or a wealthy husband. He sees Terry hand a bookmaker a fifty-pound note. "I was going to back Milzig." He watches as Terry goes to a second bookmaker and to hand over another fifty-pound note. "I have a strong tip for it."

The woman shrieks with laughter. "What! Jack's horse! Whoever supplies you with tips is no judge of a horse." She pulls a twenty-pound note from her handbag. "Here, you go put that on Welshman and on the way home you can buy me supper out of the proceeds. I only live across the road so you'll not have far to travel."

They watch the race shoulder to shoulder from the

top tier of the stand. The crowd has thinned and they have an unobstructed view of the race. Welshman is prominent throughout but though he leads between the last two hurdles he gives way timidly when challenged by Milzig and Here He Comes. Here He Comes is favourite and the crowd buzz with the anticipation of a mass winner as he takes the lead. It seems the only punter on the course who has backed Milzig is Terry. The buzz peters away to curses and sighs as Milzig forges clear in the final hundred yards.

The woman crumples her betting slip and bats it into the air. "Win some, lose some, lose some more." She slips her hand around Eddie's arm, not wanting him to slip away too. "I'm up on the night, so it can't be all bad, can it?"

He looks the woman over as he might a horse in the parade ring. Light of former years but with a pleasant conformation; paunchy but then he carries a fair bit of overweight himself. Yet with prospects.

"My friend was right," he tells her. "He said my luck would change tonight and it has. Fancy a tandoori?"

Two Sides of the Coin

They all stare down at the bed, their eyes focused on the occupant. Three pairs of eyes glued to the lifeless form of Alfie Good. The outside world is bathed by a vibrant sun that warms the hospital grounds and brings the daffodils, crocuses and tulips to vivid attention. It is a lovely March morning. Though the health of the outside world is uncared-for and irrelevant to those inside who must stand in prayerful remorse.

The nurse checks Alfie's chart, looks at her watch and adds something significant to the medical jargon that describes his condition. Noticing the concern etched onto the faces of the two visitors she tries to soften their trauma. "He'll be fine. The doctor expects him to wake soon. He is only unconscious. It is not a coma."

Mary cannot bring herself to believe either the diagnosis or the prognosis. She witnessed the fall, witnessed the half-ton of horse crush her husband into the turf. Now he lies lifeless; so unlike her sprightly Alfie. It is as if his very last ounce of energy was left on the ground between the third- and second-last fence.

"Why couldn't he listen to me? Why couldn't he be content with the hunters and the show ring? I said this would happen.

And what for? I ask you, what for?" Mary wraps her arm around her mother-in-law's shoulder, wanting to stifle her suffering, wanting to put an end to the continuous maternal strictures. But nothing will quell the storm of anguish at Edie Good's heart. "His grandfather ended up like this," she explains to the nurse. "Paralysed! Useless for anything. I said it would happen then and I said it would happen now. I warned him. Time and again, I warned him. I told his father to put a stop to it. But did he? Just encouraged him more. Wanted the glory, didn't he? Not one thought for my heartache. Now look at him. My only son."

Once again tears trickle down her drawn, pale cheeks. She makes no attempt to stem the flow, nor does she apologise for her outbreak of honest emotion. Here is her son, who she struggled for a day and a night to bring into the world, unconscious, perilously balanced between life and death, dead to those who love him, dead to his mother's touch, dead to her grief. And all because of an insane ambition to follow in the footsteps of his father and grandfather. Never considering for a single moment how fate had treated them so cruelly.

Mary leaves her mother-in-law's side and leans across the bed, kissing Alfie on the cheek, resisting the urge she has had all the while to shake him, to wake him from his silly prank. "I've got to go, love. I've left Martin with Mrs. Edworthy. He'll want feeding. You know what a greedy guzzler he is." But there is no spark of recognition, no flicker of an eyelid, no sign of life. Alfie remains inert, cut off, locked within the darkening prison of faraway sleep.

"You get on, Mrs. Good. We'll ring the moment there is something to report. Don't worry on so." The nurse resumes her duty, straightening the neat and tidy sheets, politely ushering away the visitors with the quiet conduct of routine.

"He'll be okay, won't he?" Mary asks wearily, apologetically, having asked the same question so many times before, feeling silly for asking again, but in need of information so that she can visualise how her life will be in the months and years ahead. There is the farm to consider, Martin to consider, Harold and Edie to consider. "He'll be like he was before, won't he?"

Edie Good remains defiant in her anger. A lesser woman would have succumbed to the heavy burden she has carried through the years. But not her. She is made of country stock. A woman born to suffer the toils and troubles of a farmer's wife. She sits before the roaring fire, memories of her father, Alfie's grandfather, spinning with the rapidity of a band-saw across her mind's eye: the doctor explaining why he would never walk again; the wheelchair that became the limitation of his world; the ceaseless effort to remain alive; the pitiful futility of his life, a life which was once too small to contain all he needed to pack into it: the corruption of normal living brought about by the madness of steeplechasing. She hated it. She would always hate it. And now she has cause to hate it even more. First her father, now her son. And in between the never-healing scars of her husband.

"Tea?" Mary asks, busying herself, tiptoeing around the farmhouse so as not to wake Martin, fearful and desperate for the phone to ring, all consideration of the up-coming war blown from her mind.

"I suppose so," Edie replies in resignation to life going on regardless to how she feels. She thinks to ask if Harold is back from Torquay and to enquire if the farm work is being neglected. There is a bullock ready for slaughter, ewes nearing lambing: real work, the bread and butter of true farmers. But all enthusiasm for the great minutiae of the physical life deserts her as she remembers that she has gone all day without a cup of tea.

Since the accident to her father she does not discuss horses, even though they are the stimulus of Harold and Alfie's lives. If she were to stir herself and go out into the yard and come face to face with Harold, in her present mood she knows she will accuse him of being the cause of Alfie's injuries. "Better put a drop of brandy in mine," she instructs, turning her head to make sure she is heard in the kitchen. Then she must articulate the afterthought which demonstrates the kinder side of her nature. "Make sure Harold gets something inside him. We mustn't let him go without. We can't have him keel over, can we? Then we'd be in straits, wouldn't we?"

"Dad." Mary always refers to Harold as 'Dad', her own father having died of tuberculosis when she was a baby. "Edie sent me out with this." She holds up the mug of tea and two large scones on a pewter plate.

Harold is with Peggy, the grey mare Alfie had his accident on. He is checking her over, running his hand down her back, over her quarters, feeling for pain, for a hidden injury. "You're okay, old girl. At least we can be thankful for that small mercy." He talks more to himself than to Mary at the stable door, knowing the health of the mare would not be uppermost in her thoughts.

He unbuckles the headcollar and lets the mare down,

slapping her on the neck and guiding her to the hayrack. Remaining in the stable he takes his tea and scones. Between bites he informs his daughter-in-law of his morning. "Lord Ilsington's son drove me to the racecourse in his sports car. Good of him, wasn't it? He's a nice lad. He said that a friend of his had a fall last year and was in a coma for a week but he's fine now."

It is not what Mary needs to hear; for hours and hours people have assailed her with gifts of optimism; kindnesses that in time might prove as regrettable as birthday presents too large or too small to be of use. This is just another conversation to which she cannot contribute without having laid before her the worst possible scenario.

"I was fortunate, you know," Harold continues, accounting for the time he might have been at Alfie's bedside. "I got the mare onto the train at Totnes and then Bert Flagg comes by just as I were tacking her up and we put her in his wagon with some steers he was taking to Ashburton market. I only had to lead her from the racecourse to the station and then up our lane. That's why I'm back so quick."

He knows he cannot escape from the inevitable. His absence, as important as it was to fetch home Sidney Abraham's mare from the racecourse stables, has kept him from the hospital, from seeing for himself the extent of his son's condition. "How is he, love?"

"The nurse says he'll be fine," she explains, the syllables of her explanation devoid of the professional optimism that prefaced everything the nurse conveyed to them. "I had to come home to feed Martin."

"How's Edie taking it?"

"As you would expect."

"It'll be hardest for her, after what happened at South Brent to her father."

"And you."

"I've only a duff leg. Doesn't stop me fetching a horse back from Torquay."

"It was bad at the time, though. She can't forget that. You were laid up a long while."

"Aye, but that's life, isn't it. I'm a darn sight better off than those poor beggars shipped off to France and who knows where else." Harold may be right but the accuracy of his argument will do nothing to lessen the pain of severance, the great lonely fear that nibbles at Mary's sense of purpose.

The mare, exhausted by her excursion to the racecourse, her fall and her return home, circles the stable and without preparation lies down, emitting a loud sigh once settled as if rest was all she ever craved. "There was no stopping him, you know. I had no hand in it. He asked Sid Abraham himself if he could ride the mare. It was arranged over my head. Alfie's a good lad but he's headstrong. He can never wait, you know that, love, don't you?"

Mary knows Harold is right. Alfie can never wait. Today is never soon enough for him. He married young. He fathered quickly. Since he was fourteen he has been an extension of his father, working as if an adult, showing hunters, doing his equal share on the farm, riding every type of horse brought to the farm. It is as if he knew his life would be short and he needed to get as much done as he could in the time he was allotted.

"It was the same with me," Harold continues, pushing home the bolts of the stable door, returning the plate to Mary, throwing the dregs of his tea to the ground. "My old dad knew I had to get it out of my system. If it wasn't for Edie and the farm I might have made a good show of it. I couldn't deny Alfie his chance, could I? And it's a marvellous thrill, you know, riding a horse over a steeplechase fence."

The Good family are seated around the fire, the wireless switched off now the Henry Hall concert has finished. The door into the hallway is open, allowing a cool draught to sweep in to dilute the heat from the crackling fire, the family not wanting to miss a single strident ring of the telephone. Outside the March wind is wild.

Mary cradles Martin in her arms. He is unusually restless, his quiet nature undermined by the raw emotion that sours the air he must breathe. Edie sits in the rocker, imprisoned into silence by the dreadful fear at her heart, heedlessly finishing a sweater she is knitting for Alfie. Harold is on the battered sofa, blindly scanning the local newspaper. On the wall, in the alcove directly behind Edie's rocker, is a photograph of Harold on a flashy chestnut flying the very same fence at Torquay which all these years later has claimed his son. It is a coincidence that all evening has drawn his attention. He cannot stop recalling the thrills he experienced upsides the likes of Fred Flippance, Captain Herbert, Bill Redmond and once the noble Lord Mildmay. It is the life he wanted for his son. He can still feel the pride as he watched him lead the others a merry dance, getting a tune out of Peggy that no one before had done. Everything in the future was possible until the fence adjacent the Eastfield Lane.

He can recall the compliments of those who stood beside

him; knowledgeable people who thought Alfie had the style of a professional jockey, and as his eye is drawn again to the dark-shrouded photograph tears the size of marrowfat peas form in his eyes.

"Dad! What's ever the matter?" Mary asks, noticing the tears before even Harold himself.

He stares at her for a moment, wondering what she can be referring to. Then the coldness of his uncloaked sorrow awakens him to the embarrassment of displaying tender feelings. Caught out in an act of self-pity, he fumbles for a handkerchief, hiding his face from Edie. But she too has noticed the unexpected tears and the cessation of the clicking needles is as calamitous as the wild wind. It is a silence that demands acknowledgement.

At the very same moment that Harold brushes his face dry and the fire spirals red-hot flames up the large chimney, a car arrives in the yard. It arrives in a hurry, with screeching tyres, the noise of its arrival provoking a frenzy of response from horses, dogs and cattle. Mary stands up, fear slackening her jaw, arresting her heart. Edie takes charge of the baby, her face as pale as if she had sat in the freezing cold all night. Harold buries his head in his hands, silently reciting the Lord's Prayer. All of them believe to the depths of their souls that the hospital would not impart bad news over the telephone and that at any moment they will hear the thud of annihilation at the front door.

They wait, and wait, trepidation a hurl of merciless hail that stretches taut their last strands of hope, pummelling the future into a shape only God might recognise. They hear muffled voices; conspiratorial and preparatory, and Mary is poised to respond, determined to remain calm and dignified. Edie and

Harold, she knows, will need her now more than ever. Alfie will expect her to look after his parents, to be the tower of strength he always tried to be.

But there is no thud on the door. Instead the door flies open, as if the whole weight of the March wind was thrust against it, and in breezes a smiling Alfie Good, his head bandaged, as ghostly, to his family, as if he were the headless coachman of legend. "Whatever's the matter with you lot? Thought you'd be glad to see me. The hospital have rung, haven't they? They said they would. All I need is bed rest and I can get that here as well as in hospital. So as I promised the doc, I'm off straight to my bed."

Mary needs no more convincing. It is not a ghost, it is her husband. She flies to him, hugging and kissing him, playful and angry in dispensing her wish that he never put her through such torments again. Harold, too, goes to him, more shyly than Mary, but with equal enthusiasm. Only Edie remains unresponsive to the miracle. She slumps into the rocker, her relief so enormous it has left her hollow and breathless. Then, as if to anoint the moment with memorable piquancy, the photograph of Harold on the flashy chestnut falls from its perch in the alcove and Edie realises that Alfie is destined to put the sword of torment to her heart many more times yet.

Veering Off a True Line

"Are you happy now?"

For half an hour Harriet has stoically struggled to re-hang the living-room curtains and by her taut expression anyone could see she remains unhappy. It is a battle of wills, a battle fought not so much against the curtains as against her boyfriend's complacency, the slovenliness of his home and his shortcomings as a soul-mate. The curtains had hung as if hanging on for grim life since before she entered his house as he thought they complemented the general rag-bag of his living arrangements. He lived a free and easy lifestyle; too busy living dangerously to cater for the rigmarole of domestic idealism. According to Harriet a disregard for interior design is only one of his personality defects.

"No. Not really," he jests, as usual not taking any real interest in her ambition to tidy him up.

She looks with a jaundiced eye at the disarray of the home he has invited her to join. As he gets up, wanting to put a check on her natural inclination to nest, in want of ending the small domestic skirmish, she moves away from the curtains, avoiding the intervention of his predatory token embrace.

"Until you trapped me in this cobweb of a house I considered

I had an eye for interior decoration. But where would I start, where would anyone start, to put this squalor into an order fit for ordinary human habitation?"

"Hey, don't get disheartened so easily," he jokes, keen to return the smile to her face. "You're in the company of a real professional. Wait till you see what I've achieved in the bedroom since you last saw it."

Having escaped his embrace she returns to the curtains. "Why won't they hang straight?" She tries again to even out the folds. "When did you last wash them? They feel like they are made out of cardboard."

"Questions, always questions." He pulls her back to him, wanting to make love, but she again escapes his grasp, slumping disconsolately onto the settee.

"You could, Wiz, I suppose, if you pulled your socks up, move in with me," she suggests, seeking compromise, the idea as much a surprise to her as to him.

They have veered off a true line. This is new. He too slumps onto a settee clawed almost into submission by his cat. "And what about Sophie?" he asks. "Is she invited into your Homes and Gardens bijou residence?"

"Your familiar, you mean," she jokes, still not smiling, rewinding to an old argument, whether a wizard could have a familiar or whether such a companion was the reserve of witches.

"You know she throws up occasionally, as all cats do. She's not particular where she sleeps and is in the habitat of bringing home trophies for me to admire. All of which is okay here but in your temple to the Arts and Crafts movement might not be so acceptable." He doubts if she is sincere, doubts if she is ready for such a commitment. "She also hates you, which is not good. She's not forgiven you for chasing her from the bedroom that time."

"It had a ruddy great rat in its mouth!"

"It was dead." His mobile phone interrupts the debate from developing into something meaningful and he goes to the kitchen for better reception. Out of the tail of his eye he sees Harriet pick up her hat and coat from the banister. "It's my agent," he informs her, wanting to delay her departure.

"Is that for tomorrow?" she asks as he joins her at the door. It is raining, which pleases him as his agent has just informed him about a last-minute ride on a horse in need of soft ground, but which annoys Harriet as her umbrella is in the car.

"Yes. Haydock."

"Will I see you tomorrow night? I'm busy the rest of the week. I have these local writers' groups I have to tutor."

He escorts her to the car, shielding her from the rain with the tail of his coat. "I'm schooling for Jeff Simm, so it makes sense to go straight there from Haydock." He is desperate for her to stay over but is hampered by the agreement that she stayed only if she felt like it. They have been a couple for two years and all of a sudden their careers are colliding with the regularity of dodgem cars. "I'll ring you when I get home," he tells her, though the look on her face suggests to him that the curtains might prove to be the last straw.

Wizard drives to Haydock with Mark Good, a nineteen-year-old with the world at his feet. He possesses everything Wizard once had, especially youth and vitality, but also no weight worries and a job as second jockey to one of the top stables in the country. He also has a racing antecedence that goes back into the mists of time.

"Good piece about you in the Post yesterday. 'Best of the Goods.'"

"I have big shoes to fill. What will be, will be, I suppose."

"I'll not be able to give you a lift back," he tells him, having not explained the situation when they had set off.

"That's fine, Wiz. If I can't manage a lift with one of the lads I'll cadge a ride home in the guv'nor's lorry."

"You'll go far, Mark Good. You have the right attitude. A few of the lads would have thrown the toys out the pram if I told them that."

Wiz parts company with his ride at the third fence, rolling clear of his pursuers. Wanting to retain the ride he tells the owners that he likes the horse, that it was athletic and strong but too keen. He suggests they either find a way to restrain its enthusiasm or they run it in quick succession to quieten its spirit. Wizard believes in talking to owners, bolstering their enthusiasm and giving his best advice. He is not someone to tip his cap, mumble something incoherent to the trainer and walk as quickly as he can back to the weighing room. As a professional sportsman Harriet would be proud of him.

"What happened to you? Did you wait around for a bus?" George sarcastically asks, taking the saddle from him. "The rozzers will have you one day for loitering with intent." Remembering his valeting duties George removes the girths from the saddle, throwing them onto the bench to be cleaned. "If you had hurried, Wiz, you would have seen the rare sight of young Mark dipping his hand into his wallet to buy some bubbly. Though to be accurate he wanted to get in Tizer but once I stuck his head down the toilet he had a change of mind."

Wizard shouts his congratulations across to Goody, trying to remember how long ago it was when he himself last rode a treble. George, his valet for the whole of his career, reading his mind, reminds him. "Too long ago, Wiz. Don't even try to remember. Just be thankful it happened. The world, these days, belongs to tight-arsed youngsters like Goody now."

As he crosses the Pennines he phones Harriet. She is at a meeting with other Arts and Museum directors and cannot be disturbed. Whoever took the call asks for a message. He thinks to say 'all my love' but decides on the spur of the moment to say, "Tell her that if the bedroom activity picks up I'll sacrifice the cat." After smiling at his own wit for a moment the realisation hits him that 'all my love' was all he needed to say. He rings back to leave the more appropriate message but there is no signal and the die is cast.

On Friday morning he drives straight from Malton to Exeter races for two rides book-ending the meeting. In the first race, riding an outsider, he gets a better than expected ride, finishing third. The trainer is amazed, promising him more rides in the future. "I can see why they call you Wizard now. You worked a spell on this old monkey."

His ride in the last race is his best prospect for the season. He had won a bumper at Ascot on King Sid the previous season and has looked forward to his first run over hurdles all summer. He is owned by a Cornish owner/breeder who had turned down big money for him and Wiz had journeyed down to Saltash once a week to school and gallop the horse. A bad experience first time over hurdles can spoil a horse for life and

Wiz wants for nothing more than a good educational run. It is his dream to retire in the winner's enclosure at the Cheltenham Festival and King Sid is his only logical hope of making the dream reality.

He sets off on the poached ground down the outer, tracking Mark Good. They are mid-division, travelling nicely, in a novice hurdle without incident. There is as always a lot of pleading for room at the hurdles, with everyone wanting to look after the nice prospects they are riding. Turning into the straight he follows Mark onto the tail of the leading group, both horses full of running, with those in front beginning to labour. Wiz is confident his horse is fit enough for the long pull to the finishing post and asks the horse to quicken. They ping the second-last, whereas Mark's horse catches the swinging hurdle, falling directly in front of King Sid. There is nowhere to go but over the top of the horse and jockey. It is all over in a second.

As he picks himself up from the ground, looking around for his whip, annoyed to have what he thought to be a certain winner taken from him by unlucky chance, he slowly recognises the carnage around him. On his left Mark Good is being attended to by paramedics. As he turns around he finds the prostrate mass that is King Sid. Dead. He had thought the horse had got up and galloped off. It is a kick to the guts far worse than a broken bone. Sitting upright, under the rails, looking more bemused than hurt, is a young amateur who Wiz has schooled with on occasions. Standing, observing the calm, efficient work of the paramedics, is Dave Letts. Four horses have come to grief at the second-last, though only King Sid has perished.

"Goody looks bad, Wiz," Dave tells him, taking off his helmet, as ghostly white as Mark. "He hasn't moved."

The tone of dread in Dave's voice fixes Wizard's attention. He walks across to Mark as a neck-brace and respirator are attached to him. He is connected to a drip, which serves to emphasise the seriousness of the situation. He looks as if the last drop of blood has been pummelled from his body.

"You were brought down by Goody," Dave explains. "And I was brought down by that young fellow over there." As he is talking another ambulance arrives and they go across to cadge a lift back with the young amateur. "Goody will be going straight to the hospital," Dave continued. "The first-aid room will suffice for us."

As the ambulance begins to move Wiz remembers his saddle is still on King Sid. He bangs open the doors and leaps from the moving vehicle to the consternation of the paramedics. To his astonishment King Sid is on his feet, with his owner and a vet checking him over. "That's right, look for your damn saddle, never mind my bloody horse."

With his soft Cornish accent it is never clear when Bert Rowan is annoyed. Wiz apologises and asks after the horse. "No lasting damage, I would say," the vet tells him, feeling King Sid's spine for pain. The look on Bert Rowan's face, though, suggests the same might not be said about the relationship between owner and jockey.

As he turns off the car engine in the car park of his block of flats, Wiz turns on the radio to hear of the life-changing injuries Mark Good has acquired. It is a brief headline but it is all Wiz can take. He has Mark's saddle and riding gear in the boot of the car, the memory of George almost in tears as he left the weighing room lodged at the forefront of his mind, both believing then that Mark might have died. To a jockey, enthralled by a way of life as adventurous as that of a knight at the court of Camelot, life-changing injuries can be as bad as death itself. Losing the ride on King Sid is suddenly small and insignificant.

King Sid is alive but Mark Good's career is extinct, and Wiz cannot get it out of his head that he was involved in the accident that took away the future of as nice a young man any mother had brought into the world. He sits in hopeless desperation in the dark, cold flat, waiting for something to happen, for someone to ring. And when the phone does ring it echoes like a gunshot around the flat, the sound he expected to hear earlier in the day.

It is Harriet. She is attending a writer's workshop and is worried because he has not rung her as he promised. She, too, heard the report on the radio and that he was mentioned as being involved. "I'll come over when I'm finished," she tells him, her concern touching. "I'll have another go at those curtains."

He is finishing a large Scotch when his agent rings with three spare rides for the next day, two of which would have been ridden by Mark. Life goes on, his agent reminds him. He pours himself another a Scotch and goes to the bathroom to run a bath and to tidy the bedroom in preparation for Harriet. On the bed, where she likes to sleep, is his old cat. She doesn't move as he sits beside her, in need of her loving response to his petting. She is cold and stiff. As he realises he has now lost his old devoted friend the sheer bloody awfulness of the day overcomes him and in his tears he realises that Harriet is the best aspect of his life and that she deserves more than what he has so far been prepared to give her. He remembers his mother's old wedding ring, remembering also his pledge to retire if he got married. But there is also his dream to retire in the Cheltenham winners' enclosure and as long as he had King Sid to ride he still had the dream.

He must ring Bert Rowan to ask after the horse and plead his case and he will offer Harriet the ring and ask her to wait for his vows. And he must bury Sophie in the garden before Harriet arrives. Never has he made so many important decisions without forethought and back-pedalling.

And he must get round to buying new curtains.

It is a long list of must-dos that can only get longer if he is to rearrange the future. But first he must go to the bathroom, turn off the tap and mop the floor. If Harriet ever gets to know how often he overtops the bath or burns the bottom of pans she will withdraw her offer of co-habitation.

Mrs Underwood's Pony

Mrs. Underwood stands on her doorstep inhaling the morning air. Ahh! Her senses tell her. The tea roses! The warm May has brought them on a treat and she is pleased with herself for ignoring Emmanuel Ploddy's advice to uproot them as last summer they were plagued by greenfly. Bert would have spun in his grave if he knew she had replaced his beloved roses with a hybrid. And probably come back to haunt her.

She smiles at the thought, seeing Bert in her mind's eye in one of his 'passions'. Over the thorn hedge and across the barley field she can see the Ploddys' red-brick bungalow, a spiral of white smoke coming from the chimney. Reminded that summer is not yet full-blown she pulls her cardigan tighter and rubs her palms together.

As she walks down the short path to the road to bring in the wheelie bin she notices that the lawn needs mowing. She will have to get Emmanuel in. At the gate she looks left and right. The long stretch of road is clear both ways. As she likes to do, she listens to the impatient lowing of Jack Hurworth's cows, a sure sign that he will be along shortly to take them up for milking.

She hangs around, wanting to see the cows amble up the

road. She waves as Jack appears, his collie at his side. He shouts 'good morning' as he opens the gate before commanding the collie to bring the cows on. Until his illness it would have been Bert taking up the cows. It is a sad memory but a welcome recollection.

It is still chilly and she rubs the goose pimples on her arms as she returns to the warmth of the bungalow, pushing the wheelie bin. Of course it shouldn't be in the road. Dick Ploddy should have brought it in when he delivered the evening paper. It was the routine. An unasked kindness. At an uneven part of the path she hears the sound of movement and immediately thinks she must have a mouse in the bin again. She peers cautiously in, not having Bert any more to keep her safe from creepy-crawlies and vermin. It is her greatest embarrassment that after forty years living in the country she has not overcome her fear of rodents. The bin, though, is empty, save for an ice-cream wrapper stuck to a glutinous mass. Then she sees what looks like a roll of five-pound notes. Not that it can be five-pound notes. How could a roll of money get into her empty wheelie bin?

It is a roll of five-pound notes. Slipping off the elastic band she excitedly counts her surprise bounty. Twenty-five pounds. She is a mite downcast as in the bin the roll looked decidedly more rewarding.

Over breakfast, a small bowl of porridge, she wonders how best to spend the unexpected windfall, not really caring now how it came to be in her bin. It is not a king's ransom but a useful supplement to her pension nonetheless. Every appliance that needs replacing would cost considerably more than twenty-five pounds. Certainly, her most pressing need, a new washing machine, would cost a lot more. She is still considering the matter when Emmanuel Ploddy arrives to clean the upstairs windows.

Emmanuel returns the ladders and buckets to his van and goes back to the bungalow for a cup of tea and a home-made biscuit. Mrs. Underwood has explained about her windfall and as he cleaned the windows he has given the quandary a good deal of thought. "A pony, you say," he comments, dropping his newspaper onto the table. "If it had been a monkey one might have thought it was nicked or counterfeit, chucked out of a passing car to get rid of it."

Mrs. Underwood pours the tea, unsure what he is going on about. "Why, may I ask, would anyone chuck a monkey out of a car?"

"A monkey, my dear," he informs her over the top of his Daily Mirror, "in racing parlance is five hundred quid."

"A pony?"

"Twenty-five."

They drink their tea in silence, Emmanuel engrossed in his paper. In her head Mrs. Underwood, as she is prone to do when Emmanuel is at her kitchen table eating her biscuits and drinking her tea, finds fault with him, thinking he wouldn't need to be cleaning windows and mowing lawns at his age if he had been as diligent a worker as he is at sitting down, reading newspapers. She would not have put up with it if he were her husband. She was fortunate that Bert was the complete opposite, so how the two were best friends for over sixty years is a mystery beyond solving.

"Do you think I should tell the police?" she asks, haunted by the vicar's sermon the previous weekend on how it was up to the individual to guide the lawless towards honesty and the Christian way of life.

"Why in heaven's name would you do that? Manna from the gods, that pony. Don't be soft. Haven't you heard about gift horses and not looking them in the mouth?"

"It's the first stroke of luck I've had since my Bert passed on."

"That's the spirit. Which reminds me, mentioning your dear departed, as you have. Today is Derby day. Do you remember when you and Bert and me and Florrie went to Epsom? When was it, '54?" He reaches across for a shortcake, cramming it whole into his mouth as he reflects on the day they picnicked on the Downs and had their fortunes read by a gypsy. "Your Bert bought a tip from Prince Monolulu, remember?"

"Fifty-five," she corrects him. "It was our fifth wedding anniversary."

"Yes, that's right. Bert backed the winner. What was it called? We all got over-excited. We had ice-creams and a go on the shooting range. Not that Bert spent any of his winnings. He said to me, 'This money is for Pru, Manny. She's eyeing a washing machine and she's going to get it.'"

"And he started his rose garden as well."

"He always was a jammy beggar." He reaches for another shortcake and the teapot. "He knew sod-all about horses yet he backed the winner because he was in the army with blokes called Palmer and Drake."

"Yes, that's it. The horse was called Phil Drake and the jockey was Freddie Palmer. Strange, you know, they hadn't met before they joined up, yet they ended up in the same cemetery."

"No getting maudlin," Emmanuel tells her, slapping his

hands together. "How about putting your pony on a horse in the Derby? For old times' sake. I'm off into town later." He drains his tea and as is his habit, belches loudly. "Our Raymond still works in Newmarket and he tells me to back Presenting." He pushes the paper over to her, tempting her to look down the runners.

Her eyes immediately fall on Lammtarra. The name sounds soft and delicate and she remembers Bert was always happiest when he was lambing. And she had a cousin somewhere called Tara. And then she notices the jockey is called Swinburn, the name of the avenue in Perth where their daughter lives. The name of the trainer is Arabian and her father was killed at El Alamein. She looks at the names of Presenting's connections: Asmussen. Gosden. Strawbridge. The bridge at the bottom of the road is called Hay Bridge but that is the only connection she can find. But then she remembers that her 'pony' had been presented to her by fate. "What odds will I get on this Presenting?" she asks, wanting to remain uncommitted.

"14-1, perhaps 16-1. Gosden has another runner and young Dettori is on that. People will assume he is on the better fancied. But our Raymond reckons Presenting is better suited to Epsom."

"How much will I win if I put twenty-five pounds on?"

Using his fingers as an abacus Emmanuel calculates the possible winnings. "Three hundred and fifty-four. Why, are you on?"

She glances again at the paper. Three hundred pounds would buy her a new washing machine. But her eye is drawn to Lammtarra. It is a nice name. On the mantelpiece is a letter from Alice, her daughter in Australia. Yet Presenting seems more apt, more in keeping with the way Bert had chosen Phil Drake. A pony was hardly anything. She would have spent a fiver on a return trip to town on the bus.

"Well, what about it? Just for a bit of fun. Bert wouldn't mind."

She is tempted but unsure. "What does the W stand for in Lammtarra's jockey's name?" she asks, stalling, trying to think what Bert would have done.

"Walter."

"Is he any good?"

"He's called the choirboy because they reckon he looks like one. Yes, he's one of the best. You're going to disregard my advice and back Lammtarra, aren't you? He hasn't run this year. Horses don't win the Derby first time out, you know."

She doesn't know. Most of the time she doesn't know what Manny is talking about. What she does know is that Bert's father was called Walter and that Bert was a choirboy when she first met him. "You put my money on Lammtarra. It's what Bert would want me to do and he never put me wrong in life and he won't start now."

Emmanuel shakes his head. "Looks like your twin-tub is going to have to last a wee bit longer as I see it."

Mrs. Underwood smiles. She knows better. She knows exactly the washing machine she intends to buy and who will be plumbing it in for her.

Mischievous Jack

It was not because his sire was called Scallywag and his dam Up To Mischief that he was named Mischievous Jack. At least not solely. There was no other name for him, not without using words deemed unacceptable by both the Jockey Club and polite society. Never was a son more determined to live up to his mother's name. From the moment of his breech delivery, his first breath accompanied by the midnight chimes of the church clock, Jack destined himself to a life of delinquency and altercation.

Life at Shaw Farm was always hectic. Toby Harris, Jack's owner/breeder, was smitten by the racing bug in his late teens, going to point-to-points with his fellow Young Farmers. The original fascination was as much hormonal as equine, with the Sloane Ranger types who frequented hunt gatherings in those days being as good a draw as a quality Men's Open. It was not long though before the shape of a horse's hindquarter took precedence over the curves of the Chelsea girls.

Involvement in racing became an obsession that did not diminish when he married Anne, a farmer's daughter. Somehow he shoehorned the exercise, management and qualifying of his horses into a daily life dominated by his financial need to be at the wheel of the lorry he drove for the family's nursery.

Whilst Harris Flowers prospered, and Toby became father to Alice and Graham, Jack grew obstreperous and unruly. Rarely did he accept Man's authority and at times he did his level best to convince people he was not a thoroughbred with a future but an untameable wild bronco. As a foal he fought against being halter-broken. As a yearling he was reluctant to be led anywhere, even from stable to field, without the company of another horse. As a two-year-old he took a manic dislike to stables and would barge out of them any way he could, usually by crashing out over the door. As a tall, wiry three-year-old he experimented with walking about on his hind legs and running loose, with a particular liking for destroying Anne's garden. In the autumn of his three-year-old days he was gelded. Not a minute too soon was the collective opinion. Gelding can modify a horse's temperament but it can never remove the true character of a horse. Jack was a lively personality; he acted on instinct not malice.

In the early summer of his fourth year, whilst being brought in from the field, he reared up, sparring with his front legs, acting the maggot, as the Irish will say, for no other reason than because he felt happy with himself. Unfortunately he smacked Toby in the face, removing three teeth and remodelling his nose. Anne Harris, who at the time still loved her husband, was petrified to see him prostrate on the ground in a pool of his own blood. She knew what she had to do and did it decisively; she phoned for an ambulance for Toby and Bernard Fowler, a local professional racehorse trainer, for Jack. To her untutored mind she believed Jack to be dangerous and instructed Bernard to have the horse put down. Bernard, though, would not consent to do so and Anne tearfully relented, knowing that Toby would never forgive her. Jack was, after all, Toby's first-born foal. Those that had followed, mercifully, did not possess the same mercury in their hooves as the elder brother.

It was not, as can be imagined, an easy task to get Jack out of Shaw Farm. A vet needed to sedate him to help get him into Bernard's horsebox where on the short journey to his new home he kicked and kicked until there was a hole in the partition.

Upon learning of Jack's transportation Toby was furious. Anne defended her actions and accused Toby of caring more for his horses than he did his family. Piqued by the kernel of truth in her argument Toby responded by telling Anne he was disappointed by her lack of support. It was their first marital argument; it would not be their last. In the end, though he could not admit it to his wife, Toby had to concede that Shaw Farm was more peaceful without the forceful presence of Jack.

Bernard, who trained mainly horses that other trainers would not touch, found Jack surprisingly easy to break in, though the only answer to curb the worst of his excesses was to work him hard and forget he was young and immature. Jack remained Jack, though, refusing to learn anything new until he was good and ready.

In time Bernard persuaded Toby that Jack would benefit from a couple of runs in hurdle races. He was, in fact, a natural jumper, as he proved from an early age by the ease with which he could jump out of a stable. His immaturity came to the fore at the races when the buzz and clamour of the racecourse proved too much for his temperament. On one occasion he refused to race, on another he careered off the course. Yet to Toby's unalloyed pleasure, on his fourth race, a modest selling hurdle, Jack won at odds of 33/1. It didn't matter that the twelve hundred guineas he had to pay to fend off the optimists who thought Jack had potential made the day a financial loss. Jack had won a race. He had bred a winner. Jack had redeemed himself. Toby was so relieved and proud he cried in the winners' enclosure. He also cried in the car on the way home and in the pub in front of his friends.

Declan O'Byrne was a fresh-faced young man with a burning ambition to make his mark in racing. He had ridden without success in point-to-points before he had even finished school, riding first for his cousin and then for Peter O'Riordan, one of the most successful trainers of point-to-pointers in the whole of Ireland. But Declan was a long way down the pecking order at O'Riordan's and seeing Toby's advertisement in the Horse and Hound decided to try his luck 'over the water'.

On the way back from Luton airport Toby and Declan talked of the great matters of the time, which to racing people is racing and horses. Toby, whose grandfather originated from Dublin, was easily won over by Declan's soft brogue and exaggerations. When he packed his suitcases Declan had led his mother to believe he was going to a seminary in Wales to think over the possibility of becoming a priest. To him it was not so much a lie as a kindness as his mother had always wanted to go into Kilmurrey to boast to her friends that her youngest had heard 'the calling'.

"Mr. O'Riordan, didn't he insist I ride away all the young horses. He would have no one else on their backs but me," he told Toby, taking in the foreign landscape, no doubt wondering when he too would be driving a BMW. Or a Mercedes. Or a Jaguar.

"You have good hands, then?"

"Well now, you wouldn't be buying hands as soft as these at the Kwiki Mart, would you?"

Toby could only laugh at such brazen confidence.

"You just leave Jack the lad to me. In the mornings I'll have him swinging round the gallop as quiet as your grandmother's G-spot."

Declan's first reaction to Jack's accommodation was that a barn was all wrong for a horse who thought he was the boss.

"He gets claustrophobic," Anne assured him, watching Declan struggle to put a bridle on the bay, with Jack running backwards across the spacious pen every time the bit was presented to his mouth. "He'll not stick it in a stable for a second."

"A racehorse can't be kept in a drear, draughty barn, he'll sure get cold in the bones. And isn't he the cutest divil to do anything with?"

"What about Paddy?" Anne demanded, holding Graham, her youngest, close to her side, both of them looking on as Declan led Jack away from the gloomy barn and the whinnying grey who was Jack's companion.

"Sure, he can go in the field. With his legs it'll be the grandest place for him," Declan told her, more concerned with winning his battle with Jack than worrying over the old grey.

Jack planted himself at the entrance to the stable yard, his ears flat, his weight thrust back on his hind legs. Declan flicked him with a riding crop, wanting forward momentum. Jack responded by running round in a circle as if that was all the exercise he thought he needed.

"But Toby will want to hunt him," Anne continued, still concerned about Paddy. "And you'll need him to lead Jack."

Declan, determined not to be beaten, pushed Jack backwards towards the stables. But Jack's stubborn streak was more than a match for Declan's show of bravado. He planted himself. He bucked. When his stable rug slipped round his belly he reared, pulling Declan clean off his feet. His temper frayed, Declan aimed a kick at Jack's ribs but Jack was too quick and half rearing, half spinning away, he pulled Declan to his knees. Pulling himself upright he smacked Jack across the muzzle with the end of the lead rein.

Anne, her loyalties divided, ran to the safety of the patio, putting Graham in the house. She then ran and closed the farm gate which led directly onto the main road. The last thing she wanted was to phone Toby to tell him Jack was loose on the A46.

The battle of wills continued: Jack rearing, jibbing, stamping; Declan shouting, sweating, blaspheming and bleeding. By dint of greater fury Jack was winning the battle, gradually inching his way back to the barn and the whinnying Paddy.

"For the sake of all that is holy, woman," Declan implored. "Will you not move yourself to help!"

Anne had no intention of becoming involved. The Irishman's presence in her home had come with a promise that she would never again be needed to help out with the horses; Declan would be a controlling influence. She returned to the house and her housework, leaving Declan to lose his own battles. Jack would win, he always did.

In the late autumn, frustrated and wearied by how she perceived herself and the children to be also-rans in their own home, Anne slipped away with the children to stay with her mother in Cambridge. Toby was infuriated by the inconvenience of her sudden departure; mystified by her reasons. Over the phone she argued that since Declan had been lodging in her home she had become nothing more than a housekeeper and that the children were too often upset by being told to hush when in the throes of innocent play. She was fed up with having to scrimp and penny-pinch to buy clothes when Declan got all he wanted for the horses.

Toby begged her to return and at Christmas Anne relented. He promised change. And he meant it. His family were important to him, even if they were a mite less important than his horses. His ambition was to give up the family business and become a racehorse trainer, and at night his dreams shaped his plans. Only in his dreams there was no family, only horses and success.

Qualifying was an easy matter: attendance at the Boxing Day and New Year meets, a word in an influential ear and a contribution to hunt funds and the certificates were signed. Jack, to everyone's surprise, behaved as if the whole day was a spectacle put on to entertain him. He happily cantered at the rear of the field, remained calm throughout and jumped every obstacle the uniform East Anglian countryside put before his path, including drainage ditches and tiger traps. Toby, aboard Old Paddy, had never been more proud of him.

Spring ousted winter in early January, encouraging daffodil and man to raise their faces to the sun. On a bright, cheery morning Declan cobbled together a fence to mimic a steeplechase fence, using four large blue barrels roped together and dressed with sacking and gorse. Jack hated it, hated it from the moment his eye fell on it, and hated it even more when he realised Declan expected him to go within twenty yards of it.

Declan did not pursue the matter. He returned Jack to the barn, removed the tack, gave him a pinch of hay and made himself a mug of coffee. He returned with a plan. He put down a row of telegraph poles which Jack trotted over without complaint. Holding Jack by the reins with one hand he raised the poles off the ground by placing either end on five-gallon drums. Jack cooperated as if butter would not dare melt in his mouth. And he jumped over them with the deftness of a hare. But he would not go anywhere near the steeplechase fence. He wouldn't even look at it, it so appalled him.

Declan, his ego refusing to allow him to admit defeat, reported to Toby that the schooling had gone according to plan. "He's ready to go to Newmarket to jump some proper fences," he boasted. "I made some good job of him, I can tell you."

An arrangement made prior to Declan's arrival meant that Declan would not be riding Jack at Newmarket. Hale Robbins, the area's leading rider, had phoned one evening and asked if he could ride 'that nice young horse of yours'. Toby was so flattered he would not have refused Hale if he had asked to sleep with Anne.

The understanding with Declan was that in return for working for a pittance he would ride Toby's horses whenever they raced. To jock him off would be unfair. But how could he reject the services of Hale Robbins, one of the country's foremost amateur riders? Toby was caught in the mire of a moral dilemma and had no idea how to get himself out of it without offending either Hale or Declan. So he did nothing.

All the while his marriage was in decline. Anne resented Declan's presence in the house and nothing Toby could say or do would placate her. To escape the daily disagreements Toby fell into the habit of calling in the pub on his way home, leaving Anne to eat with Declan. "Sure, you're not to worry," Declan advised, his reassurances only serving to fan the flames of her discontent. "Back home the wives wouldn't give it a second thought. They'd be thankful for the peace. But then I dare say you think Irish wives to be a bit backward in their thinking."

The annual vernal pilgrimage to the Links schooling ground at Newmarket is the opening salvo of the season for point-to-point enthusiasts in East Anglia. Toby parked the horsebox at the loading ramp, the unchanging scene sending an anticipatory tingle to course his veins. He instructed Declan to put bridles on the three horses, Jack displaying his frustration at being kept waiting by kicking the sides of the lorry, Declan berating him to no effect. "At least by being here it proves your mother stayed still once in her life!"

As Declan moved with difficulty between the three horses, Toby watched Hale and his friend Donny school Zara Thompson's horses. The two horses jumped four fences without incident and proceeded to gallop away into the distance. With Hale and Donny out of his view Toby's eye drifted to Zara and he enviously wondered if the rumours concerning her and Hale were true.

"I'll get the misbegotten son of a donkey's dick out of the lorry before he kicks it to Cape Clear and back," Declan shouted, bringing Toby back to reality.

"Lead him, don't get up on him," Toby instructed, still yet to tell Declan of the riding arrangements.

"I'd rather be sitting on him," Declan countered, struggling to unknot the halter rope as Jack tried to belligerently barge his way through the partition.

"Lead him," Toby insisted, his nose pressed hard up against a conflict only he could see.

It was a bright, cold day and Toby exchanged salutations with people he only came across at point-to-points. "The wife said she would leave me if I bought another horse. I did. But she's still here, look." "Perhaps you should buy ten more." "If he had as much money as sense he would be begging on street corners."

While Declan was walking Jack around, Toby put a saddle on Anstey Lad, a horse he had bought only a few weeks earlier. Unlike his stable companion the white-blazed, white-footed chestnut was kind and willing and although he had shown no sign of winning for his previous owner Toby was optimistic that as he strengthened he would improve.

"Morning, Toby. Fine day for it," Hale said in greeting, catching Toby by surprise. "That your young horse there? In a bit of a state, isn't he?"

"Oh, I wouldn't worry. For Jack he's quite settled."

"Donny is on his way. I said you might need him."

"He can give Declan a lead on the old grey. We keep coming back for more, don't we? But don't we love it?"

"I see you've landed the plum job with Zara."

"She's got some nice horses, mainly Opens and Maidens."

"No Restricteds?"

"Hardly."

"So you are free for the Restricted at Higham?"

Declan heaved Jack to a halt, planting his right foot on the edge of the ramp as a brake. Jack hoisted his head higher, keen to hear every sound, to see every sight, every bit of action. "Hi there," Declan introduced himself. "Isn't it the grandest day for it?"

Donny ran over, a saddle under each arm, his sudden presence enough to spook Jack into half rearing towards an expensive saloon. Hale took his saddle from Donny and to Declan's surprise walked across to Jack, patting his neck and making a fuss of him. "You ride Anstey," Toby instructs Declan. "As Hale is here he can have a sit on Jack. Donny will give you both a lead on Old Paddy."

It was not the place to argue and Declan consented to the arrangements. He had heard talk of Hale Robbins, heard him praised time and time again, but had not imagined him as a rival.

Jack, as was his custom, took control, backing away from his companions, jibbing and half rearing with excitement, unable to decide whether to go forward or to stand still. Hale humoured him, sitting quietly as Jack spun this way and that. Again and again Hale lugged him back to face the line of fences, Anstey Lad and Old Paddy circling patiently in front of him. Finally, in exasperation, his best equestrian skill exhausted, Hale raised his whip and cracked Jack on the rump, wanting to impose discipline. Jack reacted in kind, pawing at the ground before napping violently towards the golf course at the centre of the schooling ground. Hale pulled him round in ever-decreasing circles, halting his progress towards the golfers. They were the centre of attention, holding up other groups of riders wanting to school. Hale shouted to Declan and Donny to go on without him, accepting defeat.

Old Paddy led Anstey Lad to the first. Hale, resigned to having lost the struggle, relaxed and allowed the reins to slip through his fingers before dismounting. Suddenly, seeing his companions disappear into the distance, Jack had a change of heart and lunged forward, causing Hale to gather up the reins and regain his balance. If Jack was going to school it was going to be done under his terms.

At the fence Hale looked for a nice stride but Jack ignored his effort at organisation and hurdled the fence quickly and neatly, rising from the ground a stride outside the wing. They swung along at a pace far too quick for an inexperienced horse, Jack refusing to respond to Hale's subtle entreaties to ease up. At the second Jack again came off the ground from outside the wing. At the third Hale got him inside the wing, an achievement that allowed Jack to come up off his hocks, jumping the fence perfectly. At the fourth Jack had learnt enough to jump it equally as proficiently.

Scowls and curses had turned to smiles of satisfaction. "Bugger can't half jump."

The run-up to Higham went without mishap. Hale, impressed by the feel Jack gave him, schooled him twice more at Bernard Fowler's, declaring him the best young horse he had ridden for a long time, and turned down two other trainers to ride Jack in the Restricted.

Declan, his self-assurance nipped by the realisation that Hale Robbins was ahead of him in the pecking order, became less assertive and competitive and took to joining Toby in the pub. He continued to work hard, though, his ambitions drawn towards Anstey Lad, Old Paddy and Apps Boy, a new young horse Toby acquired from a friend of Hale's. He was consoled by the truth that at Shaw Farm he had three more horses to ride than he had back in Ireland.

Toby had never anticipated a season so much. It was all he could do to keep his lorry on the road as he daydreamed of what might be. In fifteen years he had trained only two winners, when Jack's dam finished alone in a Maiden and when Old Paddy won a poor Ladies' Open at Costessy. Although all four horses had improved under Declan's care Jack was the apple of his eye, the horse that would help him towards his ambition of becoming a licensed trainer. Over the years he had rejected the advice of friends and the pleading of Anne to sell him, to be rid of the bad temper and disruption. But his faith had remained undented: Jack would prove his detractors wrong.

Higham: ridden by Hale, Jack was to run in the second race, the Restricted. Anstcy Lad, ridden by Declan, was to run in the last race, the second division of the Maiden.

Jack, as was his custom, scraped, banged and sweated his way to the races. Yet out of the lorry, with the bridle and paddock sheet on, he was as relaxed as a priest at matins, the agricultural ballyhoo of a point-to-point an amusement to concentrate his mind. As he was led through the car park towards the tented enclosures, passing spectators opening umbrellas and struggling into waterproof clothing as a fine drizzle fell from a leaden sky, Declan could not believe he had the same horse at his side, the horse who would ordinarily turn himself inside out at the drop of a feather.

The state of calm repose lasted through saddling, the parade ring, mounting and the canter to the start, only dissolving into restless impatience once there. As the starter called the runners into line Jack backed away, half rearing, half cantering sideways, the other jockeys delighted at Hale's predicament. The starter quickly lost patience and dropped his flag, catching everyone by surprise.

Toby, standing by the winning post, a betting slip in his top pocket, sighed with relief, unaware that Jack had whipped around and refused to race. When the commentator relayed the information his heart sank to his ankles. Raising his binoculars to his eyes he was just in time to see Jack set off two fences behind, with Hale, undoubtedly, proposing to give him a quiet school round. The commentator, unused to seeing Hale Robbins out of contention, assured the spectators that Mischievous Jack could be disregarded.

In disreputable isolation Jack jumped neatly and fast, in harmony with Hale's feather-like communication. Passing the start line, amazingly, Hale found himself closing on stragglers. At the winning post with a circuit to go Jack zestfully passed backmarkers, with Hale hopeful of an astonishing victory. Jack joined the middle order runners, still jumping faultlessly. At the next, an open ditch, he passed three horses in mid-air, the commentator eating his words. By the next Jack was fifth, only fifteen lengths off the leaders.

Toby was now breathless with excitement. Even Anne and the children were jumping up and down with expectation. Declan, his fingers crossed, expected Jack to tire after making up so much ground. And just as the commentator was extolling the virtues of the peerless Hale Robbins, Jack fell.

"Sorry about that," Hale apologised, walking back to the weighing tent, his breeches bearing testimony to the soft ground.

"No worries," Toby said disarmingly. "No harm done."

"Getting him on the floor was not what was wanted. I should have pulled up but things didn't work out."

"Would you have won?" Toby asked hopefully.

"No. He got tired. I'd have pulled up."

"Plenty to work on then."

"He'll win a race, don't worry about that. I suppose you'll be going to Costessy next?"

"That's the idea. I have Old Paddy as well."

"Damn! I'll have to go to Thorpe Park for Zara. She's got six going there." They agreed to speak in the week, Hale hoping to persuade Toby to give Costessy a miss with Jack, desperate to keep the ride. At the tent entrance he turned to Toby and shouted after him. "He would want better ground. And a brain." He laughed. Toby smiled.

Though he pulled up Anstey Lad at Higham, Declan approached the next weekend with renewed vigour. With Hale unable to ride Jack he saw his two rides at Costessy as a probable winner and a safe conveyance. He even wrote to his mother, telling her that the seminary had closed but through divine intervention a wealthy businessman had provided a roof over his head, food in his belly and horses to ride.

Shaw Farm became a refuge of peace. Even Anne was happier, buoyed by Toby's promise of a heart-to-heart at a swanky restaurant. Jack was fit, sound and on good terms with himself. He even consented to being schooled by Declan over the dreaded dressed blue barrels. All was set fair for Costessy.

Costessy: Jack, ridden by Declan, was to run in the second race, the Restricted. Old Paddy, also ridden by Declan, was to run in the third race, the Men's Open. This required another pair of hands to lead up and Reg Swains, a retired farm worker, was recruited to lead up Jack, leaving Anne to deal with Old Paddy.

Jack behaved himself perfectly for Reg. He even remained calm and collected at the start.

Declan manoeuvred Jack to the outside to give him a clear view of the portable fences. He got too close to the second and hit it chest high. Declan slapped him down the shoulder to get him to buck up his ideas and Jack extended his stride, accelerating into the third, Declan yelling at him to pick up, making up the ground they lost at the previous fence. Wanting to curtail their charge to the front Declan eased him back. At the fourth Jack waited for instructions which did not come and the momentary indecision cost them dearly as they barely cleared the take-off rail. Declan had never hit the ground so hard.

Toby saw the fall clearly and feared for both his horse and jockey. When he reached the fence he was relieved to find only his jockey on the floor being attended to by St. John Ambulance volunteers. "Looks like a broken clavicle, love," he heard one of the ladies tell Declan. "A bit of concussion, too, I should think," her colleague suggested.

"I don't suppose anyone saw where my horse went?" Toby asked, looking down the course, unable to see any riderless horses.

"You sees them iron railing, next to road," a course worker volunteered, pointing a garden fork in the general direction, "well, they weren't bent before your horse barged his way over them. He had a huntsman in pursuit, if that's any comfort to you."

Toby scanned the broad, flat countryside with his binoculars but could see no sign of either Jack or the huntsman, displaying no interest as the runners leapt the innocuous plain fence for a second time, the uproar of excitations, the instructive slap of the whips, the crash of birch and the garrulous, profound breathing of the horses as they neared the limits of their endurance, combining to destroy the composure of a Saturday blessed by wintry sunshine. Stillness returned. No horse fell, no heroic intervention was required to keep partnerships intact. Declan groaned as he was lifted into an ambulance, reminding Toby he had to get back to Old Paddy, to find a jockey to replace Declan. "Any chance of a lift?" he asked the ambulance driver, leaving Jack, for now, for the huntsman to locate.

Dashing into the weighing tent he met Reg coming out with a saddle under his arm. "Was pondering where you might be," Reg said in his laconic way. "Donny Smith wants ride. I said he could. Hope you agrees."

Standing in the parade ring with Reg and Donny's girlfriend dressed in the silks she would wear in the Ladies' Open, Toby blanched at the announcement over the Tannoy. "Would the connections of Mischievous Jack please go to Costessy village to retrieve him as he is in someone's garden helping himself to cabbage and other sundry vegetables."

"Leave bugger there to scare off crows and pigeons. Bestest place for him," Reg advised.

"Poor thing! He must be frightened to death," Donny's girlfriend commented, placing a commiserating hand on Toby's arm.

"Never had anything to do with Jack, have you, love," Reg said, having had many past dealings with him, very few of them without incident. "Suppose it's my job to fetch the brute. It'll cost you a tenner, mind. At my age I shouldn't be doing this sort of thing."

"All I need now," Toby told them, "is for this old horse to do his tendon again and I'll go home and shoot myself."

"Why would you do that?" Donny asks.

"Why not? It was good enough for Fred Archer."

"Fit, is he?"

"No comment."

"He looks fit, doesn't he, Donny?" the girlfriend suggested as Toby took off the paddock sheet.

"He does, doesn't he," Toby agreed, thinking he had never seen the old horse so lean.

Unsupported and to the consternation of the spectators and the amazement of his owner, Old Paddy won by five lengths at 33/1.

In the three weeks between Costessy and Cottenham, the venue of Jack's third attempt at fulfilling his owner's ambitions for him, Toby enjoyed unparalleled success: Anstey Lad, ridden by Hale, won his maiden at Horseheath and Old Paddy, again ridden by Donny Smith, won the Men's Open at Mark's Tey. But success is always tempered by the nearness of tragedy and he also suffered the loss of Apps Boy who fell on the road, unseating his rider, a newly appointed temporary groom, breaking her leg in the process, and careering loose, colliding with a bus.

Declan, the point of his shoulder chipped and his

collarbone broken, continued to work as best he could, cursing his misfortune to every well-wisher. To fortify his spirit he spent more time in the pub where he had become a local sporting hero. His fame attracted girls, many of which he took back to Shaw Farm, his one-handed clatter drawing even greater criticism from Anne.

Sensing an opportunity Donny Smith volunteered to ride out for Toby.

Cottenham: with Hale committed to riding for Zara Thompson in the Restricted and Donny obliged to riding his mother's horse in the same race Toby chanced his luck in running Jack in the Men's Open, ridden by Hale.

Declan was opposed to the idea, aggrieved that Toby chose to act on Donny's advice rather than his cautionary approach. "You are casting your luck to the wind," he argued, "running a horse in a race he can't win. Isn't what he needs an educational run to help get his confidence back?" To appease his frustration Declan fitted a rubber bit to the racing bridle, believing Jack would be impossible to control.

For a short spell Cottenham was once a proper racecourse and boasted a concrete grandstand, unusual for a point-to-point course. It was considered a good track for a novice, with well-maintained turf and plenty of room at the fences.

Jack was on his best behaviour, even though he succeeded in kicking a hole in Toby's horsebox. Anne refused to lead him up and Reg was again drafted in to assist. As he was led onto the course Hale asked about the rubber bit. Before Reg could reply, as he struggled to unclip the lead rein, Jack lunged to the left, knocking him over. Jack bounded enthusiastically away, his neck outstretched, the lead rein falling free at the furlong pole.

Hale, caught unbalanced and unprepared, sat tight, gathering in the loose reins with the composure of a fisherman with a trout on the end of his line. He cooed words of impassivity, encouraging Jack to relax. To his combined relief and surprise Jack slowed easily to a canter, arriving at the start in a measured and for once coordinated manner.

The jockeys, as they milled around having girths checked and tack adjusted, reacted with incredulity when Hale announced he would be making the running. "On Lethal Weapon one!" "I'll not be sitting up your ass then." "Asking a bit much of a five-year-old in this company, Hale?" "Don't worry, I'll keep your side of Zara's bed warm while you're in intensive care!"

Hale waited as the starter called them into line. Anticipating the off he trotted Jack forward, gauging his advance just right. He led the fourteen runners, many of them the best Open horses in the East Anglian region, at a good gallop to the first. Jack, his head lower than usual, his mouth lighter, pinged the fence with gazelle-like ease, giving Hale all the right signals. They jumped the next two equally easily, gaining a length each time. Hale patted Jack down the neck, his faith restored. For the first circuit Jack led his rivals a merry dance, three lengths to the good. At the turn into the straight Johnny Hartington drove his horse upside, wanting to unsettle Jack and slow the gallop. Jack responded by lengthening his stride. At the next, Jack came off the ground a stride before the wing, his first real extravagance of the race. Hale caught his breath, enjoying the moment. Hartington's horse tried to imitate Jack and breasted the fence, catapulting Hartington over his head.

Jack galloped on. At the next fence the pace he was setting began to take its toll on his rivals. The horse in second place fell, got to his feet and charged through the plastic running rail, galloping riderless up the inside of the course, scattering spectators. Travelling a shorter route and without fences to slow his progress the loose horse caught the rest of the field at the sharp turn out of the home straight, crashing again through the running rail, broadsiding Jack.

Before Hale could gather his thoughts, to take stock of whether Jack had incurred an injury, before he could decide whether to pull up or go on as most of the field went pat him, Jack took hold of the bit and set off in pursuit. By the next fence he had clawed back ten lengths. By the following fence, an open ditch, he was back in front. He continued to lead down the length of the back straight. At the final bend his exertions began to get the better of him and Hale, determined to get him home in one piece, sat still as fitter horses passed by.

On paper, to finish seventh of ten finishers looked nothing out of the ordinary.

Yet Toby was ecstatic. "That's certainly the way to ride him," Hale told him, unbuckling the surcingle.

"He can jump, can't he?" Toby laughed, slapping Jack proudly on the neck. "He needed the race, though, right?"

"Yes, and I still think firmer ground would suit him better," Hale advised, struggling to undo the girth as Jack, although exhausted, refused to stand still. "He covers the ground so easily. I think you'll find," he continued, wanting to choose his words carefully, "that given the right ground, the right company, and better luck, he'll win next time with his head in his chest."

Toby smiled a victor's smile in Anne's direction, although

she had heard similar predications in the past.

"The rubber bit worked a treat. Brilliant idea," he told Declan.

"Sure, sometimes don't I surprise even myself with my genius?"

The exertion of racing for a full three miles tightened Jack up, delineating muscles in his neck and removing the last vestiges of fat from his belly. He ate up and calmed down and Toby scoured the schedules in search of a suitable race to enable Hale's predication to come true.

Everyone agreed that going back to Cottenham was a good option even though it meant keeping a lid on Jack's exuberance and temper for three weeks. The race was also restricted to riders who had not ridden more than ten winners, excluding both Hale and Donny.

Declan was quick to see an opportunity. He started an intensive course of physiotherapy and ignoring advice to the contrary, started to ride out again, riding Old Paddy around the roads as a lead horse for Donny on Jack.

This allowed Jack to demonstrate his new-found reposeful approach to life. Without a lead horse it was normally impossible to exercise him on the roads. When the mood took him he would refuse to walk past anything he considered suspicious – a sparrow on a gate, a vehicle any bigger than a mini, a combine harvester working several fields away. Declan recounted to Donny the litany of felonies Jack had committed: the gardens he had danced around, the cars he had dented, the traffic hold-ups he had created; all seemingly gross exaggerations as Jack tucked his head under Paddy's tail as he followed him like an articulated trailer drawn by a tractor.

One morning, as Declan's collarbone mended, Old Paddy, who had returned from his win at Mark's Tey with a cut that turned septic and who as a consequence had become fresh and full of himself, took exception to a large heap of sugar beet in a farmyard. He spun round, a devilment he was unknown for, catching Declan half asleep. By the time he had reclaimed control he was thirty yards behind Jack, wincing with the discomfort of a collarbone unhealed. He kicked Paddy forward, expecting to see Jack pirouetting towards him. Or upside down in a drainage ditch.

Ten yards past the offending sugar beet Jack stopped, bucked in annoyance at Donny's attempt to make him walk on and waited defiantly for his old friend to resume his role as lead horse. "I didn't even ask him to walk by," Donny said, shaking his head.

"Sure, hasn't he a multitude of methods of taking the Michael."

The Monday before the Cottenham race Declan decided he must test his shoulder. He rode Anstey Lad, who was due to accompany Jack to Cottenham, in a gallop with Jack, ridden by Donny. They began, as was customary, by hacking around the makeshift gallop, limbering up muscles and picking the most even ground in the sheep-strewn field: along the riverside; right-handed up the short, sharp hill; across the top – where the stables came into view; through the gateway into the cherry orchard – Jack's favourite spot for high jinks; down the swathe cut through the trees; through the next gateway; along the roadside and then sharp right back along the riverside.

Jack was eager to work, straining to go faster, his bay coat dappled and gleaming in the spring sunshine. Anstey Lad was more amenable, his ears pricked, his chestnut coat also portraying his well-being. After a circuit they quickened the pace. Along the river Anstey Lad led. Up the hill Jack extended his stride and pulled himself upside. "What are you feeding him?" Donny asked, his body contorted, in fear of being run away with.

Declan sent Anstey Lad on a pace quicker, his collarbone telling him tales he didn't want to hear. At the gateway to the orchard, having seen Jack do likewise many times, the horse cocked his jaw and ran off towards the stables, Declan powerless to prevent the escapade. Toby winced and closed his eyes, anticipating Jack to follow. When he opened his eyes, though, Jack was galloping on. After four circumnavigations he was still merrily galloping, his joie de vivre matching his energy.

"Your Irishman will have a steering job at the weekend," Donny assured him. "If he can hold him. Jesus! He's got strong."

Toby led Jack back to the stables, to let him loose in the sand-pit prior to hosing him down. Anstey Lad greeted their return with a frantic holler. Underneath him, slumped on the ground, his back to the stable door, Declan gave the look of a man tortured by defeat.

Securing a competent rider proved difficult. The obvious choice, the riding discovery of the season, Peter Alleyn-Struther, would not get off his aunt's horse, General's Fable, a horse he had won three Opens on and that was regarded as the best young horse in the area. Toby was disappointed to be rebuffed by the rider but even more disappointed to hear that General's Fable was to be in opposition. Eventually, as panic threatened to overcome logic, John Hoakes, the nineteen-year-old son of a Newmarket trainer, phoned to offer his services. After consulting Donny, Toby accepted his offer and went to bed to dream of a hat-trick of winners.

Cottenham: Old Paddy, ridden by Donny, was in the third race, the Men's Open. Jack's race was the fifth and Anstey Lad, also ridden by Donny, was in the Restricted, the seventh and last race.

It was a dull, cold day. In the pressured atmosphere of having a 'certain winner' Toby forgot his overcoat and shivered through the first two races and was forced to buy himself a new coat.

With Reg leading up Jack, Rachael, Donny's girlfriend, who had come as temporary groom to Shaw Farm, would lead up Old Paddy and Anstey Lad. Anne liked her; she was good with the children, which was a boon to Toby as her presence calmed the marital waters.

In a six-horse race Old Paddy finished last of two finishers, beaten ten lengths – the hat-trick bid over before it had started. Toby thought Donny had given the old horse too much to do and Donny agreed. Not that Toby was the sort to bear grudges.

John Hoakes strolled into the parade ring with the swank of a musketeer, his handsome young face glowing with brash self-confidence. He shook Toby by the hand and touched the peak of his cap in acknowledgement of Anne.

"He looks a tame sort," he observed, gesturing his whip in Jack's direction. "Quite the opposite to what I have been told."

"He'll liven up."

"How do you want him ridden?"

"Make all, win easily," Toby laughed, expecting his

instruction to be carried out to the letter. Seeing Anne cringe at the lofty confidence he smiled and told her the size of the bet he had already placed.

Anne asked how many winners John had ridden, a question Toby had forgotten to ask.

"I haven't," he said as if it had no bearing on the outcome.

Toby did not see Anne blush as John Hoakes brushed her gloved hand with his whip. His attention was on General's Fable, a strapping seventeen-hand chestnut with plenty of bone and heart room; the living picture of what a steeplechaser should look like. He was hard fit with not a hair out of place, and for a moment he might have exchanged Jack for him.

Jack settled nicely in front, allowing John Hoakes to sit tidily. At halfway he was twenty lengths to the good, with the others strung out like sheets on a washing line. Alleyn-Struther, realising the race was not going to plan, kicked on and reduced the gap by half. At the first in the home straight he closed to within two lengths, travelling exactly as a 1/4 favourite should do. Toby's heart was in his mouth, cursing his rider for sitting still and looking pretty.

Those who supported the favourite began to cheer him home, their glee tempered when Jack extended into the third-last and came away four lengths in front. Hoakes gave Jack a slap down the neck and they quickened again. At the second-last he was flamboyant and four lengths became six. The cheers were now groans. Jack gave them renewed hope by running down the last fence but he still landed running, galloping on to win by a majestic twenty lengths.

At the moment of confirmation Toby sank to his knees and crushed his trilby to his chest. Strangers, strangely, applauded him and acquaintances, who knew what owner/breeders go through with talented but capricious thoroughbreds, pulled him to his feet and ushered him towards the winners' enclosure. It was his fourth winner of the season; one he would cherish forever. The fifty-pound prize money and the Challenge Cup might have been all the world's diamonds for the joy they brought him.

"I would like to ride him when you get him spot-on. He blew-up going to the last, you know," John Hoakes said, defending the way he allowed Jack to veer off a true line.

Lady Harpley, General Fable's owner, completed Toby's day by telling him, "We think our horse is the best we've had in thirty years. We thought we would send him to Mr. Henderson next season."

But Toby's day was not over. Anstey Lad won his race and Anne complained about all the silverware she now had to polish.

The following week the sun shone brightly, drying up the ground. In spite of Anstey Lad and Old Paddy coming back from Cottenham with slight injuries, curtailing their seasons, Toby continued to walk on cloud nine. The only question was whether to run Jack on firming ground. He looked tremendously well; eating up and squealing with exuberance when set free in the sand-pit. Donny advised only entering him in the Men's Open at Higham, the next meeting. "If it's a hot race," he reasoned, "it will be easier not to run than if he looked a good thing in a lesser race."

On the Wednesday Jack bucked Donny off twice and he told Racheal to tell Toby to either commit to Higham or to rough him off straightaway as he was dangerously fit.

As usual Toby was not short of advice. Declan rang from Ireland to tell him not to run. Bernard Fowler drove over to say that good never came from running a five-year-old in an open race. Hale said he preferred to go to Lincoln where Zara had five for him to ride. Donny, desperate to ride Jack in a race, refused to sway Toby one way or the other.

Higham: the Men's Open was the third race. It was as hot a race as East Anglia had seen for years with people wanting to run their top horses before the ground got too firm. The course record was broken in the Ladies' race. Toby thought long and hard about risking Jack. But he kept hearing Hale's advice ringing in his ears that he would be even better on firm ground.

With the sun shining on his back Jack was so calm and at peace with himself that Anne was persuaded to lead him up, Rachael having ridden in the Ladies' race.

"I've never seen him look as well," Toby said to Bernard Fowler as Jack led the field onto the course.

"Let's hope you are as happy with yourself after the race," Fowler replied, envious of the success Toby was now having.

As was now normal, Jack jumped off in front, bouncing off the firm ground as if made for it. He stretched his rivals into Indian file. Donny sat quiet as a mouse, letting Jack dictate. By halfway he knew he was riding the best horse he would ever ride. With six fences to go seven good horses had cried enough, with only five left in contention. Each jockey thought the novice could not keep up such a stern gallop. At the second-last Donny decided to find out. Jack responded in an instant and Donny was unprepared for the huge leap he put in. At the last Jack was in full stride, galloping away to win by ten lengths.

Carrying a stone more than the winner of the Ladies' race he had broken the course record by a large margin.

It was a performance which staggered experienced point-to-point enthusiasts. "Best horse I've seen in years." "You have a Gold Cup horse there, mark my words." "A joy to behold." The congratulations came from all quarters. Toby was overwhelmed by his popularity. When he arrived home there was an offer of £50,000 on the answerphone from a leading bloodstock agent.

Never had a man needed such money. £50,000 would allow him to set up as a public trainer. He could give up the family business and live his life as he wanted to live it.

The following morning the dilemma was wrested from his shoulders as Jack was lame and no bloodstock agent would pay £50,000 of a client's money on a lame horse. The near-fore tendon was slightly swollen. It was not much. It probably wouldn't stop him running the following season. But it was enough. Toby had taken a chance with the ground and fate had bitten back.

Such is the savage and beautiful journey a man must take between dream and reality.

Jack never won another race.

As Unbelievable as a Thriller

I had ridden four winners at Newbury, my first four-timer since arriving from Oz, and I was feeling pretty good about myself. I thought at long last I had silenced my critics, the armchair jockeys who wouldn't know a whip from a piccolo. Of course at the beginning people brimmed with hospitality. "Good to have you over here, Murdo. Good to have someone of your calibre riding here." But then I won their Derby and got the retainer from the prince, in place of one of their own. It was then the knives were drawn, when I had to fight my corner. Anyway, that evening I went down to London, to the Waldorf, to a party given by the Australian Ambassador. It was there I met Belinda.

I'll refrain from describing her. Just think gorgeous and add a bit on. She had style, elegance and sex appeal. And she knew it. But these are memories which in my present position I am unable to afford myself.

What was to come later, alas, was that she was in the employ or the clutches of Vaslav Horniak, an adversary of mine from back home. Compared to Horniak a rattlesnake is trustworthy and cuddly. Horniak is villainous from his toes to the top of his bald head. In Oz I thought him just a common shark and fixer. I knew what I knew but I had to come to England to discover what I didn't know about him.

He liked to bet big and he didn't lose with good grace. In Oz he decided the profit was not in owning horses but in owning the men who rode them. For a while, until the authorities got wise to him, he had an impressive stable. Every unaccountable result was linked to Horniak's manipulations. He tried to own me but I thought my integrity was worth holding on to. It cost him a lot of dough to discover my virtuous streak is as hard as teak. It seems he has made it his life's work to make it cost me a whole lot more than I cost him.

I remember the evening I got back from Newcastle, when Horniak first turned the screw. I was tired and dispirited; my first journey to the north-east proved as useless as a politician's promise. I found the security system of my house breached, with one of Horniak's henchman waiting for me in the sitting room. He was lounging on the couch, as if he owned the place, his dirty trainers on the arm, a bottle of rather good claret in one hand, an empty glass in the other. In acknowledgement of my arrival he stood up, without introducing himself. Like all henchmen he displayed no manners or courtesy.

"Mr. Horniak is not a happy man, Murdo," he said, wagging a finger at me. "He's very displeased with you."

He was typical of the breed: tall, muscular and with the dress sense of a pimp. My first mistake was trying to seem indifferent to both his presence and the threat he implied. "I have a CD here somewhere of Naked Gun. You are welcome to it. It cheers me up every time." He dropped the glass and ground it into the carpet with his heel.

"Mind up," I said, impersonating Paul Hogan. "This is only rented, you know." I thought it a reasonable impression.

My intruder was not impressed. He swept his arm across the overmantel smashing the collection of Meissen figurines I had bought at Christie's to take home to my mother.

"Now you're not very happy, right?"

"I haven't been really happy since I walked in," I confessed.

"Mr. Horniak has sent me with a message. He's a generous man, Murdo. He wants you to know that he would like to be generous to you." He slurped good claret from the bottle like the slob he was. If he had asked I would have found him another glass. With the bottle emptied he threw it into the fireplace to create more tidying up for my cleaner. "What happens to knick-knacks can happen to flesh and bone, Murdo. Remember Lonnie Lansey? Sad what happened to him, wasn't it. The minute's silence at Flemington, though, was kind of nice, wasn't it? Wasn't an up-and-coming jockey after that, was he?"

I remembered Lonnie alright. As do the police. They are still trying to solve his apparently motiveless murder.

"I'm a foreigner here," I reminded him, reminded Horniak. "And that means I am not above suspicion. The stewards keep a close eye on me in every race. Those stories in the Sunday papers about race-rigging back home follow me around. It was too much of a coincidence that I left Sydney just as jocks were getting arrested." I needed to stall him, to say no to Horniak's advances without thuggo getting wise to my refusal.

"This isn't only about the horses, Murdo. If Mr. Horniak finds out you were behind that crap in the papers he'll probably let me kill you anyway."

If it was his intention to scare me by putting into my

mind his ambition to kill me whenever he got the chance he succeeded. Not that I was going to advertise my fear.

"Is that Horniak's message?" I asked, suspecting it wasn't. It wasn't.

"Palistrado is not to win the Eclipse on Saturday. Do as you are told and you can keep Belinda. Keep her alive, that is. Mr. Horniak has tired of her. I take it the message is understood. Not like back home when you were not clever enough to understand simple, basic instructions." I must have smiled at the recollection because I suddenly had the misfortune of him burying his fist into my solar plexus. Being a jockey there was no fat to cushion the blow.

When I returned to the vertical I was alone. Nothing was broken, which must have been as much of a relief to Horniak as me. I could still smile, though. I was not intending to ride Palistrado in the Eclipse. I had made the decision to get off the Derby winner on the way back from Newcastle. Which reminded me to convey my decision to George Blair, Palistrado's trainer. My retainer with the prince gave me the choice of all his horses trained in Europe and Jean Mallarmes was running Ambre, who I had finished third on in the French Derby. I thought the soft ground at Chantilly beat him; Sandown's stiffer mile and a quarter would suit him better. Palistrado was a lovely horse, a good Derby winner, but it wasn't a great Derby and he was a galloper, in need of every inch of the Derby distance. It was the done thing for a Derby winner's pedigree, for his career at stud, to demonstrate speed, to show breeders he could win at distances below 1 mile 4. I had advised giving the Eclipse a miss with Palistrado but Blair was not for turning.

I knew in the plane that I would be putting myself up to be

shot at as Ambre was still a maiden, I just didn't realise at the time that the shots might be for real.

Winning the Derby two years running has done nothing to improve my popularity and as I forged clear in the jockey's championship my popularity with owners and trainers further alienated me from my fellow jocks. I was seen as poacher-cum-mercenary. I was here for the money and the kudos and when I'd milked the sport for all I could get out of it I would hightail it back to Oz. That was the generally held view and I allowed them to think it. It gave me an advantage. I was living rent free in my opposition's heads and it made beating them in the top races that little bit easier.

Make no mistake, what I have I've earned the hard way. In Oz and over here I have always given 100 percent. Cheats and crooks leave me cold. And I have no sympathy for those who think the sport owes them a living. I hoped the articles in the Sunday papers would have allayed any suspicion about my honesty and commitment. But mud sticks. The race-rigging scandal back home was big news, my name kept being mentioned, and I was here in their midst. And of course I had the Ferrari, the Cessna and Belinda.

Belinda catalogued Horniak's involvement in crime to me in alphabetical order. D for drugs tied in with R for racing. He was in league with a Colombian drugs baron and needed to win big bets to launder the dirty money into squeaky clean money. Ten thousand pounds' worth of drugs money could be turned into twenty or thirty thousand courtesy of Ladbrokes, Hills or the spread-betting boys. He only needed to bet on even-money shots to do his business.

He envied the sheikhs with their never-ending supply

of oil money. The notion of a harem fascinated him and he had Belinda arrange it for him. It was her job to manage the harem in much the same way a stud manager runs a band of broodmares, though pregnancy was thought of and dealt with as the greatest of failures.

Belinda hailed from the same Sydney suburb as Vaslav Horniak. They attended the same school and lived on the same street. She made her way out of there by the more legitimate method of nude modelling and the fashion catwalk. She was honest, intelligent, witty and the best company a man could expect in the sack. She wanted to leave her past behind, to build herself a respectable reputation. She used to say, "To sin in secret is not to sin at all." She also said, "Crime is not a sin, Murdo, not when it is a necessity to live."

After Palistrado proved me wrong by winning the Eclipse (Ambre finished lame) Horniak began to lean more heavily on me. My Cessna was sabotaged at Sandown and Joe Fecklam, a fellow jock, surprisingly offered me a lift home. Just before the motorway Joe stopped the car and apologised. Before I had chance to ask why I found out. Two of Horniak's nastiest henchmen got in the car. I was told that unless I started to cooperate with their enterprises my ex-wife would be cut up into little pieces and posted to me.

Joe squirmed in his seat, wanting to be invisible, wanting to be walking the hard shoulder. I couldn't blame him for looking after himself but that didn't mean I intended to let him off scot-free.

"She's been bleeding me dry for years," I told them in a show of bravado. "You'll be doing me a service. Sydney's a big place, you'll never track her down." I had no doubt they were serious. In Oz they had shot my dog, burned down my brother's house and destroyed a garage where I stored my vintage cars.

"Murdo, who do you think you are dealing with? A boy band? We know the suburb and the street, the number, the time of day she takes the kids to school and when she arrives home. You know that, so stop messing with us." The second clause of the sentence was shouted in my ear to emphasise their point. It made no difference, though, because I knew that Roselyn lived in Auckland with her new husband, a Maori prop-forward.

A week later I received a severed finger in the post with a note suggesting the rest of Roselyn's body would follow in instalments. I buried it in the garden. I didn't even bother the police with it. It was laughable, so Godfather imitating. I was expecting a horse's head on my pillow for an encore.

Instead they shot me. It was only a flesh wound but it cost me six winners at glorious Goodwood. I had my agent release a statement saying I had broken a finger playing golf. They wanted me to stop a two-year-old of the prince's in a race at Newmarket. I told them they would do better by laundering their money by backing it to win. But my fellow jocks knew I hated golf and had refused to play in one of their charity tournaments and Joe Fecklam experienced a crisis of conscience and told the security unit about the incident near the motorway. So instead of having five days in the sun with Belinda I was with the police telling them everything I knew about Horniak.

He has won, though, I have to admit it, even if he has fled the country.

It resembles a poor novel I read on the plane over here. It is the sort of nightmare only a writer of pulp fiction could dream up.

I am tied to a tree, lured here by Belinda's screams. My arms are behind me, my wrists taped together, my feet manacled. Around my crotch is an iron contraption which resembles a chastity belt. With every minute movement the device digs into my groin as if searching for my balls.

I too would like to scream. But screaming would involve movement and I cannot risk the excruciating pain of possible castration. I have been here since early light. It is now dusk. No one has come. No one, I suspect, will. The security fencing and prohibition signs work too well.

It is as unbelievable as a thriller, and a cheap thriller at that. Surprisingly I have never met Vaslav Horniak. He may not even exist. Belinda may have made him up. For all I know Belinda might be the Mr. Big Australian police are desperate to arrest. I keep remembering what she said about crime not being a sin if it is necessary to live. Last night she suggested I cooperate with Horniak once in a while, to make life easier for everyone. It was said in her innocent fashion, as if she spoke in concern for my welfare. My views, though, are plain on this matter. She above all others should know me better than to even suggest I would stop a horse or help someone who would harm the integrity of the sport. I should not have slapped her face. I know that. It was wrong. But how was I to know she would call the boys round? I just hope she looks after the Ferrari. I love that car almost as much as I love her.

The Crux of the Matter

"Please sit down, Mrs. Meek."

His formality surprises her, irks her, even. Of course she had not known what to expect but the use of her married name increases her nervousness and makes her suspicious of his motives. And should she in kind call him Mr. Maddocks and not Tim? And refrain from mentioning their shared past? After all, it has been a long while since they last spoke.

She sits down as instructed, on the visitor's side of the impressive desk. She looks around and must admit that he has refurbished the old study to good effect. The king is dead, long live the king, she muses, admiring the newly stocked library shelves and the fresh decor.

"How is Duncan? Is the vending machine market still strong?"

She watches as if she were a juror at a trial as he seats himself behind his father's old desk and thinks how lacking he looks compared to his father's domineering presence. Why ask about Duncan, she muses, wanting to keep him out of whatever business this happens to be.

"Fine," she answers. "Holding its own."

She continues to stare across the void of walnut, at the third button of his expensive shirt, at his gold cuff-links, at the flecks of dandruff on his shoulder, hopeful that her reply will prove closer to the truth than the lie she suspects it to be. Not that Duncan and his business are at issue. So why mention him? Curiosity? Polite conversation? She is summoned as a tenant of the Overstock Estate, a mere commoner forced by official document to prostrate herself before the new Lord of the Manor. She feels disadvantaged. Duncan could have been here but it is not his business.

"Good. He was a clever man to give up the saddle before the saddle gave him up. I wish I had the foresight to have followed his lead."

She is tempted to make a remark about him not needing to, that the family fortune was always in wait for him around the corner. But she holds her tongue. She knows from experience it will do no good to antagonise him. He now has too much authority, too much influence. And she cannot know how much animosity still beats at his heart. To effect an appearance of sangfroid she brushes imaginary dust off her corduroy jodhpurs.

"My father's unexpected death has wrought changes to the estate, Mrs. Meek, as perhaps were foretold."

She has wondered since the funeral how the heir would use his new-found status. Until that overcast November morning she had not been so close to him in nearly ten years. She has heard the gossip and seen him from a distance at the races. He always was a local celebrity, riding in the big races if not actually winning any of them. And she will never forget the day he was airlifted from Larkhill, his life in the balance. Yet for the four years she has held a public trainer's licence they have sidestepped each other, even though she is a tenant of the family estate; his career on a steady decline, her career on the gradual up.

"Death duties have been punitive. My father lived in the past, wanting the world to march to his drum. He made no provision for his death, for the future of the estate."

She wonders if it is too late to offer her condolences. She had liked Dudley Maddocks. "Your father was always fair, always civil and polite. He introduced me to several of my owners. I will always be in his debt for that." She suspects the son is not intending to be as helpful. Rumour is rife that at the next review of farm and land rents there will be a huge increase.

"If only the Inland Revenue were as lenient as my father was to his tenants, Mrs. Meek."

Here it comes, she forecasts: the crux of the matter. Her innards knot at the thought of being put out of business by a large increase in rent and she wonders why he has changed so much. She had known him as shy, without pretensions: a home-boy who preferred the company of the local kids to the children of the gentry, refusing to attend boarding school, wanting to remain at Overstock with his friends. Somehow in manhood he has achieved a reputation for overzealous merrymaking and a liking for fast cars and even faster women. This man is not the Tim Maddocks she grew up with; the boy she once loved.

"Times change and we must change with them or perish, Cath ... Mrs. Meek."

She can feel again the big wet tears running down her face when she read the letter obliging her to attend a meeting at Overstock Hall regarding her tenancy of Apple Fields and Dobson Acres.

It was the unfriendliness that had hurt. She knew the other tenants were addressed by the land agents, yet she had been singled out for a personal audience with the owner of the estate. The implication was obvious. The men she had seen with theodolites and maps in the fallow next to her gallops were in the employ of Tim Maddocks. He had some sort of development planned for Apple Fields.

"I'm sure Duncan must always be looking towards the future, searching for new markets, new sites for his vending machines, replacing those he must lose to his opposition. You cannot survive these days by taking one day at a time. It is an on-going proposition these days, business. You cannot just sit back and expect money to come to your door."

"I'm in business, too," she reminds him. "I'm forever scouting around for new owners, for horses to sell to them. Money comes to my door but it is never long before it is off again." She feels her body tensing, waiting for him to ignite the conflict that will separate them forever.

"It's odd, isn't it, that as a professional jockey I never rode for you? Yet when you trained point-to-pointers and I was an amateur I rode for you all the time."

Odd? She cannot believe him. It was perfectly reasonable in the circumstances. "I have a policy of staying loyal to jockeys who come and school. You never did."

"It must have been a blow to Duncan, the demise of the business park. One by one the units emptied. I'm sure he saw the inevitable coming, made good the shortfall in income. Duncan was always blessed with foresight. He was one of the first claiming jockeys to hook up with an agent. It got him a reputation he did not deserve as being too ambitious for his own good. Too flash."

The craving to fire some home truths at him wells in her heart. But she remains quiet, her legs crossed, her hands between her knees, a prisoner to fate. If he knows, she reflects, why doesn't he say so and offer his regrets? Not that it is any of his business. Duncan is her concern. It is her marriage. Apple Fields and Dobson Acre is the business at hand. "He's left me," she blurts out through clenched teeth, the indiscretion palliative, an emotional weight lifted from her shoulders.

She has told no one about Duncan's absence, yet she has told Tim Maddocks! The man with the power to take away her stables, her home, her horses, the bread and butter of her life. "I didn't chuck him out, if that is what you think. He cannot accept that I am successful whereas he is struggling to keep his head above water."

She uncrosses her legs and softly stamps her foot on the deep carpet. This is not about Duncan she reminds herself. This is about what she loves most in the world. "I'm sorry. You can't be interested in my domestic problems."

"How many horses do you have in at the moment?"

The changing of the subject matter catches her by surprise, releasing more of her private life to him. "Three for the summer, plus a couple of young horses to get going." For a second she wonders how closely he has followed her career, how much he knows about her. "I had the dreaded virus in the yard last autumn. Then, just as we were having a few winners, I lost my best two horses. The owner turned up with a horsebox and whoof! They were gone to another trainer. No warning, no explanation. Things have picked up since the New Year, thankfully. I have had twenty winners, so we're okay. I think Assassi will go close at Uttoxeter tomorrow. I have Liam Lazenby riding."

"We are not always architects of our own fate, are we? We do not always reap the reward we deserve. I hope Liam does the business for you. He's a good man for the type of horse that saves a bit for himself."

"Yes, I like him." The crumb of comfort is easily digested, not that she is certain he is talking wholly about her own circumstances.

"My own position, for example, as it is facing me, is not of my making. You remember my father as courteous and generous. To those who advised him, though, on matters of business he was annoying and troublesome. Take the land he sold to your father. A classic example. He practically gave it away. I am sure you are pleased he did. Your father built an excellent range of stables."

She must interrupt, to protect her father's reputation. "He paid the price asked by your father. They were friends and ..."

"Exactly, they were friends. My father only conducted business with friends and always at a loss to the estate. This is the legacy I have inherited."

She would like him to stop. She will not stand for any criticism of her father. She needs him to get to the matter in hand. She needs to be put out of her misery. Unable to remain seated a moment longer she stands up and walks to the window, in need of calming her nerves, to be able to think more clearly. Her Land Rover is parked amongst the rubble of destruction. The old farm buildings of her childhood are already razed to the ground and she wonders what he will put in their place. His white Porsche nestles incongruously under a ramshackle corrugated lean-to, staring back at her like a harbinger of calamity.

"Do not get me wrong, Ca—"

"Oh, for pity's sake," she lets fly, turning to face him, to square up to him. "Call me Catherine. It is my name. It is the name you always called me. When we were children I was Catherine to you. When we rode in point-to-points I was Catherine. Never Cath or Cathy. Even in your sleep you said Catherine." She bites her lip. She has invoked the past, wrenched it into the present where it does not belong.

She cannot gauge his reaction: the boy who she loved into manhood. He leans back in the black leather chair, his dimpled chin supported by interlocked fingers. Once he was an open book, now he is encrypted. "Have you refurbished the whole house?" she asks lamely, wanting to deflate the ball of excitation in her head that threatens to run out of control.

He shakes his head and smiles.

Stranded by the window she feels even more vulnerable and curses her inability to walk nonchalantly back to the desk.

As he gets up her heart skips a beat. Instinctively she recoils, her heart fluctuating between treachery and the safe house of common sense. As he opens the door of a lacquered cabinet she dives back to the chair. It is a shock to discover that she does not really trust him any more. "Would you like a drink, Catherine? A sherry, perhaps?"

She looks across to him, her hands clasped together to prevent him from recognising that she is shaking. She cannot decide if alcohol is a good or bad idea. He takes her silence as an affirmative and pours a small sherry, pouring himself a large whiskey. As he sits again behind the walnut desk she notices he has put on weight. It is another surprise. She has only ever known him as slim and fit. She had not noticed when Duncan had put on weight. She had thought he played squash twice a week.

"I was about to say that my father has left me with a dilemma. The estate is on the verge of bankruptcy. Death duties are the problem. To ensure its future the estate must be made commercially viable. Too much of the estate assets have been allowed to slide into disrepair. Urgent action is required. I have already sold the house to a property developer. The part of the building we are in is all that remains that is mine. It is a sad state of affairs."

She places the untasted sherry on the desk and watches as he gulps down his whiskey. They have, at long last reached the bend in the road that might lead to the abyss.

"I must also sell off land."

"Apple Fields and Dobson's?"

"Yes. If there was another option I swear I would prefer it."

She is almost relieved to have it out in the open. She is also relieved that she believes in his regret.

"I cannot criticise my father for the mess he has left me and then leave my own son with a similar mess."

"Your son?" The revelation travels like poison to the pit of her stomach. She reels from its reality and half stumbles from the chair. Her only thought is to terminate the meeting and get away. He rushes to her aid and she squirms from his touch.

"You wouldn't know about him. He's in France with his mother. It is where I lived when I quit racing."

She pulls away, stubbing her foot on something hard. She bends down and picks up an old flat iron. "I'll fight, you know.

One of my owners is a barrister. You cannot take away my living without compensation."

"Catherine, we must be adult about this." He reaches out to her, to take the flat iron from her, but she steps away from him, holding the flat iron to her chest as if it is all she has left in the world. "The county must build ten thousand homes. Apple Fields and Dobson's and the land to the east are heaven-sent as far as the authorities are concerned. They will pull out all the stops to build a new village there. It is the only solution, believe me."

As he goes back to his side of the desk she throws the flat iron towards him. It lands heavily, knocking the sherry glass over and gouging an ugly scar into the polished walnut.

"Same old Catherine, I see. Whenever you can't have your way you must cause damage."

"Damage! You have the nerve to say that to me. You take away my gallops and then you accuse me ..." She rushes around the desk to slap his face. Her hand still stinging from the assault she picks up the flat iron, knocking over a lamp. "My father died building Apple Fields Stables. Do you remember?" Once more the flat iron is raised aloft, neither of them knowing in which direction she will throw it. "Do you think I could sell the stables? It is dad's place. He died there. Even Duncan would never ask me to do that."

Seeing her flag, as if the last ounce of defiance has left her, Tim steps forward and takes possession of the flat iron. "Go home, Catherine, cool down. Have a long bath and we will talk again later. Of course you will be compensated and with the money you could move to Lambourn or Newmarket."

As she is leaving, as he opens the door of her Land Rover,

she asks. "Would you be doing this to me if I had not left you for Duncan?"

"You broke my heart, Catherine. For a long time I could not get over it. But, yes, I would be doing this because I have to. This is about love, not hate. My love for Virginie and Fabrice and my love for my father and the estate and those who built it and cared for it over the centuries and who died here and are buried here."

As she turns out of the bumpy drive onto the main road a home truth demands she stop the car. She can cry now for her loss and the predicament Tim's cold business sense has saved her from. She could not have stayed, not with Duncan gone to a woman who claims to love him, and with Tim, the only man she has ever loved, married and seemingly happy. That is, and always will be, the crux of the matter.

Christmas Surprise

It is a cold morning. The church clock has just finished chiming seven. Two degrees of frost coats the grass a translucent white. Ordinarily Liam would be concerned by the frost, by the crisping over of the exposed molehills. But already the naked sky is dotted with grey clouds. Consequently, as his dogs hunt scents and torment the lake's wildfowl, there are many permutations going around inside his head. Tomorrow is an important day in his career. Tomorrow is King George day at Kempton.

His season is jogging along nicely. Twenty-two winners is a big step up on his first two seasons as a jump jockey and he has The Stratagem to look forward to in the big race. The horse is a novice on a winning streak of six ordinary races and contrary to the view of so-called experts he believes he has a golden opportunity of creating a Christmas surprise.

In the weighing room he is known to all as 'Lacks', a modification of the slighting sobriquet 'Lackadaisical Lazenby' imposed on him by a racing journalist unimpressed by a ride he gave a well-backed favourite at a wet and windy Plumpton in his first season as a fully-fledged professional jockey. His approach to his big ride, though, is as far from lackadaisical as can be imagined. Little else has occupied his mind for several days. It is his idea to run The Stratagem against more seasoned steeplechasers in the biggest race of the year outside of Cheltenham and Liverpool. In fact he had to twist the trainer's arm and then practically beg him before he agreed to the audacious plan.

Not that they agree on tactics. "He's untried at the distance, Lacks," Ben keeps on saying, defending his instruction that Liam should ride a waiting race. "We don't want to make asses of ourselves."

But the young horse is a swift, uninhibited jumper. Bowling along in front, blazing a trail and putting the opposition to the sword at every fence is what Liam believes gives them the edge. It was what they had done from Hereford to Fontwell and every race in between. To Liam it makes no sense to change tactics.

He is weighing up his options, rehearsing scenarios in his head, when he is aware of a commotion. It is Christmas morning, the air is tranquil, the nearby housing estate at peace. Yet the ruckus pollutes the serenity of the day.

At the top of the lake, behind a screen of willows, he finds a woman clutching to her chest a distressed miniature black poodle, protecting it from a snarling, agitated fox terrier. In and around the reed beds a spaniel, two Jack Russell terriers and another fox terrier are engaged in a frenzied search for sport. At Liam's heel is his faithful Alsatian.

Liam apologises profusely, snatching up the snapping fox terrier. "He hates poodles," he explains, securing his hand around the dog's muzzle. "The Blue Cross warned me when I got him." The terrier continues to struggle, shaking his head to free himself from Liam's strong grip. To restore calm, to the astonishment of the woman, he throws the dog underarm into the lake. "Don't worry about Bertie, he can swim like a duck. He'll probably come out with a trout in his mouth."

The woman's distress modulates to an expression of amused shock as she watches the fox terrier swim towards the shore. Then, as Bertie joins his friends in the reed bed, she smiles and Liam finally recognises the woman. "Sandy Leyton! By all the saints! Where have you sprung from?"

The woman drops the poodle to the ground, looking across to Liam's dogs to make sure they are a safe distance away. "It's a long time," she answers, not at all surprised to catch up with him again.

Sandy Leyton presents Liam with a new dilemma. She was his first love, a girl who still makes guest appearances in his dreams. "I live across the way," he tells her, wondering what she is doing walking her dog around the lake so early on Christmas morning. "Would it be inappropriate to suggest a cup of tea and a warm-up? I think it is time I got my reprobates out of the way of respectable people and their respectable dogs." As if to prove his damning description of them the spaniel trots into view, a mallard limp in its mouth, with two contented Jack Russells and two fox terriers in tow. "It seems duck is on the menu, if that helps you decide."

"I watched you from across the lake for a while," she admits, slipping off her coat, her eyes roving the nice yet obviously unappreciated fitted kitchen. "You seemed particularly occupied."

The semi-detached is warm and she places the heavy coat across a high-backed kitchen chair, adding to the general state of untidiness. She is uncomfortable with the unsterile worktops, the grubby hand-towel and the muddied quarry tiles. It is the complete opposite of her own kitchen. She removes her silk scarf and pushes it into the pocket of her coat, keen to give the impression that she is no hurry to move on to somewhere else.

"It's the King George," he tells her, filling the kettle. "I have a fair chance if I get the tactics right. It's not so hot this year. It tells you everything you need to know that Pitching Debate, who hasn't won in two years, is favourite."

As he searches the cupboards for his mother's old china tea service he wonders if Sandy has kept up to speed with racing from her loftier perch in the fashion world.

Amused by his inability to find whatever it is he is looking for in his own kitchen Sandy tells him a mug will do. "I bet you have hundreds. All dirty, all in the dishwasher."

"Voila!" he surprises her, pulling open the dishwasher, regaling her with the cleanliness of his crockery and dog bowls. As he makes the tea he thinks to recall their days together, when betting against one another kept what they had fresh and entertaining. 'Bet you a fiver I can muck my three out faster than you can do your lot'. 'Bet you a Bar Six I can do ten stone by Friday'. 'Bet you a tenner I can get this horse over those parallel rails'. Then he notices the sparkling ring that looks remarkably like a wedding ring and decides the past is best left to look after itself.

Belatedly slipping off his muddy wellingtons Liam notices the Alsatian at the window, her paws on the sill, wanting to know where her breakfast has got to. "Okay, Sasha. It's coming. Go into the living room," he tells Sandy. "Make yourself comfortable. I'll not be a moment."

But Sandy does not move from where she is standing. She watches Liam as he goes to a shed at the bottom of the long, barren garden, though it is plain it is not a garden in the sense his neighbours have gardens. It is an exercise paddock for the dogs. She is impressed that though the garden is littered with old bones, dog toys and matting, there is no dog mess.

"Is that where you keep them?" she asks as she opens the back door, pointing to the two Wendy houses either side of the shed.

"Yep. The planners wouldn't allow me to put up a range of kennelling. Max Jacobs gave me the idea. The neighbours couldn't object to a Wendy House, could they? I had to reinforce them but they are as snug as a bug in a rug."

The living room is as unkempt as the kitchen. The settee is home to countless copies of the Racing Post and one of the armchairs is uninhabitable due to a pillar of form books and a saddle perched on one arm. The pedestal dining table has become home to a holdall that has various pieces of riding equipment escaping its hold. Sandy inspects the random negligence with a curious and slightly disgusted eye. There is no yuletide festivity about the walls, no tree, no cards, only photographs of dogs and horses. Liam, she decides, has not changed one bit.

As if to prove her hypothesis Liam comes into the room bearing mugs of tea and talking horse racing. "So I take it you aren't optimistic of my chances tomorrow." In the kitchen he has speculated on why she is here, what possessed her to walk around the lake so early on Christmas morning. Her nifty sports car suggested she did not live in walking distance of the town. "Nine runners," he continues, handing her a mug, suggesting she sit on the settee, "two of which don't get the trip. Toby's horse gurgles when under pressure. Bobby's horse doesn't do a tap if he can't get his head in front and Pitching Debate is not the horse he was. I've got a right chance, no mistake."

Sandy settles herself amongst the Racing Posts, amused by Liam's enthusiasm and wishing she could join in as she once would have done. She looks across to him as he sips his tea and is gladdened that he has not changed and that his soul remains totally connected to the thing he does best in life.

"I live in Philadelphia these days," she tells him, offering him a clue to her present life. She knows how important a big win on television is to Liam. She is aware that his unflustered style of riding does not suit everyone and he is frequently asked by the stewards to explain why he did not pick up his whip or why he was not more vigorous in riding out for fourth or third place. She even wondered when a tabloid newspaper devoted a double page spread to allegations by 'vague insiders' that he was not above fixing results, if he had betrayed the sport he loves so much. "You know my husband owns The Stratagem, don't you?"

He didn't. It is a bolt from the blue. "He's owned by a company. Gestalta Fabrics."

"Gestalta is owned by Limprini. My husband's family own all the shares. My husband is Guido Limprini. They have their own stables in Philadelphia, Textus. They had a runner at the Breeders' Cup this year."

"In the two-year-old fillies' race. Finished fourth or fifth." He is animated now; Sandy is talking his language. The anonymous people he is riding for have turned out to be more influential and wealthy than Ben Lacy has allowed him to believe.

"Third," she corrects him, putting her mug of tea on the floor, aware that the conversation is digressing and that soon she will have to get back to her mother and stepfather.

"Do you want to come to Kempton with me?" he asks without forethought. "I'm going on my own, so you'll not have to put up with stupid jockey talk." As his face broadens with the anticipation of tomorrow he notices Sandy's face shrink into a portrait of sadness.

"I couldn't. You see Guido is having an affair with Ben Lacy's wife."

As he holds open the car door Liam notices the poodle asleep on the back seat and he thinks to apologise again for the trauma his dogs caused it. But too soon Sandy is starting up the engine. "Shouldn't you spruce up the house? It is Christmas, you know."

"Next time I'm suspended," he promises, adding to the humour. "Won't be long, now. I'm such a regular down at Portman Square there's talk of allocating me a parking space."

It is still cold and he has come out to the car without a coat or body-warmer. A shiver distorts his smile. If he knew what needed to be said he would say it and damn the consequences. He just knows he does not want her to leave. "Perhaps we could get together to celebrate my pillar-to-post Christmas surprise?"

As she drives away guilt harrows a path across her heart. If she had known he lived locally she could have rehearsed what as a friend she should have told him. Yet the truth would spoil his Christmas. Why, she keeps on telling herself, wanting to salve her conscience, should she take away his hope and expectation by telling him that Ben Lacy has not had The Stratagem ridden in a week and that in the New Year he will be shipped to the States to be trained for the Maryland Hunt Cup? He must know, she tells herself, that Ben is behaving oddly, that he is moping about like a man with nothing to live for.

Her mind is elsewhere. It is not on her driving and at the next junction she must jump on the brakes as the white line looms up in front of her at the same time as a van zooms across her front bumper, the urgency and violence of the preventative action throwing the poodle from the back seat. The thump and whimper collects her thoughts together and she knows instantly that Liam deserves to be told the truth. If she had his mobile phone number she would ring him. She will return and share his spoilt Christmas.

The Fairisle Mystery

Rogers and Heatley, jockey and trainer respectively, were summoned before the BHB's Disciplinary Committee to explain the running and riding of Fairisle at Newmarket in a ten-furlong handicap and the subsequent discovery of traces of cortisol, a banned stimulant, in a post-race urine sample. Both Rogers and Heatley vigorously denied any wrongdoing. Dominic Finbow, owner of Fairisle, was also summoned to the enquiry, having removed three horses from Heatley's Lambourn stables two days after the Newmarket race. He explained the removal of the horses to the Racing Post as 'protecting my interests'. Islay and South Uist were sent to be trained in Ireland. The whereabouts of Fairisle is unknown to this day.

The race in question was an innocuous 0–90 handicap run on the July course. Fairisle started fourth favourite at 8/1 (his owner having bet £1,000 on him at 14/1) He finished third, beaten a length and 2, running, as everyone agreed, including the BHB's senior handicapper, up to his best form. The race was won by Torsch, the subject of heavy support off-course, plunging from an opening price of 20/1 to 3/1 by the start of the race. The 2/1 favourite Anglo-Iqbal, finished last, his apprentice rider pulling him to a walk in the last furlong. The horse was considerably distressed and the racecourse vet reported that he had an irregular heartbeat and a general unsoundness. Clayton, his trainer, commented that he had never experienced one of his horses finishing a race in such a condition. Exhaustive tests failed to determine the cause. Anglo-Iqbal never fully recovered and died a few days later under a surgeon's scalpel after suffering an attack of colic.

Rogers said at the enquiry. "I was happy throughout the race. At the 2-furlong pole I looked round and thought 'Rogers, this is in the bag'. But then I picked up my whip and found him running on empty and I was fortunate to hold on to third." Asked if the horse felt different to the other times he had ridden him, he answered. "The strange thing was that the horse normally needs hard riding, he doesn't give a lot of his own volition, and then runs on as game as a goose at the finish. He's no world-beater, though we thought as he strengthened into his frame he might make a useful handicapper." The official handicapper concurred, adding that as a two-year-old Fairisle had been tried in blinkers.

The whole affair was riddled with intrigue and confusion, with many theories circulating for what had gone on and why. It was obvious that the BHB were as mystified as everyone else.

The waters were further muddied by an anonymous female claiming on the BHB's Raceguard hot-line that Fairisle was not 'off' that day and that Jill Rogers, Milne Rogers' estranged wife, had been seen in a London betting office on the day of the Newmarket race placing a substantial bet on Torsch. This led to Rogers having his licence temporarily withdrawn and having to go to the High Court to gain an injunction. The tabloids added considerable weight to the controversy by pointing out that at no time did Rogers pick up his whip in earnest in the final furlong. Rogers countered: "Find one occasion when this horse responded to the whip. He'll only give his all if you kid him along." At the enquiry the official handicapper had agreed that Rogers had ridden the horse in a similar manner as previous occasions. Journalists, though, clung to this shred of evidence against Rogers.

It was a baffling case with no rhyme or reason. Nothing could be substantiated except that Fairisle had been doped to win, not to lose. The BHB's security division could not name the anonymous female informant or identify the betting shop that Jill Rogers had allegedly used to place the 'substantial bet'. The owners of Torsch made no secret that they had backed their horse to win a six-figure sum, though one of them had also backed Fairisle. Jill Rogers said she could not have been in London on the day of the race as she was ill in bed with a stomach complaint, an alibi that also could not be substantiated.

Who administered the cortisol and where was also a mystery. The situation was made more perplexing by the theory that he could have manufactured the stimulant himself. Predictably the Hill House scandal of the sixties was retold by virtually every tabloid newspaper.

And why was Fairisle tested in the first place? There was no requirement for him to be dope-tested; winners, beaten favourites and horses that run inexplicably poorly are required by BHB rules to be routinely tested, plus a minimum of twelve horses per meeting. Copeman, in charge of the testing unit that day, said that as the first five races were won by favourites he chose to test the placed horses in the last two races to make up the required quota. "It was either fortunate or unfortunate, depending on which side of the table you are sitting," he said at the enquiry. "If Fairisle had finished fourth he would not have been tested."

Basil Heatley, who in forty years as a trainer had never before been summoned to Portman Square, was of the old school and was incensed by Finbow's disloyalty subsequent to the Newmarket race. He reacted angrily when Finbow insinuated that only the trainer or one of his staff had the opportunity to administer cortisol. Heatley threatened Finbow with a libel suit unless he retracted his accusation. Finbow refused, even when asked to do by the Senior Steward. "Blame will be apportioned in the direction to which the facts point," he added, refusing to say where Fairisle had been hidden away.

The BHB had no alternative but to adjourn their enquiry as they were unable to apportion guilt or explanation. They were unanimous in the belief that foul play was afoot but could not point a finger in any direction with any degree of confidence. It was a paradox encircled by an enigma of confusion. Why should a jockey stop a horse doped with a drug to improve its performance? They were suspicious of Rogers, with good reason given his poor disciplinary record with regard to suspensions. In his youth, as an apprentice, he had been found guilty of betting while a licensed jockey, and while riding in Germany he was suspended several times for 'not riding to make every reasonable effort to obtain the best possible placing'. In focusing their efforts on proving guilt on Roger's part it was argued that the BHB overlooked the possible guilt of the other suspects in the case.

The season rolled into autumn. Rogers continued to ride for Heatley, though it was rumoured around Lambourn that the partnership was upheld despite pressure from many of Heatley's more influential owners. One owner did move his horses from Heatley at this time but when questioned said it was for personal reasons unattached to Rogers. Rogers was convinced there was a conspiracy against him and became ever more truculent with journalists when asked about the case.

At the end of September two events occurred that heated up the story once more. The Rogers' divorce became absolute and the body of a hunt kennelman was discovered in a shallow grave half a mile from the home of Dominic Finbow.

The Rogers' divorce would have been a minor affair in comparison to the murder but for the revelation that Jill Rogers was co-habiting with Ian Baker-Blyth, one of the co-owners of Torsch. This twist in the tale gave rise to the theory that Finbow, a frequent player at the casino owned by Adam Hill, the other co-owner of Torsch, was in debt to Hill and that the coup was his way of settling the matter. Baker-Blyth was a research chemist and that he too owed Hill a substantial amount of money.

The murder of Ivan Anderson was solely a police matter, though like the Fairisle affair there seemed no motive. Anderson was well liked. He was a family man, with a devoted wife and two sons. He played cricket for his village and collected for a children's charity. His widow revealed that months before his death he had received a present of £500 from a local horse owner for humanely killing a horse with a broken leg. The man in question, Fred Ditchum, denied employing anyone from the kennels to shoot a horse. To Ditchum and the police £500 seemed a large amount of money as payment for dispatching a horse.

In December Finbow claimed that Fairisle had been sold

to a stud in Mexico where the horse met with an accident. He produced a bank statement to support his claim. Miquel Moreno, the agent he dealt with, confirmed that he purchased the horse on behalf of the Hispañola Ranch. The owners of the Hispañola Ranch denied ever doing business with Moreno. Finbow said that £25,000 was too good a deal to turn down, which was why he asked few questions. He insisted he kept the deal secret as he did not want certain people (Adam Hill, perhaps) from knowing about it. By this time it was clear that Finbow and Hill had fallen out and the journalist who interviewed Finbow reported that he looked haggard, as if he had the troubles of the world on his shoulders.

At the Newmarket sales Finbow disposed of all of his equine assets: Islay sold for 12,000 guineas, South Uist for 9,500 and a mare in foal realised 11,000 guineas. He then emigrated to Australia.

In February Ian Baker-Blyth went to the Bahamas to marry a fashion model half his age. Jill Rogers, jilted and humiliated, took her revenge by selling her story to a Sunday paper. She claimed she had phoned the Raceguard hot-line under instructions from Baker-Blyth. She was told the Newmarket race was set up and that they needed a 'patsy'. She cooperated as she had a grudge against her former husband as he had fathered a baby born to one of her friends. The phone call was a smokescreen to make the trail as cloudy as possible. She claimed that Baker-Blyth had contrived to nobble three horses in the race and that two jockeys were under duress not to win. She named the horses as Torsch, Fairisle and Anglo-Iqbal. The jockeys she refrained from naming. She claimed that Hill and Baker-Blyth won over £250,000 and that Finbow was led to believe that his casino debt would be overlooked if he cooperated by disposing of Fairisle. The murder of Ivan Anderson was not mentioned.

The new season began without Basil Heatley. During Cheltenham week he wrote to the Senior Steward and demanded that his name be publicly exonerated. The BHB declined to do so and Heatley handed in his licence to train, only to hang himself a few weeks later.

Rogers, in the eyes of the Stewards the most likely culprit, was advised not to reapply for his riding licence. He was forty-two. He was told they would look favourably on an application to train. He smiled and walked away, having already accepted an offer to rent Heatley's stables.

By now it was apparent that Baker-Blyth, not Finbow, was the linchpin in the business, though all the evidence against him was circumstantial. It was the same with Hill. The BHB hoped the police might link one or the other with Anderson's murder.

On the culpability of Finbow the jury remained out. In some quarters it was felt he had to be one of the conspirators. The disappearance of Fairisle remains the only real evidence against him. He was, they believe, under Hill's thumb and that his debts made him malleable for blackmail.

Like the disappearance of Shergar, the Hill House affair, the Flockton Grey incident and the Running Rein Derby scandal of 1844, the Fairisle mystery will go down in racing folklore. The powers-that-be would like it to go quietly away but Rogers, in particular, will not allow it to disappear completely. He feels hard done by and at regular intervals, whenever he gleans a sliver of possible information, real or imaginary, or when Baker-

Blyth's name appears in the financial sections of the meatier newspapers, he approaches a journalist friend and receives a small payment for a few column inches. Training is not proving to be his métier.

It is a sad and hard-to-understand business: Fairisle is thought dead, perhaps shot by Ivan Anderson, subsequently murdered to keep him quiet; Anglo-Iqbal is dead, his death no doubt as a result of whatever he was administered with by Baker-Blyth or an associate; Rogers is nearly penniless, hamstrung by alimony payments and an inability to train enough winners; Heatley is dead; and Dominic Finbow died in a car accident within weeks of arriving in Canberra.

Ian Baker-Blyth gets richer by the day and Adam Hill owns casinos all around the world. They believe they have got away with whatever they achieved that day at Newmarket. But I know different and now that Finbow is dead I can reveal that he gave me Fairisle in exchange for a horse with similar markings which he sold to Mexico. I call him Fresco and he is as safe a hunter as any man could wish for. Finbow had doped Fairisle to try to get his own back on Baker-Blyth and Hill for going back on their word to absolve him of his debts. Baker-Blyth had doped Torsch to win and Anglo-Iqbal to lose. To cover himself Finbow had to back both Torsch and Fairisle.

Where Finbow went wrong was that he could not get into the racecourse stables and had to administer the cortisol, injected into a slice of apple, as the horse came off the lorry prior to entering the racecourse stables, which meant the effects of the drug were wearing off come the time of the race. Baker-Blyth did not need to get into the racecourse as he had an accomplice. Me. Husband to a gambler as easily blackmailed as Finbow.

Not that I shall supply my name or what occupation allowed me access to the racecourse stables that day at Newmarket. Though as it is with everyone else involved in the business, except Baker-Blyth and Hill, of course, I have gained nothing but a good hunter for my trouble, a pastime I now must give up due to the pancreatic cancer that I am informed will kill me sooner rather than later.

And, of course, ironically or not, it is Fairisle, or Fresco as he is now known in hunting circles in these parts, who will eventually give me up to the authorities, and though I will be either too ill or dead to contribute to any further enquiry or investigation, Baker-Blyth and Hill will not be afforded the same immunity from prosecution.

Heaven and Hell

Lads come and go from Skilbeck with a frequency that perplexes and infuriates Adrian Bone. He only asks of his staff what he is prepared to do himself and it is not as if his methods are unsuccessful. He has trained six winners in two seasons. All he asks of people is that they learn his ways. It is hard work but horses are hard work.

He offers employees a job situated in splendid, peaceful countryside, in a village with a butcher, a supermarket and a pub. He has also given up occupancy of his late parents' bungalow in the centre of the village so that he can provide first-class accommodation as part of the remuneration while he boards with his brother above his carpet shop.

His own business takes him away from his horses every weekday from nine to five and he needs to have someone responsible to do the work in his absence. He just cannot employ someone who is lazy or incompetent. He has invested too much of himself in Skilbeck, both bodily and financially. It is a problem that in three years he has not come close to overcoming. He has tried lads from racing yards, hunting yards and on one occasion someone fresh out of the King's Troop. He has employed girls and boys, men and women. He has even tried a man and wife. But they either leave of their own accord or he is forced to fire them.

"Adrian, you're such a perfectionist. Why not lower your ideals a little?"

Laura means well, he knows that, and if it was not for her he might have given in and sold the horses by now. She is his rock, his constant, his fiancée. He removes his arm from her waist and walks to the other end of the concrete frontage of his stables to pat Disquisition, his best horse, on the neck, and wonders how he can reply without upsetting her. "What is the point of relinquishing the standard of work that has brought about the improvement in Disquisition since I've had him? Or Preacherman? To drop standards is to go backwards. You know that?"

She watches as he glowers at the scarified concrete as if he is inspecting each groove and ridge for cleanliness and precision. She smiles. Even angered he is dark and handsome and sometimes she cannot believe her good fortune at wearing his engagement ring. She has never loved anyone before and the feeling of Christmas it affords her is a gift she hopes to never have to return. It would though make life so much easier for both of them if he could find someone that he trusted and believed in to look after the horses.

He does not want to be angry with her. She is, in her way, only trying to help. But it is not the first time she has called his judgement into question.

He turns his attention to his car, laden with the computer equipment that represents his business. The boom in the economy is spent and he is working full throttle just to stand still. More and more he must tender lower estimates and argue his skill with greater force. He is, he knows, a good businessman. He knows when to cajole and when to charm. But he is wearied by the sprints up and down the motorway, the meetings long on promise but short on conviction, the deals that prove not to be good deals. He is tired. He would love to give it up and train racehorses for a living. And Laura would make a perfect trainer's wife.

"Are you saying I am wrong?" he hears himself say, not intending to sound accusatory.

"You know I'm not," she tells him, placating, throwing her arms around him, kissing him. "What you need is a holiday. We both do. You said we would this summer as a reward for my B.A."

His brow furrows as he remembers the promise. He pulls away from her, turning again to Disquisition for distraction. "How can I? I have this chap starting tomorrow. It'll be months before I could think of leaving him on his own. You know how important this year is for me." He turns his face from her, biting his lip as he sees disappointment register on her face. He had not meant to be so dismissive, to break his promise. He had thought to break the news to her more softly. But she always understood; deferred to his greater priorities.

She tries to hide her disappointment but for once frustration prevails. "How could you! You know how much I was looking forward to being alone with you. It was the same last year. How will you ever find the time so that we can get married? You have to trust people, that's all I am saying." And she must rush away, up the steep drive and across the lane to the security of home.

He does not rush after her; confident she will return and apologise for acting so childishly.

In the nearby wood a fox barks and the horses race to their stable doors, their ears as rigid as gun-barrels. Adrian is unaware of the fox and does not respond to the excitement of his horses. He is lost in disillusioned speculation. It is their first real quarrel and he has absolutely no idea how to react.

Joe Currie is tanned, slender and muscular, with close-cropped hair and the look of a young man who will grasp any opportunity that comes his way. In defiance of the Cumbrian summer he wears pale blue shorts and a t-shirt. His only luggage is a small suitcase, a holdall with the flap of his racing whip sticking out and a lightweight racing saddle. Laura does not need a photograph or for Joe to be wearing a carnation in his hair for her to recognise Adrian's new employee.

"You travel light," she observes.

"It's all I'll need for three months."

"Three months?"

"That's the agreement Mr. Radford made with Mr. Bone. It's a cross between a working holiday and work experience. Mr. Bone has promised to give me rides, which will give Mr. Radford's owners more confidence to give me rides next season."

It is not the arrangement Adrian told her. But what can she do? It is Adrian's business.

Adrian is eating a salad as Laura reports in to tell him she has completed her task.

"Where is he?" Adrian asks, stuffing lettuce and cress into his mouth as if in training for a competition.

"At the bungalow. He seems a nice sort."

"What do you mean 'a nice sort'?"

"Pleasant. Well-spoken. Open. I like him." She sits on the arm of the old settee and watches as Adrian devours his lunch. He is still dressed in his riding clothes, giving the appearance he is not going off anywhere. "You said nothing about him only coming for three months."

"Didn't I?" He is still eating against the clock, his devotion to salad greater, seemingly, than any responsibility to furnish Laura with the details of Joe's employment. "Radford said something about his girlfriend ditching him and wanting to keep them apart. Radford seemed to think more of the girlfriend than Joe. I said I would give him a ride if the opportunity came up."

Laura is surprised by the depth of her disappointment. Adrian had employed people in the past that she liked and thought likely to tolerate Adrian's regime, people Adrian was enthusiastic about at the beginning of their stay, and Joe seemed the nicest, even if he had said nothing about a girlfriend and a break-up. "I picked up some brochures when I was in town. The Greek Islands look nice."

Adrian stops eating and pushes away the salad bowl. The grimace on his face is the shape of disappointment. "Let's not count our chickens. You can't trust people to be what they say they are. He might be a drinker or a sluggard. When we go on holiday I'll want to relax, not worry about my horses."

On their first morning riding out, as the landscape huddles under an everlasting grey, damp cloud, Adrian informs Joe that Cumbria is the wettest county in England. "If you wait here for the rain to stop you'll never get a horse out of its stable."

"That's why you have those wonderful lakes up here and not down in Surrey. There are always compensations."

Already Joe is confronted by the unorthodoxy of Adrian's methods. They have just worked the two horses in a sheep-strewn field, with Adrian insisting he take hold of Preacherman's head and urge him into the bridle, a practice at odds with Radford's way of training which emphasised relaxation and patience, to have the horse drop its head and bit. With Adrian, from the moment the rider is on the horse he should be making it work, even on the road, pushing it forward, making him use all of its muscles. But everything is different at Skilbeck, everything from mucking out to brushing a horse's tail. And Adrian shows no latitude, no deviation, not even for someone new to the regime.

"Shouldn't think you know about strapping, do you?" Adrian asks as they dismount back at the stables. "Straighten their coat with a body brush and throw on their rugs, I expect. That's the way at Radford's is it?"

"When there's sixty horses it will always be different than where there is just two. But I'm always willing to learn. Mr. Radford said things would be different here."

He has already learnt that his day must begin at five-thirty and that he is expected to completely clean out the stables of the two horses, barrelling the muck several hundred yards to a muck-heap he is expected to keep squared-up and flat. He also must lightly groom and have tacked up the two horses in readiness for Adrian's arrival at six-fifteen. Exercise always lasts two hours. After breakfast he must groom both horses again, inspect their legs for cuts and sores and in turn lead them out for a twenty-minute pick of grass. The mangers are to be scrubbed clean twice a day and the tack saddle-soaped regularly. Then there is hay to be ferried from the barn at the end of the plot of ground on which Skilbeck stables stand, put into haynets and stuffed into a water barrel to soak before being hung up to dry. He must also cut squares of turf for the horses to lick. The regime is endless. And then there is something called strapping, and Adrian is addicted to strapping.

"It stimulates the blood, lubricates the skin and encourages natural oils to be secreted from the horse's glands. It's a process of cleaning the skin by applying friction and massage," Adrian explains, enthusiastically demonstrating the art with forceful glancing blows on Disquisition's hindquarters with the palm of his hand. "Good healthy exercise for man and horse. Nothing better for building up your pectorals and biceps. Half an hour both sides from neck to tail."

Joe watches in bemused silence from the open stable door, wondering what Kelly, his girlfriend, a chiropractor, would make of Adrian's grooming technique. The two horses look undeniably well but then Mr. Radford's horses also looked well in their coats, though perhaps not as fantastic as Adrian's.

"Stand with your feet apart, your left knee slightly bent and put your back and shoulder muscles into it," Adrian instructs. "And a cushioned blow downwards, along the muscle."

For five minutes Adrian works on Disquisition's neck, beads of sweat rolling down his cheeks, exhaling on every downward sweep of his open palm, the burly chestnut seemingly enjoying the massage.

"Have you thought any more about Preacherman?" Joe asks, grabbing the chance to intrude as Adrian returns the cloth he is using back to a perfect square.

"About his back?" Adrian queries, inflecting derision.

"Mr. Radford expects us to draw his attention to anything we think might be wrong."

"With sixty horses he would need all the help he can get. I think I am able to know the well-being of my two. Unless you think you know better."

"I didn't think he was using himself properly this morning. I know it's the first time I have ridden him but that's the impression he gave me."

"So you said."

"If you stand behind him you'll see that he falls away slightly on the near side. I also noticed he wears his off-side shoe unevenly."

Adrian will be late for his ten o'clock appointment. He knows he will be late but the opportunity to put Joe in his place is too inviting to pass up. He gives him a cloth to use as a pad and instructs him to strap Preacherman while he continues to strap Disquisition. Both horses methodically munch on their hay. Over the dividing wall of the stables Adrian presents his defence of Preacherman's muscular condition.

"If you are after the chance to get your girlfriend up here forget it. That gobbledygook doesn't wash with me. He needs building up. Good grub, hard exercise and a lot of strapping. You should have seen Disquisition when I bought him. You could have hung your shirt from his hip-bone."

On his first day in the village Mr. Cleghorn, the butcher, had told Joe Cumbria could be heaven and hell in one day. At the time he thought the remark was exclusively about the weather but experience is telling him that heaven and hell is an apt description for working for Adrian. Heaven when he is at work and hell when he is at the stables. His shadow, though, always lingers in his absence like an omnipresent and all-seeing CCTV camera. Laura, too, he suspects is used by Adrian as a snoop, reporting on what she observes on her daily visits.

"Do you like it here?" is a difficult question to answer as he does not want to hurt her feelings. So he tells her he is finding it interesting. When she asks if he thinks he will stay on for the winter he makes it clear that it is not his decision. Laura is nice; the complete opposite to Adrian, and he cannot see how she could love the guy.

"His grandfather taught him how to look after horses," she explains to Joe as he ineffectually straps Preacherman. "He used to be a carriage groom up at the castle. When he retired he wrote a book on the old methods of looking after horses. It's Adrian's bible."

When Joe asks, more to get a breather than out of sincere interest, how she met Adrian, she confesses. "I have known him all my life. We were born in the same ward of the same hospital on the same day. It is fated. We are the perfect match."

Sensing she is unresponsive, Adrian pulls away from the embrace. "What's wrong? Don't you love me any more? You're not falling for Joe are you?"

Laura straightens her skirt and licks her dry lips and asks herself for the first time whether it will always be like this, with Adrian's jealousy at the periphery of every aspect of their relationship. "No. Don't be so insecure."

"So what is it?" he demands, playing with the car ignition keys, toying with the idea of driving straight home.

"Why don't you tell me your plans? Joe thinks you already have someone lined up to take his place."

"I'm being prepared. He's only here for another six weeks."

"Will you give him the ride on Disquisition next week?"

"No, he'll be too hard a ride for him. He's not up to it."

Laura opens the car door and stares down the dark line of limes, noticing her father's car in front of the house, her own parked in front of the garage doors. On any other night they would have made love at the stables, in the car or in some sheltered spot in the woods. But tonight her father's negative comments about Adrian have disorganised her mind, ravaged her adoration of him.

"Where are you going?" he asks, his ardour unsatisfied.

"You should always honour your promises. That's what I have been taught."

"Tell me, Laura. Why are you so keen on him staying? I remember you said you liked him when you picked him up from the station. Do you like him a bit more now? Is that why you don't fancy it tonight?"

In the dark Adrian does not see the hurt disfiguring her face. He only feels his own loss and the sense of betrayal that he is certain lies at the heart of the change in Laura. As she walks from the car, rifling her pockets for the door key, he angrily starts up his car, revving the engine to startle Laura's parents into wakefulness, stifling the good side of his character, determining not to run after her.

He cannot decide what to do. He has always been so certain of her and her disloyalty cuts him to the quick. It is unforgiveable for her to interfere, yet he loves her, cannot live with the idea of someone else having her, taking what rightfully is his.

His software business is struggling, placing a strain on his finances and reducing his hopes to one day train racehorses for a living. He is too reliant on one big customer and there are rumours that the company is close to folding. He is relying on Disquisition and Preacherman to win him enough races to get him noticed by prospective owners, to be able to apply for a full training licence. Laura's championing of Joe is a distraction he can do without.

To placate Laura he has decided to give Joe a few days' break. "The ground is too soft to run Disquisition and Preacherman is lame," he explains to Laura over supper at the local pub. "I can manage for a few days."

"Aren't you worried he won't come back?"

"If he doesn't he doesn't. I have someone lined up for when his three months is up, remember."

Laura knows that unless Adrian changes his ways he will never be able to keep staff happy and that will haunt him if he ever becomes a public trainer. "I'll drive him down," she volunteers. "At least then we have a better chance of him coming back."

"No," Adrian tells her, the plea involuntary and more forceful than he intended.

"I can visit my sister in Reading," she tells him, refusing to be dissuaded, acting in Adrian's best interests.

Laura's car pulls up outside the bungalow. Adrian watches from behind the curtains of his bedroom, a glass of whiskey in his hand, the empty bottle on the window sill. It has been a long weekend. The vet has diagnosed Preacherman with a pulled muscle in a hindquarter and advises box rest. And still it rains. He is maddened by Joe's happy demeanour, by the way he talks with Laura instead of going straight inside the bungalow. The familiarity appals him.

As Laura drives away he makes his way out into the street, wanting air, to think. He sees Joe jog up the short path and into the bungalow. He walks away, down the hill, stalling at Pixton's house with his expensive classic cars arranged in a large glass-fronted garage and his sense of loss intensifies. Pixton has the wherewithal to collect classic cars whereas he only has Laura and his horses, one of which is lame. He decides there and then that Joe is to blame, that his life was everything he wanted it to be before Joe Currie appeared with his swank and know-better attitude.

Using his spare key he lets himself into the bungalow. The only light comes from the master bedroom, formerly his parents' bedroom. His anger grows as he imagines Laura in bed with Joe. He looks about the scantly decorated front room, with only the black figurine and the old radiogram remaining after it had been cleared by the auction house. This is the first time he has been inside the bungalow since and it feels like an empty, abused mausoleum.

"Anything the problem?" Joe asks, surprised to see Adrian in the bungalow at such a late hour, realising that it can only mean trouble and disturbance. He is naked to the waist, a toothbrush in his right hand.

Again Adrian imagines Laura in the bedroom, waiting for Joe to return. The whiskey is really hitting him now and he can feel himself sway as he walks towards Joe. "Nice day?" he asks. "I thought I'd welcome you back."

"Is there a problem?" Joe asks, weighing up the situation and deciding that the problem is Adrian.

"What would you know about problems? Did you do any rutting when you were away? How did Laura measure up to expectations?"

Joe cannot find the words to reply. There is madness about and he wishes it would go away. He should say something though; defend Laura if he cannot defend himself. But the confusing situation ties his tongue and his silence is evidence to Adrian of guilt. The madness must either escalate or dissolve. It escalates. Adrian picks up the figurine and tried to crack Joe over the head but Joe is too quick and instinctively lands a straight jab on Adrian's jaw.

"What's got into you?" he demands, looking down on Adrian sprawled on the floor. Once, in a stable lads' boxing tournament, he had knocked an opponent unconscious and he hopes he has not achieved the same fate again. He looks at the clock. In five hours he will have to go to work, to work alongside someone who is impossible to please.

Adrian staggers to his feet, feeling his jaw, walking slowly to the door. "You're sacked," he tells Joe. "I want you gone by morning."

He is not surprised. "Laura got me back with Kelly, you know. She's a wonderful girl, Laura. You are lucky to have her. She's asked Kelly to come up and look at Preacherman. She just wants you to be successful, you know, to make good your mistakes of the past."

Adrian looks at Joe as if he is a specimen in a jar, unable to make out what he is or what he is saying. Somewhere something, some aspect of the evening, of him, perhaps, is wrong. He feels an upwelling inside of him to apologise for something unsaid or undone but cannot decide which and he walks away, leaving the front door open, blood trickling from a broken tooth, his life changed forever.

The Golden Boy

"Any calls?"

Her eyes do not rise from the sewing machine.

"Any calls, Jude?" he repeats, annoyed by the obvious demonstration of where her priorities now lie. Noisily he closes the door and looks around Judy's sanctum, at the debris of a flourishing business, at the neatness and order of the paperwork and finished product.

The breast pocket stitched, she turns her attention to Bart, her significant other half for five long years, covering the monogrammed V.T. with her hand. "I thought you were picking up a new phone today. Why should I neglect my business to look after yours?"

Bart is ripe for argument. "The answerphone does not say thank you. It is impolite and impersonal. And why is it such of a hardship all of a sudden to get up to answer the phone? You answer your own calls, I suppose?"

"I don't have to get up. My mobile is in my pocket."

Bart looks again at the room that is the hub of Judy's life, focusing on the put-you-up bed that Judy more often these days prefers to sleep in than sleep with him. It looks as uncomfortable as their relationship.

"Your father called," she tells him, telling him all she wants him to know.

"Really."

"He has something he must discuss with you." As she expects, as she fears, Bart turns on his heels, slamming the door the only compromise he is prepared to make. "Talk with him," she shouts, her hostility heightened by the heavy-footed upswell of his departure as he descends stairs that remain as uncarpeted as the day they began cohabiting. But she knows he is as likely to speak with his father as he is to finance the carpeting of the stairs, his unflinching belief in his father's culpability in his mother's death as disuniting as the Korean ceasefire line.

He looks to the heavens, seeing for himself if the weather is living up to expectations. It is dry, with cumulus clouds scurrying by. Drying weather, exactly what he requires. He lights up a cigarette and leans against the house wall, staring down the garden, ignoring the neglect, the broken fork testimony to his short-lived attempt at domesticity.

"Why aren't you riding? Nobody want you any more?" It is Tiffany, the young girl from next door, sent out by her mother to bring in the washing. She sits on the low wall that divides the two properties, hitching up her skirt to allow Bart an unrestricted view of her inner thighs.

"No racing today, waterlogged," he explains, pulling the cigarette packet from his top pocket. "Want one?"

"I've given 'em up. My gran died last week. It was cancer. She used to smoke like a chimney. Apparently she's left all her money to charity. Talk about family upset." She looks up to the bedroom window above where Bart is standing, smiling and shaking her hennaed hair as Judy looks down on her.

"Why aren't you at school?" Bart asks, stubbing out the cigarette on the heel of his boot. "Been caught with your knickers down again?"

"No. That was our Sharon, anyway. You've had too many knocks on the head, your memory's going. And I ain't a schoolgirl no more. I'm waiting to join the Wrens."

He notices a cobweb attached to her hair and sits next to her to remove it. He looks up at the bedroom window to see if the coast is clear.

"I've cleaned out our Joe's toy cupboard. It pays to keep mum sweet. And it keeps me fingers out of me knickers." She laughs out loud, throwing her head back and thrusting her chest towards Bart.

"You need a boyfriend, Tiffany. I would not have thought the Wrens a good place to find one."

"I'm fed up with boys. They only want one thing and I'm too mature these days to provide it. Done it, been there, got the t-shirt. I want a proper bloke now. I need to move on, if you know what I mean."

Bart laughs at her impudence, at her naivety. If Judy was not home he would be tempted to invite Tiffany indoors to see if she is as uninhibited as her sister. He does not pretend to himself or anyone else that he is a saint and it is a constant struggle to remain faithful to Judy, especially with the Monroe girls living next door.

"Are you riding tomorrow?" she asks, getting off the wall to stand directly in front of him. "It must be dead nice going different places and meeting new people."

He kisses her forehead. She will play on his mind; a fantasy that might help him over the torment of separation. For a moment he toys with the idea of taking her to Somerset, the idea only repulsed by not knowing how the Rammages would respond if he turned up with a girl nearly half his age. Don Rammage likes him, employs him on a regular basis. They have promised him the ride on Cool River in the Grand National; an outsider, a no-hoper to some people, but still a ride in the world's greatest race. Sex with Tiffany would be fun but not worth sacrificing a ride in the National for. "Schooling tomorrow," he tells her, knowing that not for the first time he will have to explain what schooling a horse entails.

"Polly took him hunting the weekend. Perked him up no end, hasn't it, Pol?" Don Rammage tells Bart as he hoists him into the saddle. "Well, come on, Pol, tell Bart he bucked you off yesterday morning."

Polly gets down from the fence and walks towards her father, shooing from her path the curious Charolais steers that are the Rammages' bread and butter, their playfulness enough to send the chestnut gelding bounding away to the centre of the field, allowing Bart to demonstrate his balance, his ability to sit still, to gather up the reins with the deft efficiency of a croupier shuffling cards, not looking for a moment like he might fall off.

"Well done, my boy," Don shouts, putting an arm around his limping daughter. "If you could sit like that, Pol, you wouldn't have a twisted ankle."

Bart steers Cool River back to the Rammages, pulling up the girth and zipping up his anorak against the cold wind, asking for instructions, his eye straying to Polly.

"Twice up the hill, I think. Go a third if you want but Polly has done plenty with him lately, haven't you, Pol? No need to jump him today."

"I'd do three, Bart," Polly advises. "Punishment for dropping me."

Conical Hill is a natural feature of the landscape, after which the farm is named. It stands sentinel over the flat terrain, separating the Rammage farmland from the ancestral reaches of the large estate beyond. The hill climbs for two hundred feet, the all-weather surface as good as any found at any of the large training centres around the country.

Bart lets Cool River lob quietly away, his head, as is his habit, low to the ground. He is now accustomed to this idiosyncrasy, to the sensation of being a stone in a slingshot. He enjoys riding Cool River and cannot wait for April and the Grand National. Wary of doing too much, he works the horse twice up the hill and is pleasantly surprised by how fit he is.

After the work is done, as he prepares to drive home, they discuss plans and availability, where to run Cool River next and how many times before Aintree. Bart is aware that luck and the weather will determine where they go and how well the soft-ground-loving Cool River will run. But at least he can still harbour the dream; the downturn in his fortunes, caused mainly by there being so many younger jockeys making a name for themselves, yet to kill that most essential part of a jockey's life.

Arriving home he is as relieved as he is saddened to find Judy missing. On the answerphone there is a message from his agent. He takes his new mobile from his pocket to return the call. It is a ride in a novice chase at Towcester. It is nothing special but it is a ride. Tony harangues Bart about not having a mobile phone for the past few days but they part amicably. He then phones Don to make sure Cool River is okay after his exertions and is invited down for supper and to school some young horses. "Bring your girlfriend, we're broadminded down here."

Not that he would want to take Judy within a stone's throw of Somerset as her knowledge of him is now her secret weapon. He scans the kitchen for a note. He also looks in the bedroom and the lounge. She is a slave to the nine-to-five routine and it is unlike her to go off midweek on a whim. As he fries bacon and butters bread he wonders about phoning Judy's mother, even though that would involve an interrogation on the state of their relationship. Instead he phones her brother to chit-chat about racing, hoping he might offer a clue to his sister's whereabouts.

All evening he sits in front of the television, answering his phone, re-establishing contact with those who thought he had been mugged, waiting for Judy to appear. Believing she has left him he is confused to find her clothes in the wardrobe and uncompleted work in her studio. At ten o'clock he rings their mutual friends but no one has seen her. At eleven he goes to bed, resigned to losing her.

Don Rammage is descended from an unbroken line of beef farmers, all of whom over the generations have developed and improved Conical Farm. In a quiet manner he is proud of his contribution to the Rammage heritage, having trebled the farm's acreage and established an accredited and prize-winning herd of Charolais cattle. Phillip, his son, has already graduated to overall control of the business, allowing his father the time to extend his passion for horses and racing. It is his ambition to train for other people, to give, in time, a career for Polly now she has turned her back on eventing and show jumping.

At supper he announces his plans, suggesting to Bart that he will be first in the queue for rides. There is a full complement around the table and two of the guests promise to send Don a horse presently trained elsewhere. "Isn't it exciting," Polly suggests to her mother.

"As long as you and Phillip don't get in each other's way."

This for Bart is the life, perhaps even the life he was born to, except that this family are united and work in harmony with one another. Phillip does not seemingly resent losing some of the farm acreage to horses. Don Rammage is devoted to his children, to their future. The opposite to his own father, a man who must dominate, who brooks no argument but his own. He could give his son everything Don Rammage has given to his children but chooses to only give if he can offer up lectures on how disappointed he is with his whole family.

Noticing his expression change from happy to something else Mrs. Rammage suggests Polly take Bart out to where they intend to put up a new range of stables, to ask his advice on design and construction. "I'll tell you my life story," Polly promises, pulling him from his chair.

"Bring him back in one piece," her mother laughs, knowing her daughter to be a replica of herself when the same age. "He's got work to do in the morning."

"I had twelve months back-packing in Australia," she tells him, dragging him along, eager to be away from her parents and their friends. "I worked at a sheep station and did some shark fishing. I rather like danger, testing my nerve. I grew up in Australia. I was too much a child before I went."

"Somerset must be dull compared with the outback."

"What a thing for a jump jockey to say. Horses and danger are a package. I intend point-to-pointing next season. Follow me, I'll show you danger."

They go into a horse barn, with five stables either side of the passageway. As she goes past each stable she names the horse and removes an item of her clothing. By the time she has reached the place where they fill hay nets she is down to her underwear. Bart follows. "What about your parents?"

"They are quite conservative. They'll not want to join in. Why, aren't you interested? Or do you have a girlfriend already?"

"No, that's not it." But before he can verbalise his unease she is clawing at the buckle of his belt and pulling his shirt from his trousers.

Stan Leeman lies sprawled on the ground, his left foot pointing in the opposite direction to his left knee, his agonised moans confirmation that his interest in the day's racing is at an end. Bart and Dave Letts notice Leeman's predicament at the same time as the paramedic. Both were brought down by Leeman, or more precisely by his horse falling at the hurdle. Both are aware that he was due to ride one of Ben Wain's in the next race and as they both regularly school for Wain they race each other back to the weighing room to take Leeman's place. The steel plate holding Dave's right thigh together gives Bart the advantage and the ride.

But the day is determined to be miserable and Bart parts company with 'his spare' at the second fence. Two rides, two falls: just the sort of day to take the gilt off anyone's gingerbread.

Getting out of the car his back gives a twinge, a twinge that amplifies as he walks up his garden path. Tiffany notices his discomfort. "Do you want me to give you a massage? Loosen you up. Our Sharon's a qualified masseuse. I let her practice on me. I know what to do."

He winces as he pushes open the door, emphasising his discomfort.

"Stiff in all the wrong places, wouldn't you say?" Tiffany laughs, delighting in her own wickedness.

"Had a couple of falls. A good soak and a sleep, that'll put it right."

"You know where I am if you need me." She sets off to wherever she is going, stopping at the gate. "By the way, she's back. I thought I'd warn you."

"Jude? Where's her car?" He looks into the hallway, expecting to see her lying in wait for him and without warning his back is not his primary concern.

"A flash git in a flash car brought her home. They didn't snog goodbye, if you are worried."

"Dave Letts reckons he's never seen the ground as bad here. He reckons if it wasn't being televised they would have abandoned," Bart tells Polly as she leads him around the parade ring. The meeting has survived two inspections; much to the relief of the Rammages as four miles in heavy ground are exactly the conditions to bring out the best in Cool River. Polly has discarded her waterproofs to show off a tight-fitting pair of stone-washed jeans and a woollen sweater matching her father's racing colours, green with a white hoop and brown sleeves. Her blonde hair is rolled up under a leather Stetson, a memento of a holiday in Arizona with a boyfriend who preferred Arizona to her.

"Come down next week," she tells him, unbuckling the lead rein to let the horse walk free. "I'm keeping myself pure for you, if you want to know." She puts her hand high up on his thigh. "There isn't anyone else, is there? You would tell me, wouldn't you?"

They are the last to leave the parade ring and the horse jig-jogs, keen to be out on the racecourse. Bart and Polly have not seen each other since their romp in the barn and he can see no benefit in telling her about Judy and the five years that has come to nothing. She has packed her belongings and gone to make her symbolic bed with his father. He tightens the girth as they go out onto the racecourse to follow the others down to the start, concentrating on Cool River and the race. "Look after him," Polly shouts as they canter down the course.

He settles Cool River at the rear of the field, wanting to conserve as much energy as he can in the early stages. The pace is slow, befitting the arduous conditions. By halfway the pace has hardly changed and with Cool River's only attributes being his sound jumping and stamina Bart has no choice but to give his mount his head, to take up the running and try to stretch the field. Cool River obliges, taking each fence economically, stringing his rivals out behind him. One by one the competition pulls up. At the fourth-last fence only four remain, with only Cool River and the favourite, The Cave of Fingal, looking likely to win.

At the next Cool River slips going into the fence and catches the birch. Bart sits tight and they survive. But The Cave of Fingal is now closer and Bart can hear O'Sullivan urging his horse on. O'Sullivan is a talker and likes to broadcast how well he is going to his rivals. Going to the second-last he pulls upside Cool River. "I'm going plenty fine. Plenty fine. I should win now by five or six lengths."

Bart is not one to be undermined by propaganda and asks Cool River for greater effort, cracking him one, two, three times, bawling encouragement. He is receiving two stone from the favourite but Cool River has not run for several months and the gruelling conditions are getting the better of him. At the last they are still together, O'Sullivan allowing his horse to veer towards Cool River, wanting to put him off his stride. But they both land safely and a hundred yards later O'Sullivan accepts defeat. Bart pushes Cool River out to the line, not daring to stop riding in case his mount stops to a walk. At the finishing post he clenches his fist. It is his biggest prize for over three years. His account at the petrol station can now be paid.

Six winners leading up to Aintree has put a smile on Bart's face. And while it is dry in the south of the country Lancashire is decidedly wet, causing the better-class horses to drop out of the Grand National.

But on the eve of the great race, as he prepares for his journey north, his life descends into shocking madness. "We must ask you to accompany us to the station to answer questions pertinent to your relationship with Tiffany Ruth Parr." The two plain-clothes policemen are the last people he expected to answer the door to. As he is led to the police car a bouquet of flowers is delivered. One of the policemen intercepts the flowers, reading out loud the card. "'The Rammages have done all they can, it's up to you now. Love Polly'. Quite the lothario aren't you. How old is this Polly?"

Tiffany, apparently, is pregnant. Bart is baffled. "She's sixteen. What's it to do with you?"

But Tiffany is not sixteen and she is not waiting to join the Wrens. It is the often absent Mrs. Parr who has made the complaint. Tiffany has refused to name the guilty party and has told the police she only went round to Bart's house to massage his back, though as her admission was made with a smirk on her face the police are making two and two an easy conclusion.

At midnight Bart is released and after advising his accusers to back Cool River each way he drives to Liverpool for his first ride in the Grand National, his excitement and expectation still strong enough to overrule the ruination of his character and the prospect of a long prison sentence.

Amongst the forty runners he is finally alone, left to do what he does best. There is only the challenge of emulating legends ahead of him. Tiffany and her lies no longer form any part of his existence. For the next ten minutes, if his race should last that long, he will be living his dream.

The starter calls them to line up. As he pulls down his goggles there is a roar from the grandstand that sends a shiver down his spine. This, he realises, as a more famous jockey once said, is not sex but something all the more stimulating. It is how he has dreamed it. Only now the goose pimples and the rising heartbeat are real. Never has he dreamed of falling at the first.

"Here we go," someone shouts and the tape springs up and away, casting forty dreams to the fates.

Cool River drops his head between his knees, unable to lie up as the field gallop like maniacs towards the first fence.

Bart is happy, though. He wouldn't want to be at the front. He wants to take his time. They clear the first without obstruction, landing on a patch of turf untroubled by fallen horse or rider. Bart blows out his cheeks and concentrates on the second fence, concentrating as he has never done before. Because of Tiffany, today, this race, this moment, is all that remains of his career. If he falls they might as well bury him at the very spot.

He is going down the centre, allowing himself options to go left or right to avoid the danger of fallers. All he expects of Cool River is that he will jump round safely. At the second he gets in close but gallops on. Bart is a horseman, he knows how to give a horse confidence by leaving it to find its own stride, to trust it at the big ditch. They meet it on a good stride and Bart knows that with luck they will get round safely.

He wants more of the same. They jump four and five boldly and Bart pats the horse down the neck. Becher's Brook comes and goes, as do the Foinavon and Canal Turn. As they go towards Valentine's Bart assesses who is around him and how many are in front. To his surprise there are only a dozen horses ahead of him, with only half a dozen behind him. Crossing the Melling Road he counts ten horses in front of him. His horse will stay out the distance; he wonders how many of those in front of him will do the same.

The Chair looms up with the animosity of a predator. Cool River picks up his head and reacts like a coiled spring. The exhilaration and relief is so spine-tinglingly perfect that Bart wishes he could go back and jump it a second time. The water jump is a relaxation, a timid little mouse compared to the leonine rapture of the Chair. As they pass under the starting gate to begin a second navigation of the course Bart has never felt as in control of his life.

As he lands over Becher's for the second time he is tempted to ask Cool River to improve his position. Up ahead there are four horses, with only the same number behind him. But the mantra of his dreams is always 'Let the race come to you'. At the Canal Turn he is fourth with a real possibility of being placed. At Valentine's Cool River jumps up to his old foe The Cave of Fingal. "Where have you popped up from?" O'Sullivan asks, amazed to see him travelling so strongly.

And then the most magical thought of his life comes to him. O'Sullivan has not offered up any propaganda. O'Sullivan does not think he will win. And then O'Sullivan shouts across to him. "Take your time. Those in front are holding onto thin air. Nothing will quicken." And then Bart realises it is possible he might actually win the Grand National.

Crossing the Melling Road he is second, with only the Irish horse Super Highway in front of him. Everything else is toiling. He has two fences, a long winding run in and Tim Bourke to beat. This is his chance in life, his one chance to be the golden boy again. Confident Cool River will keep finding he nudges him forward, upside Super Highway. They jump the second last in unison. There is a large gap knocked out of the last fence and Bart tries to seize the initiative but Bourke has the same idea and leans into him, forcing Bart to alter course. Super Highway skips through the gap, using less energy, while Bart must ask Cool River for a big jump to keep him upsides.

Cool River responds and they set off for the elbow where the course goes around the Chair fence. Bourke is the first to pull his stick through. He gives his mount a crack and they go half a length up. Bart too must go for his whip and at the elbow it is nip and tuck. Second place will now and forever be a dagger in the heart. Both riders bellow and cajole. Their whips are a hindrance now. No whip will make tired horses go faster. Suddenly Super Highway has run his race and Cool River goes a length, two lengths up. Bart has the National at his mercy. But then, just as the image of Judy and his father come to mind, a roar of ominous thunder appears at his withers. It is The Cave of Fingal gasping for the breath which will steal him victory, with O'Sullivan shouting him home. Bart has not stopped riding and Cool River responds again as he is asked to win his race a second time. At the line no one knows who has won, who will take the dagger to the heart. The Cave of Fingal is the favourite, Cool River a 50/1 outsider.

Neither Bart nor O'Sullivan has the strength to anticipate triumph with a raised fist or to salute their connections. They clasp hands as they pull up and Bourke slaps Bart across the shoulders as he joins them.

As the seconds elasticise into the agony of the unknowing, Bart throws his arms around Cool River's neck, embracing him, thanking him for a thrill which will never be replicated: a perfect end to a less than glorious career.

"You've won! You've won!" It is Polly. He has never seen anyone so happy. She takes the reins, certain of her victory. Cool River's head is high now, as if he can sense the achievement he has brought about. "You done it," he is told. "You are such a star!" If there is a heaven on earth Polly Rammage has entered its mystery. Emotion leaks from her like water from a holed bucket. Bart leans down to embrace her, to kiss her head. But to Polly the hero is her horse.

From out of a scrum of photographers Don Rammage runs

across to greet them, trying to jump as he runs, his binoculars bouncing against his chest, his hat crumpled in his hand. He embraces his daughter, kissing her on the cheeks, his tears dripping off his smile. They look at one another in a way no words can ever express. He too believes he has won. Bart is unsure. The connections of The Cave of Fingal are also reacting as if they have won.

Next door to Bart's house Mrs. Parr switches off her television, her five-pound each-way winning ticket tucked safely away in her purse. "He's worth some brass now," she tells her daughter. Play your cards right and it can roll your way. You owe that babby to give it the best start you can and that Shane Simmons ain't going to provide it, is he? Bart Thomas is a golden boy now. Sleeping with him was the best advice I could have ever given you."

Tiffany buries her head in a cushion. She likes Bart. He is always kind to her and took precautions against her getting pregnant. But her mother is right. Shane will never amount to anything.

"What about DNA? It'll prove the baby isn't his."

"He slept with a minor. People saw you coming out of his house. It's why that Judy left him, isn't it? If he contests it he'll go to prison. What choice does he have?"

Emily's Smile of Wonder

Emily was traumatised at birth when her mother suffered a fatal heart attack during labour; in consequence she has only known life as something unrelated to her own existence.

Yet she has struggled against the odds in her own subdued way, sustained by the steadfast love and supervision of her grandmother and the diehard resistance of her father. She is helped in her day-to-day struggle by a photograph of a grey horse who her daddy talks about to her and who sometimes appears on the television. "They are kindred spirits," her father tells Emily's disbelieving grandmother.

On her bedroom wall, footside of her cot, is a large print of Desert Orchid. The grey horse is captured cantering to the start, the extravagance of his character illustrated with perfect clarity. Dessie's vitality is in stark contrast to Emily's languor, lying as she does in her cot, staring, seemingly without blinking, a wispy smile on her pale lips, her conscious spirit so obviously parted from her sick and dysfunctional body.

The picture was bought as a birthday present. It had seemed an inappropriate gift for a six-year-old and Jim, her father, could not explain why he had bought it, though as he sadly knows all gifts to children with the difficulties Emily must endure are of little or no consequence to their lives. She cannot speak or walk and she needs regular massage to help her breathing and swallowing. The experts offer no hope, no expectation of a breakthrough in curing her condition. They have warned that it is unlikely she will survive into adulthood.

"No, I'm afraid not. My son is on holiday next week. My apologies. Yes. Even taxi drivers must have a break." She dislikes disappointing people, turning away trade. But Jim is adamant, he never works Cheltenham week. She looks at the diary, with the five days scored with red lines. Yet there on the Thursday is Mrs. McCallister, The Vicarage, Rudford to Oxford Road, Cheltenham, 10.45: the destination compounding her guilt.

Pauline had lost track of the passing months and thought the Festival was in April. The diary should have alerted her, and it was not as if Jim had pencilled in the sacred three days of March. The red lines were her red lines and she had still made the mistake.

The cause of her lapse, though she is loath to admit it, is that caring for Emily is becoming a strain; she is getting heavier by the day to pick up, harder to minister to. Next birthday she will be seven. Not that she begrudges the responsibility and she is as determined as her son that Emily should remain solely in their care. She is, after all, her only grandchild, with the likelihood being she will remain so as Jim shows no inclination to remarry and Angela, Jim's sister, lives on a commune in New Zealand, fervent in her dedication to saving the planet.

"You okay, my lovely," she coos, always hopeful of receiving a glimmer of response. But Emily remains expressionless, ensconced in her own world, her eyes trained on the fingers of her left hand. "I'd better get you changed before Daddy comes in for his lunch. Bread and cheese, with spotted dick for afters. But there is steak and kidney pudding for tea." She chats on as she pulls clean underwear and incontinence pants from the tallboy kept in the living room so that fresh clothes are always at hand.

"Perhaps you'll get to see your Aunt Angela soon," she tells Emily, hoisting her up onto the sofa. "Your daddy has asked her if she can come home to help look after you because you are getting a big girl now, aren't you?"

"Is that you, Jim?" she shouts from the living room as she hears the kitchen door scrape against the tiles. It is habit that prompts the enquiry. Her late husband was also a Jim and she greeted him for twenty years with the self-same words.

"It's the milkman come for his dues," he jokes, hanging his leather coat on the back door.

"Then he's called at the wrong time as my son is due home any minute." She pulls a chair free of the table in preparation for him, throwing a shovelful of coal on the fire as she waits for him to wash his hands. "Hasn't it been a lovely morning? I suppose we could have made do with the electric heater but Emily enjoys the flames."

"Let's hope it keeps up for next week," Jim replies, cutting a chunk of Cheddar for himself.

"Oh, yes, next week." Still she has not told him about Mrs. McCallister.

"Em in bed?"

"I put her down early. She's been niggly all morning."

"Not sickening, I hope."

"I massaged her chest before I took her up but she seemed okay. You can go up to her while I brew the tea and serve up the spotted dick."

Jim stops eating, his round, honest face distorted by thought. Rubbing his bald head he looks at his mother. "You'd say if she was getting too much. I've written to Ange but I don't hold up much hope."

"I nursed your dad for three and half years. Little Emily is nothing by comparison." Her reply is instinctive, her tone indomitable. Yet Jim is not convinced.

"How's my sweetheart?" Jim leans over the cot, tickling Emily's belly even though his pleasure does not register with his daughter. She stares up at her picture, her brown eyes alive to a wonder only she can experience, the grey horse the only stimulus that can ignite a smile to form at her lips.

He steps back from the cot, as always thrilled to see her smiling. Her smile fascinates him as much as Emily is fascinated by her picture of the grey horse. He knows there is something significant, even mystical, about her connection with Dessie and in her smile there is both wonder and hope.

"You stay there, my sweetheart. Keep that smile of wonder forever," he whispers, kissing her forehead. "Stay with the grey. Let's hope he gives us more memories next week."

After two glorious days of spring sunshine that has painted Cleeve Hill in the purest of natural colours, the third day has dawned snowy and cold. The transformation is astounding, deceiving weather forecasters and racegoers alike. Against his wishes Jim drives Mrs. McCallister to Cheltenham on roads which are slushy and verging on dangerous. Mrs. McCallister, as is her custom, babbles on about her family and the surprise trip to London her husband has planned on the sly, unconcerned by the threat to the day's sport.

Jim is quiet, resentful of the snow and Mrs. McCallister for dragging him from the comfort of his living room. He had wanted to take Emily to the park to show her the ducks and the swans and then to sit with her on the settee to watch Desert Orchid win the Gold Cup. Now it is almost impossible to envisage, with the abandonment of the meeting the only possible outcome.

As he drives home, wanting for the first time in twenty years for the Cheltenham Festival to be abandoned, not wanting his beloved grey to be subjected to the heavy ground he hates, he suddenly thinks that his mother's mistake might prove prophetic, that if the third day is cancelled it would be rescheduled for April when Dessie would be more likely to get the firm ground he thrives on. The thought gives him hope, the disappointment of having his holiday spoilt by the weather made easier to bear by knowing that he can now take Emily to the park.

"Do you know, Jim," Pauline announces cautiously, not wanting to create false hope, "she's trying to say daddy."

"Em? No. You're imagining it. She can't be." He glances at his watch, then across to Emily propped up with cushions on the sofa, a doll held limply in her right hand. "You trying to say daddy, Emily? Daddy. Who is daddy?"

To their surprise she lifts her expressionless face, her mouth forming a saliva-spread O. Then, to the joy and shock of her admirers, she expels a sound shaped midpoint between a guttural cough and a split lower-case d. It is the first time she has ever responded to anyone's voice.

"She said it even clearer this morning," Pauline tells him. "More like da. Fair caught me by surprise."

The moment is too momentous for Jim to comprehend. He has waited six years for a moment of hope. He has listened to pessimistic reports on her prospects and had all his hopes dashed by paediatricians and healthcare workers. He puts his hand to her mouth and encourages her to make another sound. He wants confirmation, further reason to believe in miracles.

"Say daddy, Emily. Come on, honeybun, say daddy." He pronounces the word phonetically, touching her wet lips with his fingertips. He has done the same a thousand times before, though never with such expectation. He repeats the exercise but Emily cannot respond. Yet a prayer is answered, a spluttered fragment of a miracle has been achieved.

"It is improvement, isn't it?" Pauline asks, also in need of confirmation.

"That'll show them doctors." Jim slumps onto the settee, the day already triumphal.

The clock on the mantelpiece strikes two o'clock. Jim and Pauline look to Emily to see if she responds to the chimes. But she doesn't. In her world there is no need of time.

"Do you want the telly on?" Pauline asks.

"Might as well. If it's off it's off and we'll go the park." He reaches for the morning paper, the optimistic headline resounding back at him like a distasteful April Fool's Day prank. "I'll ring Ange tonight and tell her about Em. It might help her to make her mind up about coming home."

The opening sequence of the television coverage shows

Desert Orchid's owner walking the course, digging the heel of his boot into the sodden ground, his face bathed in disappointment and gloom. Usually only too pleased to face the cameras Mr. Burridge looks like a man enduring torture. He wants to be left alone, to run the gauntlet of indecision in private. "Will you allow him to run?" the interviewer presses. "I don't know," Mr. Burridge answers honestly. "He'll hate it, won't he?"

Jim sits on the settee with Emily on his lap. His mother is asleep in the armchair, the fire reduced to embers. He has watched the preceding races without his usual enthusiasm, half his attention on Emily in hope of hearing another ill-defined sound fall from her lips. All of his bets are losers, further dampening his mood. He has backed Dessie, of course, though with the ground so unfavourable to him he doubts if he will be collecting any winnings.

"Dessie next," he tells Emily, forcing himself to be jolly, bouncing her up and down on his knee. "Em's Dessie is next." She responds by forming her mouth into an O shape and emitting a fractured but clearly audible upper-case D sound.

Jim's heart leaps with the sheer joy of it. He stays silent, hoping Emily will repeat the sound. Then, like a rare flower turning its petals to the sun, she smiles. Jim follows her gaze. The camera is on Desert Orchid walking jauntily around the paddock, oblivious to the ordeal that he must conquer, pleased as always to be the focus of attention.

"Da," Emily spits out.

It is a disbelieving and stupendous moment in Jim's life. Emily has spoken. Not a grunt or a belch but a word bordering on the understandable. The doctors are wrong. The

Cheltenham Gold Cup, the wet ground, even the great Desert Orchid, abruptly become superfluous. He calls his mother but she sleeps on. He asks Emily to repeat the sound but she is held transfixed by Dessie as the jockey is hoisted onto his back. Jim picks up Emily's ragdoll and throws it into his mother's lap. She, too, deserves to share the triumphal moment.

"Was I snoring?" she asks, straightening herself up, noticing an almost beatific glow on her granddaughter's face.

"She said da. As clear as clear."

The smile dissolves as the camera switches from Desert Orchid to his rivals. The commentator has only positive things to say about Carvill's Hill, Ten Plus, Yahoo and Charter Party. He emphasises how much Dessie hates soft ground and that he has never won on soft ground or on a left-handed track and that he has never won at Cheltenham or over a distance as far as the Gold Cup. Jim can only agree with the pessimistic outlook but as he strokes Emily's shoulder-length hair it no longer matters that Dessie will not win the Gold Cup. "There's always next year, isn't that right, honeybun?"

As the horses canter to the start the camera returns to Dessie, his rider wearing waterproof leggings. The grey, usually so imposing and commanding, looks small and vulnerable under the threatening, dark sky. Emily's face brightens and she splutters 'Diz,' adding greater joy to her father's day.

Pauline begins to cry.

"Dez," falls from her lips, her face aglow with a smile that is the mirror-image of the scene at her father's heart.

"It's not daddy she is trying to say, Jim. It's Dessie."

"Yes, isn't it bloody marvellous?" And Jim too must cry or burst with the happiness of it. "He'll probably defy everything and win too, you mark my words if he don't."

"Dezzz," Emily almost sings as Dessie jumps the first fence, setting out, as usual, to make every post a winning post, Jim's knee is now an imaginary horse for her to ride, faith and belief toppling, at last, the adversity of defeat predicted by the experts. Much the same as Desert Orchid is attempting to do.

Printed in Great Britain
by Amazon